M000295739

SUFFER
With ME

A NOVEL BY:
ROBERT LABOO

MTW
More Than Words
P U B L I S H I N G

DEDICATION

This book is dedicated to all who saw my potential, believed and supported me throughout this process. This book was motivated by all who didn't. Thank you! Both parties are equally appreciated although for entirely different reasons. Without you I would have been given up. I hope you enjoy our story, because I was just the pen but y'all faith, or the lack of it, was the ink that saw it completed.

- Baghdad Jig

SUFFER
With ME

CHAPTER 1

"**S**IR, I'M BEGGING YOU TO drop the weapon," the woman states in an assertive tone.

The young Caucasian man, with the piercing blue eyes, searches for any trace of a bluff in her features, as he holds the old man in front of him at knifepoint.

Where did she appear from?

What was supposed to be a simple robbery, to acquire the necessary funds to feed his habit, has become a hostage situation. His eyes dart back and forth trying to spy an exit from this potentially deadly scenario. Seeing none, he ups the ante.

"Aaagh!" screams the elderly man as the tip of the knife digs in his throat.

"Next one the blade goes through his neck, bitch. Now, I'm going to release him when I get to my car. If you attempt to follow us, his blood will be on *my* knife and *your* hands. Okay?" The man states with more aggression in his voice than he actually feels. *POP!* The car backfiring causes him to jump and mistakenly leave enough room for the three shots that tear into his torso. Suffiyah Adams remains in a shooter's stance, though the perp lays motionless. She's deaf to the commotion of the gathering crowd.

"...the weapon!" The commanding voice snatches her from her state of shock.

"Ma'am, drop the weapon!" One of the many South Orange police officers, that now have her surrounded screams. While doing as told, she explains,

"I'm, I'm a—" The gunshot that robs her of consciousness is deafening.

Later

"In other news, an Essex County Homicide Detective was shot this morning on Valley Street in South Orange, a New Jersey suburb. Witnesses and the victim of the robbery say, the female officer shot and killed a 21 year-old Seton Hall student as he attempted to rob the 64 year-old man. South Orange police swarmed the Valley National Bank parking lot and allegedly shot the detective unjustly, as she was complying and laying down her weapon as commanded. The status of the shooting as well as her condition are unknown. More to come later..."

The tension in the hospital is palpable as the Newark officers stare daggers through the few South Orange officers who dare to show their faces. Today the "blue code" they follow disappears and only colors which remain are black and white. A black woman, shot by a white officer is enough to create a blood feud between the departments that will rival the Hatfields and McCoys. The doctor's approach interrupts the standoff.

"Chief," the baby-faced doctor says acknowledging the commanding officer, "she pulled through surgery and all is well. You should be proud, she's a survivor."

Nine Months Later

The reddish-brown leaves flit across the ground as Detective Suffiyah Adams steps out of her Maplewood condo's entrance. The fall breeze lightly caresses her beautiful face and sifts through her shoulder length auburn hair. At 5'3" and 127 lbs., her model looks and curvaceous body lends her the air of an actress instead of a cop. The almond shaped brown eyes paired with her Meagan Good lips are traffic stoppers. She inhales the fresh air as she watches the kids on their way to school. Zipping her waist length leather jacket over her "Black Lives Matter" shirt, she makes her way to the parking lot. The windshield of her Honda Accord is plastered in leaves. A sight which a year ago would have aggravated her, but today feels like a blessing. She now embraces and appreciates every season as if it's her last. As she exits the parking lot, she turns right onto Valley Street. Approaching Parker Rd., she makes a left. From her parking lot, making the left turn down Valley Street is a much quicker route, but even looking in that direction brings back bad memories. It's the scene of where she took her first life and where her life was almost taken in the process. The day that she realized that blue wasn't as great a color as she once believed. She drums her fingers on the steering wheel to the music, as she mentally prepares herself for her first day back at the department. Out of all the things to come, what she's anticipating most, is her appointment with her psychiatrist. After three years of celibacy, these past seven months of therapy have been the closest substitute for her lack of intimacy. The mere thought of Dr. Jackson relaxes her immediately.

Homicide HQ

"Sufee!" the officers yell in unison.

Balloons and streamers litter her cubicle she observes while drowning in the embraces of her co-workers. An overwhelming sense of love washes over her and spills from her eyes.

"Knock it off, before y'all mess up my mascara," she whines.

"Okay, okay. Y'all mofos leave my baby ay-lone," Sonya kids. "Welcome back, Mama. Don't scare me like that no more, you hear?" Sonya whispers as she guides Suffiyah to her cubicle. The desk is loaded with cases. She gently nudges her forward, "I love you. Now get to work!" Suffiyah laughs at the sudden change of tone. Plopping down in her office chair, she just relaxes and re-familiarizes herself with her surroundings. She shuts her eyes only a couple of seconds before she feels an eclipsing presence over her and jumps slightly.

"Whoo! Lou you scared me," she says touching her chest.

"Quit daydreaming Adams! Hope you enjoyed your months in the big house, now it's back in the field for mas'sa," Lt. McFarland mimics a slave. "How are your sessions with the residential quack coming along?"

"I'm progressing nicely, Sir. As if you haven't already checked my files thoroughly. I'm completely sane and able to work," Suffiyah says sarcastically while smiling.

"That's a girl. Well, I'll leave you to it." He exits her cubicle. *Home sweet home,* she thinks.

CHAPTER 2

"RELAX." THE HUSKY BARITONE OF his voice is the candlelight to her dinner. "Forget the world's expectations of Suffiyah Adams. Forget the world's perception. Forget everything that that day took from you." He continues. "What did it give you? There is a gift disguised in every curse. What was yours?"

You. Suffiyah says in her head, but her mouth says, "Life."

"I realized how much I truly want to live. To smile. To love. How much I truly want everyone else to live," she admits sadly. "But the curse is greater than the gift. Death snuffs out my every smile. I fear loving anyone that will be taken from me suddenly. Most of all I'm afraid to live outside the box, out of the fear of being placed in a box."

Dr. Jackson is a handsome man and not what many would expect from a psychiatrist. At 36 years-old, he stands at 6'1 with a muscular, boxers build. His wavy brush cut hair and high yellow complexion coupled with his looks are neck breakers. But they come a distant second to his perfect white teeth and green eyes. The same striking eye that are staring at Suffiyah, as he furrows his brow in contemplation. His stare renders her speechless.

"Something wrong, Detective?"

"Huh? No. Uhm, I was just gathering my thoughts." She smiles.

"Okay, let's continue."

"Dr. Jackson, I guess what I've really come to understand is this job, as much as I love it, is the source of my fear. It is literally composed of death. I'm seriously considering quitting." This admission catches Dr. Jackson off guard and a brief look of surprise registers on his usually unreadable face, which causes Suffiyah to smile. *Got you gorgeous!*

"Uhm. You should really reconsider that decision. Weigh the pros and the cons in totality. At the least, allow me to do my job before you quit." He smiles, which is a pleasant rarity.

"I think its best, Doc. But, I'll take a day or two before coming to a decision."

Later

A little girl cowers in the corner of the attic, as the monster frantically searches for her. She silently prays to God that he doesn't look behind the boxes of clothes stacked in front of her. "Suffer! Suffer!" He screams as he flings objects out of his path. "Here you are!" But his voice is coming from across the room, directed at someone unseen. "Now you must suffer with me..."

"Aagh!" Suffiyah's scream awakes her. The cold sweat has her nightgown clinging to her breast. Her short, heavy breaths, as recurring as this nightmare she's been having since being shot, are uncontrollable. The doctor's professional opinion is, she either invented this image or she's been repressing memories that are trying to make their way to the forefront. The clock on the nightstand reads 4:28 AM. She has to be up in two hours anyway and after that nightmare, sleep is very unwelcome. She swings her small pedicured feet over the side of the bed. With much effort, she stands and heads to the bathroom. Undressing to shower, she admires her body in the mirror. At 33 years-old her body can rival and beat out most 20 year-olds. Her C-cup breast sit perfectly above her toned stomach. Explosive hips compliments her equally explosive rear. This unbelievable package in front of her, yet no man behind her to hold her on nights such as this. *Get it together.* She shakes the thought from her head as she steps in the shower.

The water feels so good as it cascades down her naked body. Feeling like a million tiny fingers teasing her in places that have become a "no man" zone. The sudden tautness of her nipples lets her know that her mind is wandering. She swiftly washes and evacuates the shower, before she succumbs to her desires. The towel and terry cloth robe hug her like an old friend. Taking away the last lingering effects of the nightmare. In the kitchen, she puts on the tea kettle and grabs some turkey bacon and an English muffin. The nagging growl of her stomach led her here. Her finger absentmindedly rubs the bullet wound in her head, as she stares at the white wall with the blue trim. *So much has changed.*

Homicide HQ

"Got a live one, Su. Hit the interrogation room." That's her and Sonya's code for informants. It never ceases to amaze her how they build up the heart to commit these brazen crimes. But soon as the handcuffs bite into their wrists, they lose all the heart, their codes and laws and moreover the loyalty. "On my way, Mama."

The young dread head man with the face full of tattoos, runs his mouth freely with little coercion.

"I don't owe no man shit, feel me? This 'bout me and my kids."

"That's exactly right brother, think about those babies." The detective conducting the questioning further persuades him. "But why was the driver shot? Wait, who shot him, you? I'm looking at the witnesses' account of the incident and they have the shooter matching your description."

"Hell no! That was Merko. We just look like brothers."

"He can't look that much like you. I ain't running with that. I gotta see a picture of y'all." The detective leans back feigning disbelief.

"On the set! I don't have no pictures of us but watch; pull up his pic, he been bagged before. His name is Marco Jacoby. Watch, we look just like twins. I bet you!" The young boy smiles foolishly.

"Okay, you got a bet. I'm about to go see. You hungry?"

"Hell yeah!"

"Okay. I'll be right back. Ay, remember I didn't cuff you because I trust you. Don't try to escape and make me look bad, killer." He smiles at the kid. As he exits the room, he spots Suffiyah. "Hey, baby girl. I don't know if it's the schools or the drugs, but these kids get dumber and dumber." She shakes her head as he strides away triumphantly.

The rest of the day passes uneventfully. Around twenty minutes to shifts end the fatigue sets in. The phone rings. "Homicide division, Detective Adams speaking."

"Suffiyah," The way her name leaves the callers mouth gives it a vulgar feel. "There's been a murder. A young woman needs you on Ridgewood Avenue. Hurry, she's suffering."

"Who is this, Sir?"

"The murderer." The phone goes dead as the caller hangs up. It's something eerily familiar about the voice. Though his tone was so dead and devoid of emotion. Whoever in this office decided that they should play a prank on her would regret it.

Clock out time. Finally. Suffiyah gathers her things to head home.

"Adams! One hundred block of Ridgewood Ave. Get there and explain to me why your name is there."

"Excuse me, Lieutenant?"

"Your name is at the scene."

Ridgewood Avenue

Butterflies flutter rampantly through Suffiyah's stomach as she pulls her department issued Crown Victoria to the crime scene. Her imagination paints vivid pictures of the scene that lays in wait for her inside the house. Taking a deep breath, she puts her game face on and exits the car. A lone patrolman stands at the front door of the two-story townhouse. He nods at her as he glances at the shield around her neck. The unmistakable smell of blood invades her nose and turns her stomach. She pauses to put the booties over her shoes to prevent crime scene contamination. Walking pass all the blood spatters on the wall and floor, her imagination once again shows her the carnage she can expect. A dismembered corpse or a disemboweled woman. Maybe a woman with multiple stab wounds to the head, face and torso. Of all the horrible images that flooded her mental, none prepared her for what she walked into. The head CSI man, Ronald Eastman, kneels over the corpse. "Ronnie?"

"Good evening Detective Adams, I see you received your invitation to the party." Eastman says without looking back once. She stands over his shoulder, glancing pass his balding dirty blond pate. In front of him lays a beautiful young woman. The ugly bruises around her throat look profane on her otherwise flawless body. As she lays there completely nude, one thought comes to Detective Adams mind.

"Were there more victims?"

"No. The asshole splashed the house with someone or something else's blood. Hell of a promoter. Decorated the place and everything for us. Cocksucker."

For the first time she realizes the woman bears a striking resemblance to herself. Height, weight, complexion and hair color. She instinctually wraps her arms over her breast, feeling suddenly overexposed.

"Where do I come into play, Ronnie?"

Saying nothing, he points a latex gloved finger towards the victim's shoulder. A small white card is tucked slightly under her shoulder. She doesn't need to kneel down to see it's her name on the card.

Down The Street

The camera captures the flustered look on Detective Adams face as she exits the house. Her expression screams, "Get me outta here!", but her posture remains stoic. If you had to judge the severity of the crime from her demeanor, you'd believe it to be unintimidating. But not to the trained eye of Benji Cooper. He reads the subtle telltale signs her body sends off. The glassy eyes and faraway look. The shaky hand that swipes the loose hair off her face. The greatest indicator is the way she refuses to look back, as if whatever is behind her needs to be escaped. And like most people being pursued, she's running away. Again, her body doesn't say that, but her face is telling a totally different story. Benji's camera is the recorder catching every word her face speaks.

"Subject is leaving a crime scene. She appears to be taken aback by the incident but carries it well. She's approaching a blue Crown Victoria and—" Benji Cooper stops mid-sentence as Detective Adams appears to look right at him.

He slumps down in his chair as soon as her head swivels in his direction. The act in itself proving superfluous, given the dark tints on his minivan. Realizing his brain fart or lack of thinking, he returns to his proper sitting position. Just as suddenly as she turns towards him, she turns away. His heart flutters, her eyes hold such sadness in them, it is unmistakable. In that look they exchange in that brief two seconds, the stranger with the face of an angel and eyes of a widow, had grabs his heart. With the grace of a ballerina, she dances in and out of his world. In what seemed like a lifetime but only lasted a few seconds. The brake lights of the fleeing Crown Victoria stops his meandering. He tosses the camera and starts his car to follow her. Pulling out of his space in a manner as not to garner attention, as he stalks his prey. *They say everyone has a twin in this world somewhere and here is hers, in the living, breathing flesh.*

CHAPTER 3

B ENJAMIN 'BENJI' COOPER. ONCE KNOWN infamously in the
bullet riddled, pothole infested streets of Newark as "Benji
Ru". Mr. Cooper has carved the excess fat from his character and
become a somewhat model citizen. Throughout his career as a
gangbanger, for a lack of a better word, he sought out B.L.O.O.D.S
to define him. But In defining B.L.O.O.D.S., he found the
contradiction. The Acronym means Brotherly Love Overrides
Oppression of Destruction of Society. Yet, he and his cohorts were
the parasite of society. Newark, NJ was built on savage tales of
horrendous crimes and murders. Not much unlike his predecessors,
he was one of the architects of this carnage. His realization came
in the form of Sakinah. They say behind every good man is a great
woman. This cliché personified Sakinah. She was the "yin" to his
"yang". For everywhere he was aggressive she was passive. When
his soul was angered she was his calm. In times of confliction and
doubt, she was his surety. So, to call her his "everything" would
be an understatement. He thrived in the underbelly of society by
pillaging and exploiting the inner city. Born into poverty and strife,
he felt he was unable to lose or moreover, scared to lose. So, with his
affiliation came status and he took all that he felt the world owed
him. But his "college girl", as he called her, proved to be the undoing
of that outlook. Sakinah taught him that fearing to lose is fearing
to live. She discovered his love of writing and sought to exploit
it, in his favor. He told her of being Blood and she never judged

him. She didn't acknowledge "Benji Ru". She knew Benjamin, the gentleman who picked up her dropped school books at Starbucks. The 5'10 155lb. superhero. His complexion was like peanut butter and his hair he wore in a taper with 360-degree waves. In the looks department he was average, but his swagger increased him to irresistible. He could fit in inside any crowd but manage to stand out in the same instance. He was her superhero because he made her not fear living, so in turn, he saved her from herself. During their times of early courting, she talked him into getting his GED. From there, college was next. He majored in creative writing. His intelligence coupled with his street edge was daunting. His writing style could captivate her and chill her in the same sentence. He was her drug. Balancing school and the streets were proving to be a burden. He needed to quit one but couldn't choose. To leave the streets was to let down the "set" and to leave school was to let down Sakinah. He couldn't do either. Sakinah never tried to talk him out of "banging", it was a part of him. Her only advice was "bang" better. *"Bang better?"* He didn't understand. Before winter break was scheduled to begin, he had a term paper due. He wrote about how insurance companies paid out funds to slave traders in England, for loss of slaves during the voyage, being they were only cargo. Going in depth on how a boat load of slaves were diseased and thrown overboard by the traders. Unable to make money from the market with sick slaves, they opted to drown them and make an insurance claim. This way they could still obtain profit for the dead slaves, thus not rendering the travels fruitless. These events were one of the major ones spearheading the abolishment of slavery in England. His paper earned him the highest grade in his class. He couldn't wait to share the news with Sakinah. Benji went home to await her arrival. He had to practice self-control, so he wouldn't call her every two minutes. Out of fear that he would expose the news over the phone that he wanted to give in person. He forced himself into slumber to stave off his anxiousness. Waking up sometime after midnight to an empty apartment, his anxious state was replaced with jealous anger. He snatched up his phone, no messages from her. Immediately he dials her number. After the third ring an answer, "Hello?" the man said…

~ ~ ~

Benji raced through the streets of Newark, breaking every motor vehicle violation in the process. The tears blurring his vision, not a strong enough deterrent to keep him from speeding through intersections. With either God or the devil on his side, he arrived at his destination. Hurdling out his car, he burst through the front door and raced to the elevator that was closing. "Stop! You…" security screamed, but it was too late. He was inside the elevator and the doors had closed. The doors showed the reflection of a madman. Unkempt hair, winter coat with no shirt underneath, on his feet one sneaker and one boot, no socks. The door opened and he ran out. Three security guards tackled him, struggling to restrain him as he screamed, "Sakinah Rogerssss!" repeatedly. A burly detective ran to the commotion and plucked him out of the pile. The detective looked him deep in his eyes and in that moment he did something he never fathomed he would do in life. He wrapped his arms around the detective and cried like a newborn baby. In her father's eyes he saw the truth. The life that motivated, believed and loved him, was gone forever. Sakinah Rogers was raped and killed two blocks from her work place. As he stood in the hospital being held up by her father, reality set in.

~ ~ ~

Benjamin Cooper sat in his office space that he rented in downtown Newark. Silently staring at the picture of Sakinah on his desk, his eyes glazed over as they often do. This office serves a dual purpose. He's a private investigator that moonlights as the editor of his own magazine. Both businesses are housed here. He became a private investigator in the course of looking for Sakinah's killer. Unable to quaint his own pain, he found peace in sating others. By answering question for others, he is able to quell the ones he can't answer for himself. The revenue from this job created his second business and the love of his life. After Sakinah's death, instead of leaving "bloods" behind him, he decided to take her advice and "bang better". He took everything positive that B.L.O.O.D.S. was created to stand for and sought to embody it. Writing numerous editorials on oppression, rape, murder, drugs and poverty, he created a magazine in Sakinah's memory. He called the magazine *Why We Bang*. He writes his articles under the pseudonym "Just Benjamin" and dedicated each issue to a woman he never expected to see breathing again for the rest of his life. That was, until the day he saw Detective Adams.

CHAPTER 4

AN OVERWHELMING FEELING OF QUEASINESS threatens to overtake Detective Adams. Not willing to shoulder the embarrassment from her lapse of professionalism, she excuses herself from the scene. She is the master of her body, because as bad as she wanted to run away screaming, she leaves calmly. As she steps into the chilled evening air, she becomes aware that she's sweating profusely. Her clammy hands shake as she fixes a strand of hair. She breathes deeply needing to feel the fresh air enter her lungs and the smell of the streets to invade her nostrils. A sense of humiliation sets in as she realizes she's abandoning her coworkers. *But this isn't my case.* She thinks as she descends the steps. *Only reason I was called is because my card was there. But, why was my card there?* Suffiyah turns to the right and stares down the street. There is no one there, but it doesn't change the fact that she *knows* she isn't alone. She hastily enters her car and places the scene in her rearview. As she pulls away from the scene and turns the corner, the flood gates break. The hot tears soak her face as the emotion that tried to fight its way out at the scene, finally escapes. Her body is racked with sobs. It was as if she just witnessed her own death. How could this ugly world extinguish the beauty of life so easily? How does she explain the call she received at the office? That coupled with her card by the body, is more than coincidental. So, what will her superiors think?

~~~

"Sufee, fuck that job honey," advises Alicia.

Alicia and Suffiyah go back to third grade together. She's the only person outside the department she would discuss the case with and the only one in the world she'd expose her feelings to.

"You've been through enough traumatic shit to get you through two lifetimes. Your blessings' bag is filled, bitch retire already!" she says with a stare that reads "I dare you to argue with me".

But Suffiyah calls her bluff.

"But if I quit Lee Lee, how am I gonna find out why they called me? Or who killed that poor girl?"

"Look, God bless the dead and all that," Lee Lee says doing the cross like the Catholics, "But this ain't no damn movie! *Somebody* wanted you to see that girl. *Somebody* wanted you to understand the significance of the resemblance. *Somebody* wanted you to know that, if permitted, the next beautiful dead girl at the scene would be you! Maybe you can sleep at night knowing that but I can't. So I'm spending the night," she says with finality as she sips from her glass of apple Ciroc and apple juice.

"Well, you sleeping ya naked ass on the couch I could tell you that much!" they both burst out into laughter. Alicia has been sleeping in the nude since their high school days. She's too proud of her body to hide it. Whenever they leave the country, it's as if her clothes remained in the states also.

"My naked ass going on that bed, just stay on your side. I know you're on a three-year sex drought".

"Ha ha, ya momma!"

Suffiyah's day off couldn't have come at a better time in the work week. After yesterday's events, she desperately needs every second of this day. She walks around the mall with Alicia laughing and gossiping nonstop. It feels like her high school days, back when everything was simple. Suffiyah knows this trip is about distracting her, but she can't help but feel her heart skip a bit with each shadow lurking the corner or accidental brush of the shoulder. She and

Alicia have on matching waist length *Polo* pea coats in different colors. Hers is an olive green while Lee Lee's is red. Lee Lee's thick body and flawless chocolate skin, complement Suffiyah's caramel complexion and petite frame. The skin-tight *Citizen of Republic* jeans they wear, fall over the traditional green and red colored *Gucci* tennis shoes perfectly. The pair look more like video vixens, with their long hair flowing under the berets they wear to match their pea coats, instead of being seen as the cop and accountant they are. Their day started at the spa, where they received massages and facials. Next the nail salon for mani and pedis. Last stop was the beauty salon, where the Dominican women washed and groomed their long tresses. Now they're ripping the runway of the mall, all courtesy of Lee Lee's credit card. She would do anything to assuage her best friend's distress.

"What you wanna do now, Sugar Plum?" Lee Lee asks.

"I'm good, Cherry Pie. I just want to spend the rest of the day with the person that means the world to me."

"Aww!" Lee Lee exclaims as her eyes mist.

"Thanks for pampering me, boo. Now, what time you leaving so I can pick that person up?" Suffiyah says as she stops and places her hands on her hips.

Slap! "Heffa!" Lee Lee smacks her playfully.

"You just assaulted an officer, Miss. Buy me a Hermes bag or you going to jail." They interlock their arms as Lee Lee pulls her laughing.

"You better bring your gold-digging ass on."

"Don't be pulling—"

Suffiyah words catch in her throat as she locks eyes with the man smiling at her. His style was most attractive to her. He wore a pair of light blue skinny jeans (but not too skinny), a light blue jean jacket with a pink and blue rose on the back over a white V-neck t-shirt. To top it off he wore a pair of navy blue Vans and a New York Yankees snap cap to accentuate the blue inside the rose. The icing on the cake, the navy blue stitched "True Love" under the rose. As he passes by her she can't help the cheesy smile that spreads across her face. The fresh, simplicity of the outfit was a turn on by its self. His face matched it. Not over the top or gorgeous, just genuinely satisfying. Real.

"Uhm, uhm, uhm. A damn cop getting drawn in by a drug dealer," Lee Lee says, snapping her out of her reverie.

"Huh?"

"*'Huh?'* Nothing. Him," she says pointing at the man walking towards the exit.

"Nobody's 'drawn in' by anyone. I just was appreciating his style. And excuse me Judge Judy, but how would you know he's a drug dealer?" Suffiyah inquires.

"Oh my poor, naïve baby. Sit down so I can break it down to you." She really waits to get to a bench before continuing, "Eyes and posture. Eyes can lie but the posture will reveal the lie the eyes tell. Then, posture can lie but the eyes will reveal the lie the postures telling. They will never tell the same lie concurrent. But they can tell the same truth. When eyes and posture are in agreement, they create the true presence. Your little boy toy's presence was the streets. He is the embodiment of the 'hood. Tighten up, Virgin Mary, and let's finish shopping."

Benji walks to his van feeling like a new man. After following Detective Adams and her friend to the mall, he couldn't resist getting close to her. Her *1Million Prive* perfume by Paco Rabbane still lingers in his nose. His stride or smile hasn't faltered since he saw the way she inadvertently blushed and smiled at his amorous intentions. He feels he deserved that moment after sitting in the car for hours. Running from nail salon and spas, to beauty parlors and the mall, he needed to stretch his legs. Yeah, exactly. He needed to stretch his legs and what better place to do so than the mall?

Suffiyah and Alicia sit in Zin Burger awaiting their food. She is extremely and genuinely appreciative for God placing Lee Lee in her life. Days like today are a perfect example of that blessing. "Okay. So tomorrow it's back to the real world. Today's fairytale is expiring oh so quickly and the ugly world will be waiting for you. What you gonna do, Sufee?"

"Speak English, Lee."

"What are you going to do, Suffiyah?"

"I'm going to play it by ear. I need to work and prove to the world, especially our world, that all cops aren't 'pigs'. That was the dream that I joined the force with. How could I give up on my dream, Lee?"

"Baby, hear me and hear me clear. You have to be as realistic with yourself as possible. You sweat at night and jump in your sleep. You can't even rest properly. Sweetie, living your dream is all good. But be real enough to accept when a dream becomes a nightmare."

CHAPTER 5

"**Y**OU ARE KILLING ME."
The woman says as she wiggles out of her skin-tight jeans. Her beau is insatiable. At a time in her life when she needed someone the most, he appeared. In her twenty-five short years of living, no one has been more attentive or loving then him. There is nothing she wouldn't do for him. If he asked for the Sun, she'd become Apollo and bring it to him on a chariot. So, as they drove through Newark in his van and he asked her to show him her wild side, she agreed. She held his hand as he led her through an alleyway to a backyard. She doesn't know anyone in Newark, so she isn't as nervous as she should be. If caught, she'll never see her captors again. So, the embarrassment will be temporary. This ideology is what now has her on a picnic table with her pubis exposed. The cool night air causes her nipples to stiffen as she removes her bra. His hand caresses her breast immediately as he covers her mouth with his own. His kisses create a fire in her that combats the chill. His hands rub from the nape of her neck to the soft, ample flesh of her buttocks. Gently he pushes her down flat on the table. Her sex pulsates in anticipation of his entry. Tilting her head back as to give him access to her throat. He loves to choke her when they make love. It turns her on just knowing she's turning him on.

"Mmm," she moans as he slides into her walls.

He accustoms her to his thickness before picking up speed. Just as his thrusts quicken she feels his fingers wrapping around her neck. She lifts her pelvis to meet his rhythm, heightening her ecstasy. Suddenly his grip tightens. *I can't breathe.* She thinks. She slaps his hand to signal him to loosen up. She now realizes she's feeling a gloved hand. This causes him to squeeze harder. Her ecstasy swiftly changes to panic. *Why?* Attempting to flail and get away proves futile as he overpowers her and continues to sex her. She tries to scratch him to get him off her, but to no avail. The jacket he's wearing protects his arm. *Daddy!* Her eyes are wide as possible as her father opens his arm in the background. The closer he gets the less she fights. As he wraps his arms around her everything becomes calm. Her father passed away and left her when she was six, she always knew he'd come back for her, someday.

~ ~ ~

Love? Thinks the killer as he enters his van. *Why does everyone feel that they deserve love? She was so needy. I could see the love in her eyes. I bet she won't look at anyone like that again.* He chuckles out loud. *Love was stolen from me, didn't I deserve it? Didn't I deserve better? I suffered, now she has to suffer.* His mental rant continues as he drives aimlessly with no destination. Twenty minutes later he stabbed the tire of the car and as the air fizzed out of the tire, so did the frustration in his body. The silence as he gets back in his car seems ominous. He turns on 102.7 Fresh FM and bops his head along to Taylor Swift.

Early the next morning the light but steady flow of rain gives the day a dreary feel. Looking out the window at the slick streets and muddy curbs, makes Suffiyah want to call out. It's been three weeks since that peculiar phone call that served as the prelude to a murder. Alicia's words resonate inside Suffiyah's head, tugging at her conscience. A sense of hopelessness washes over her. Whether it's the weather or life in general, only God knows. But it's weighing her down, whatever it may be.

~ ~ ~

Officer Walker patrols the area lazily, regretting the decision to come in today. The high rate of shootings in Newark as of recently has him on the beat. So not only is he on his feet all day, he's on his feet all day in the rain. He can't smoke a whole cigarette without it getting soaked to the filter, which has him beyond cranky. Taking a mental assessment of his current condition, he realizes he's cold, hungry, tired, wet, craving a smoke and worst of all, only one hour into an eight-hour shift. Just as that thought plays in his mind, a group of kids rush from an alleyway and turn in the opposite direction. But he doesn't miss the look of shock on their faces. If they set anything on fire back there he's going to track them down and kick their asses!

~ ~ ~

"Hello?"

"Good morning, Suffiyah," comes the emotionless voice. "Don't hang up or Alicia can be next," he promises. Suffiyah's breath becomes ragged at the mention of Lee's name. "I see I have your attention. Perfect."

~ ~ ~

Officer Walker announces himself as police as he approaches the alley.

~ ~ ~

"If you tell anyone about these calls, it's to your detriment. Or the detriment of those you love. If you change your number, I'll find you. If you don't believe me check the back tire. No one's invisible, Detective."

~ ~ ~

"Police! If anyone's back here speak up!"

~ ~ ~

"There's another body suffering somewhere, can you help it? Do you feel her suffering? Can you find her? There are so many ladies who look like you."

~ ~ ~

Officer Walker runs to the backyard as he sees a woman sprawled out. He draws his gun as he approaches. He spots the woman on the ground move. She shakes her head as if to regain focus.

"Ma'am?"

"Some kids knocked me in my head and snatched my fucking phone."

~ ~ ~

"But only one you, so I'll find everyone who looks like you and wipe them out. When they're all gone and it's just you and me, I'll make you suffer as you made me suffer." The call ends.

~ ~ ~

Life is funny sometimes and not like "ha ha" amusing funny, but funny peculiar. Or funny contradicting or better yet, funny heartbreaking. Yeah, funny heartbreaking. That's the exact funny that Detective Suffiyah Adams is experiencing. Is she unworthy of happiness? She's never met her birth parents, so that bond is nil. According to her third set of foster guardians, she was taken from her first foster parents at the age of four. Then placed in an orphanage for two years, before ending up with the Richardsons.

She appreciates there sheltering her, clothing and raising her. Granting her a life of normalcy from six to eighteen years-old, when she was old enough to be considered grown and shipped off to college. They were financially well off, but morally poor. They didn't exhibit a parental love for her. It was like a forced attachment. She was treated as a charity case, cared for but with very little affection. In her mind she believed she was adopted only as a means to atone for some sins they committed. Sort of a tax write off to God. So, at the tender age of fourteen she lost her virginity to a sixteen year-old boy who promised her love. A love she could hold and cherish, as she never remembered being held or cherished. His promise broke with her hymen. Her life became a testament to looking for love in all the wrong places. She doesn't regret her actions, but she does wish she could amend them. After a high school friend was murdered and she saw the sorrow in his mother's face months after his murder went unsolved, she decided on law enforcement. The appreciation and love she would get, from the families that she brought closure, would be priceless. She could make a difference. Then she was shot in the shoulder and head. *Heartbreak.* The job she loved almost killed her. She healed up and returned to work with elation. Then came the phone call. *Heartbreak.* The same heartbreak which now has her balled up on the floor, bawling her eyes out. How can things be so out of control? What kind of hate could motivate someone to be so evil? Unbeknownst to most, therapy has been required throughout most of Suffiyah's life. Through bouts of depression, Alicia pulled her from the darkest moments. So, to hear of her life being placed in jeopardy for her has broken Suffiyah. Refusing to be a victim or allow Alicia to, she stands up. On wobbly legs but a renewed sense of determination, she faces the day. Correcting her momentary lapse of courage, she dresses and heads out. Arriving at her car she walks around giving it a thorough inspection. No scratches, busted windows or more importantly, flat tires. She looks up at the camera, which watches over the parking lot and wishes the caller would have been careless enough to have slashed her tire.

She pulled out her parking spot with an abundance of confidence. Her lieutenant could help her with this problem. Her phone rings startling her, but she smiles when she sees Alicia's picture on the screen. Switching to the cars Bluetooth, she picks up.

"Talk to me, Boo!" she sings through the receiver.

"What? You had sex or something?" Lee Lee asks.

"What?" Suffiyah laughs, "Why you say that?"

"You all happy and shit. Singing out at 7 o'clock in the morning. Lay your ass down, it's too early." Alicia's words drip attitude.

This makes Suffiyah laugh harder. "Well no, I still didn't have sex and apparently from your tone, neither did you. Now, I'm happy because your call just made my morning. I love you, my sister."

"Sorry Sufee. I love you too. My morning has been going from bad to worse. First, I caught my period two days early all over my good sheets. Then, I realize I've overslept. So, I have to rush and get ready for work. After showering, I have my outfit all planned out, so I can at least look cute. I throw my clothes on and guess what? I can't find my shoes." Suffiyah giggles because she can envision Lee Lee's exaggerated hand motions while she tells her story. "I search all over the apartment. They're gone. Why? Because I left them at your house. Now I'm running late and dressed funny. I get outside and jump in the car and pull off. I notice that it's driving funny. I guess I rode over a nail, because my tire just went flat. Now, to make me even later, I have to go to the tire shop. I get there and try to get the dude at the tire shop to hurry but he's stuck staring at my cleavage. Sidebar, as bad as my day's going, my girls," she says referring to her breasts, "are on point! Poppi changed my tire for free!" she cackles. "But anyway, this the icing on the cake. Wasn't no nail. He said somebody stabbed my fucking tire…" *If you tell anyone about these calls, it's to your detriment. Or the detriment of those you love. If you change your number, I'll find you. If you don't believe me check the back tire. No one's invisible, Detective.'* Heartbreak.

CHAPTER 6

THE CEMETERY IS A PLACE which signifies an end to life. Most visitors pass through and never come back, but not Benji. He's here so often the grounds keeper knows him on a first name basis. He walks through the graveyard as if it's a park. A blanket in one hand and food in the other. No matter the weather, he spends most of his lunch breaks with Sakinah. As Benji arrives at her gravesite, he kisses his fingers and presses them to her headstone. "Good afternoon, baby girl," he says as he lays the blanket down. Taking a seat with his back to the headstone, he places his head in his hands. "It's never been an easy life, period. But without you here, I swear it's much harder. How can a city ever be good enough when you've had the world? Remember you made me watch that movie with Ashton Kutcher and Bernie Mac? *'Guess Who?'*" Benji laughs at the memory. "It's so funny because Ashton Kutcher says the girl is the fifty to his hundred and without her he can never be whole. You remember what I said? Ha ha, I said 'That's some movie shit'." The amused look fades slowly from his face as a tear slides down his cheek. "But it wasn't because I haven't been whole in two years, Ma. I saw a woman who looks so much like you in every way, and it made me cry. I'm not going to lie, I be so mad. Mad at you for leaving me, mad at me for not being there for you, but mostly mad at God. If He loves us how could He take you? Get this though, she's a cop, *Boo*. Ironic right? The woman who looks just like you, is one of the people who still haven't found your killer. Just got your file sitting around collecting dust, but I swear on your memory I won't stop searching. I was just working a case for Ferming but I'm done. It's weird because..."

Benji talks to her non-stop for two hours. As he drives away he feels a mixture of relief and sorrow. Relief because he spoke to his only love and sorrow because no matter how much he speaks his only love will never speak back.

"Detective Adams, if you don't open up how can I help you?" Dr. Jackson, asks.

These session are one of the mandated orders given to Suffiyah. But this is the very first one where she is being unproductive. She's so unsure of what to say, and not to say, that she decided not to say anything.

"I'm just feeling so much better that it's not much to talk about."

"Oh? So why are you crying?" Suffiyah, touches her face and to her surprise it's stained with tears. Alicia's words comes back to her, *"Posture could lie and the eyes will reveal the lie postures telling."*

Benji, steps into his office and grabs the stack of mail. He throws his coat on the sofa as he sifts through the mail. Getting behind his desk, he sits and powers on the computer. All this activity as of lately has sidetracked him from preparing this month's editorials. He tosses the bills one piece at a time until he gets to an envelope which is heavier than the others. The return address is Benji's apartment, but it isn't his handwriting. Curiosity gets the better of him and he picks up the letter opener. Allowing the contents to spill out, the pictures fall out on the desk. The last thing out is a letter.

Dear Just Benjamin,

Excuse my forwardness, but I'm an avid reader of Why We Bang. Your journalistic skills are above average and makes your stories transcend the boundaries of the paper and become part of our life. The problems are our own, the victims are no longer just names in an article. Instead, through the vigor of your pen, you render us unable to abscond from the harsh realities we avert our eyes from. Your work makes us empathize with the oppressed, battered and murdered in contrast to sympathizing with them for a second then forgetting them the next. I applaud your dedication and craftiness but still, I remain befuddled. Why is it you so eloquently and aggressively attack and express the problems of the world, but elude your own? Pardon the frankness of my words, but I'm under the impression that they must be said. You are like Superman, in the sense you left your world to meddle in affairs of others elsewhere. Nothing of our world can hurt or harm you. Superman's home planet was Krypton and it was destroyed. Blasted into small chunks of rocks, some which landed on earth, and labeled "kryptonite". He was too strong for everything in this entire world. But the tiniest bit of his world renders him powerless and can kill him. So my analogy is, your world is to you, what Superman's world is to him. Believe me? No? Okay, well here are fragments of your destroyed world.

Sincerely,
Just A. Fan

His eyes fell immediately to the pictures which lie face down on his desk. With a trembling hand, he grabs them collectively. Sakinah, lies nude in each picture taken from various angles. Her beautiful face contorted into an ugly sneer, forever frozen. All the pictures are postmortem and the bruises around her neck are very light. Which means these images were taken right after the murder. Which also means this is her murderer taunting him. As he sit back drained of everything and feeling faint, the analogy begins to make sense. A little bit of his world kills him the same as superman.

After this morning's session with Dr. Jackson, Suffiyah left his office with more stress than she came in with. There were so many shooting and murderers this year, that she and the rest of the detectives hardly see the inside of the office. So as she sits at her desk and looks over the mountains of paper work, it saddens her. Each file is a life taken and relocated to the purgatory which is her job. A double homicide on Johnson Avenue. A body in an apartment in East Orange. A couple set on fire in their car on Dayton Street. Murder after murder after murder.

"Sufee," Sonya calls out as she pokes her head inside the cubicle. "Mcfarl ... what's wrong young lady? You look constipated."

"Nothing." Suffiyah forces a smile. "Just thinking."

"Well food for thought. If it's a man that has your face tore up like that, act like you took a laxative and let that shit go." Suffiyah can't help laughing. "That's my girl! Now anyway, McFarland wants to see you pronto."

Suffiyah gets up and walks to her supervisor's office and knocks before entering.

"You wanted to see me, sir?"

"Adams, come in and close the door." *Close the door?* She thinks, *that's never a good sign.*

She takes a seat and waits and waits to hear why she was summoned. Lt. McFarland, stares her down for a full two minutes in complete silence. This is an interrogation tactic used to unnerve suspects. Suffiyah's familiar with the methods, but baffled by its use on her. Sweat involuntarily rolls from her underarm and down her sides. Leaving a cold wet trail.

"Adams," he begins, "this office is like a family. Don't you agree?" The inquisition rhetorical apparently because he continues as if he asked nothing. "In a family, there should be no secrets. So I'm giving you the opportunity to help me help you. Before that doodoo you're standing in goes from ankle high to your neck." If she was only confused before, now she's utterly stymied.

"I don't understand, Lou." *Could he know about the caller? If so, how? He said tell no one, so why would he tell?*

"Do you know her?" He passed a photo from a crime scene to her, she takes a moment to study it.

"No but she favors the other woman. Almost exactly." ... *so I'll find everyone who looks like you and wipe them out.*

"Exactly. But look closer, in her left hand." Suffiyah, stares at a photo of a young woman naked on a picnic table and feels guilty. She now sees the card tucked in her fingers. As if he was following her eyes, the lieutenant speaks, "Your card again. Different scene, same m.o., assumedly same perp and as the last time, same card. So I ask you for the second time, do *you* know her? Internal Affairs is all over this, all over you. We as a family can keep a secret from I.A., but as a family, we can't keep secrets from each other." Sliding the picture closer, he asks once more, "Who is she?"

"I don't know, honestly."

"God dammit, Adams! Cut the shit, is it a coincidence that they both favor you?" *He's really using all of his interrogations tricks on me.*

"Lou, what are you implying?" she asks, becoming angry.

"What am I implying? What am I! Fuck it, give me your shield. I tried to help you but no. Believe this though Su-fee-yah, when the shit hits the fan, and it will hit the fan, it's going to blow right in your face. And I'll be right there grinning. You're on leave. Get the fuck outta my office."

A glint of anger lingers in her eyes. As much as she would like to display her bellicosity, she refrains. Sometimes the best weapon against the ignorance of others is to remain dignified. Suffiyah stands and adjusts her blazer. "Yes Sir, Lt. McFarland," she says gracefully allowing her submissiveness to manifest.

Next Morning

Benji gives himself the once over in the full length mirror. His smile brightens his aura immensely. As he stands there, in a pink dress shirt that fits the contour of his torso to perfection, navy blue trousers and brown ostrich skin shoes with the belt to match, his pride soars. So far removed is he from the menace that he once loved to identify with. He places the plain face, brown band Movado watch on his left wrist. This every day, run of the mill time piece is his most valued treasure in the world. As he adjusts the band his mind drifts. *"My dream man? Hmmm?" Sakinah contemplates the question. Benji rolls over on the bed to face her and props himself up on his elbow, awaiting her answer. His eyes roam over her exposed body as she lays there. Her skin is flawless to the point of faultlessness. Her breast full with a set of always erect nipples that have a pinkish brown hue. Now down to the flat stomach with the sunken in belly button, that he always kisses. With her knee bent and perfectly pedicured foot flat on the bed, the upper part of her love box's pinkness stares back at him. Stirring a longing in the pit of his stomach that transfers to his heart and crotch. His gaze backtracks until it's again on her face. Her hair is splayed on the pillow, but not in a clumsy fashion. It's almost regal, like a crown around her head. Her eyes are closed as she thinks. Her nose is the right proportion for her face. The lips full but the bottom a little fuller, lending them a heart shape. "What?" Sakinah asks as her cheeks take on a reddish tinge. Her hand wiping at her mouth embarrassed at what she imagines is dry slob. Benji meets her gaze and the brownish green eyes pause his heartbeat.*

"Nothing," he says as he kisses the tip of her nose. "Stop stalling and answer the question."

She smiles and snuggles closer under the warmth of his body. "My dream man? Well he's your complexion and physical stature. He's aware of the world around him, all while never losing sight of the world in front of him. Brave enough to fight everyone, but intelligent enough to realize he doesn't need to. He'll make me feel as safe under him, as

I feel right now. His swaggers unmatched because it's not an act, it's just him. He'll be debonair and gentlemanly, not street." She feels his body tense with jealousy. She continues, "Yeah, definitely not street, but still his own boss. And..." Suddenly she leans over the side of the bed and searches for something on the floor. "...he'll be wearing this." Her hand produces a watch as she settles back in her spot. "To signify that no matter where he is in life." She looks at Benji with unbridled affection. "He'll always have time for me. My dream man has some characteristics you don't, but I know in my heart, you will someday. That's why, you are my dream man and in the future my reality man." Benji straightens his tie as the lone tear finally finds its way to his chin.

Suffiyah rides the elevator down from the fourth floor of 50 West Market Street, which is the Veterans Courthouse and home to the prosecutor and homicide departments. She forgot to grab some things from her desk yesterday, being she was so upset. She's balancing everything in one arm and conducting a conversation with Alicia via text when the doors open. She's so busy in her phone, she's unaware of the man backing into the elevator until they collide.

"I'm so sorry," they say simultaneously.

He swiftly kneels down to collect her things. As he rises and looks up in her face, his smile intensifies. Suffiyah's smile, on the other hand, subsides and is replaced with a look of disgust. She rudely snatches her belongings that he proffers to her. What she assumed was a hurried attorney turned out to be a drug dealer late for court.

"Thank you. But you should hurry upstairs before you get a contempt of court," she says not even understanding herself why she was being so evil.

"Excuse me?"

"Contempt of court, you know? They can revoke your bail and re-arrest you, then who's going to sell your drugs?"

"Contempt of court? Drugs?" he asks growing agitated, "Shorty, miss me wit' that goofy shit. Every black man in a courthouse isn't a criminal. I'm actually a witness for the defense. Uppity ass females," he mumbles as he enters the elevator. "And for the record, Miss. Drugs are a toxin and main factor of the poverty and lowly family structure in this city. That being said, I'm averse to drug dealing. But enjoy your day, your honor," he says sarcastically. Suffiyah rolls her eyes at the closing elevator doors.

Benji rides up to the ninth floor still fuming from his encounter with Detective Adams. He never pegged her for the judgmental type, but looks can be deceiving. He tries to mentally get back where he was before his unexpected collision.

Suffiyah kicks herself as she watched the elevator stop on the ninth floor. The building frustration of the past weeks, were spewed at the first person she encountered. Alicia's assessment coupled with her own distaste for drug dealers, fueled her outburst. She found herself on the elevator again and sitting in the back row of the courtroom in minutes.

"...so being that one camera on the store sees Weequahic Avenue and the camera on the apartment building, facing Clinton Place, never captures their likenesses. It would be impossible for the statement that the officer gave to be plausible. If he was indeed sitting in Dunkin Donuts parking lot on Lyons Avenue, as I sat, and watched the defendants as he said, they would have to be on either camera. Physical evidence doesn't correspond with his reports."

Suffiyah exits the courtroom as he's dismissed from the stand. When he comes through the door, his face registers surprise and then displeasure as he attempts to push pass her.

"Wait! I apologize." Suffiyah says pleadingly. The man stops and looks at her. "I've been having the worst week and I unfairly took it out on you. It was unjust of me to form an opinion on you with no facts to back it. You only get one chance at a first impression and mines was an utter contradiction to who I truly am. So will you grant me the opportunity to buy you lunch and replace your assessments of me and my preconceived notions, with better ones. Please?" And with that she smiles. If he had any qualms about her request, the sincerity in her smile deleted them.

"Apology accepted. Benji Cooper," he says, extending his hand.

"Suffiyah Adams," she replies accepting his clasp gently.

"Let me take that for you," He offers, taking her belongings.

"Thank you. Even though I don't deserve the chivalry, especially after my performance."

"Nonsense. Every woman is deserving of at least one chivalrous act in her lifetime."

Benji cuffs his shirt sleeves up on his forearms before digging into his food.

"I've honestly never come in here," Suffiyah admits as they sit in Queens 2 Pizzeria on Halsey Street.

"You've been cheating ya self. This the best pizza in Newark, hands down. It used to be across the street on that corner," he says, pointing out the window. "But I guess that building was too dilapidated for them or the move was part of the gentrification that's taking place down here."

"So, since you aren't a drug dealer. I'm gonna take a wild guess and say you're Newark's official tour guide. Am I right?" she jests.

"Ha ha." Benji laughs putting a napkin to his mouth to prevent food from flying out. "So you cute and funny? Nah. But on the real I'm a private investigator. I do mostly freelance work for law firms, but I take on pro bono cases on hate crimes, kidnappings and rapes. Things of that nature, for families who can't afford my services. But I also have another business that I'm not entirely comfortable with disclosing at the moment," confesses Benji.

"I love how you flip the switch. You speak 'hood when you want and in the same breath you make the transition and speak like a professor with little effort. I don't know if you remember but I saw you in the mall, staring at me," she mentions, rolling her eyes playfully.

"I was actually looking at your friend," Benji interrupts.

Embarrassment flushes Suffiyah's face as she regrets her assumption. She doesn't know how she didn't consider he was looking at Lee Lee. "Well, I, you see-"

"See, you're not the only one who knows how to be funny. But I was looking at you though."

She narrows her eyes and flicks her straw wrapper at him. "Anyway! I swore I had you pegged as being in the streets."

"Why?"

"Your aura reeked of the gutter. You looked like a dapper hood rat," she kids.

"What about now? What does my aura *reek* of at the moment?"

"Honestly? Even after hearing you on the stand and talking to you now, your demeanor oozes the streets. It's in your movements, your lingo, your posture and even your eyes. They're like hard and soft at the same time, how? You're an enigma."

"An enigma? Okay, well I'm gonna stick around and let you try to figure out the riddle of Benji. Well, that's if you feel up to the challenge?"

"Challenge accepted." The rest of the lunch went perfectly.

Suffiyah sticks her key in the door and enters the living room. Lee Lee sits on the couch Indian style reading a book. Suffiyah spends majority of her week here after the tire incident. She can't divulge the situation she's placed Lee Lee in, but she can stay to protect her from it.

"Let me have some," Lee says as Suffiyah lays her head on her lap.

"Some what?"

"Of the money." Lee Lee states matter-of-factly.

"Lee Lee, if you smoking crack, we gonna fight," she jokes. "Now what money?"

"It has to be money. This morning you left out looking as miserable as a dog with worms. Tonight though, you walk in showing all 58 teeth and gums. So I figure you had to hit the lottery. Now give me some or stop smiling like the Cheshire Cat."

They both giggled. "How was your day though, Sufee? You look much better."

"Good, Lee. No, great actually. He's not a drug dealer."

"He's not?"

"Nope."

"Well, that's good. Now, let's stop playing 'fill in the blanks', because I don't know what you talking about and you got me fucked up like a black man in Nazi Germany."

"Where do you come up with the things that you say?" Suffiyah laughs. She goes on and tells her the details of her day. By the end of the story she's excited as a kid on Christmas morning.

"That smile is contagious, Sweetie. So what you gonna do about Dr. Love?" Lee Lee asks.

"Dr. Jackson's cool. But he's too extra cute for me. He looks like the type who I'll have to compete for the mirror with every morning. But Benji on the other hand, is cute by default. It's like he's not even trying. At first glance you like, 'He's alright.' Then he starts talking. His vocabulary? Superb! Not like he just heard a word and used it, but he actually *understands* it. He's so articulate. What makes it that much more attractive is he's from the number blocks. Smack dab in the middle of the ghetto! Yet he still grew beautifully, like the rose in the concrete. Do you know how strong that rose has to be to bloom from the harsh, coldness that is the concrete and still retain its essence?"

"Strong enough to hold your heart?"

"Exactly." Suffiyah snuggles into Lee Lee's lap as she plays in her hair and slowly drifts into slumber.

CHAPTER 7

A LITTLE GIRL COWERS IN THE corner of the attic, as the monster frantically searches for her. She silently prays to God that he doesn't look behind the boxes of clothes stacked in front of her. "Suffer! Suffer!" he screams as he flings objects out of his path. "Here you are!" But his voice is coming from across the room, directed at someone unseen. "Now you must suffer with me." The girl peeks from behind the boxes as the monster lifts someone by the collar. "Where is she?" the monster barks. She sees a little finger point in her direction. The monster turns...

Suffiyah wakes up, her heart beating erratically. She looks around expecting to be in the attic. To her pleasure, she's in the bedroom. The clock reads 2:00AM. *Zzzzzz Zzzzzz*, her phone vibrates on the nightstand.

"Hello?" she answers the private number.

"I'm so glad we have come to this understanding, Suffiyah," came the voice. "I was so tired of killing. I'm glad you're finally mine. Come open the door, I'm here."

Suffiyah has given herself over to the killer in exchange for him to cease the murders. She walks to the door and unlocks it. Pulling her door open, she looks down the hallway which is empty.

"I'm here."

"So am I. Look down."

She looks at the floor and her phone drops to the ground at the same time she does. Suffiyah gathers Lee Lee's naked body in her arms and shakes her as she cries. Lee Lee's eyes open slightly as she reaches out for Suffiyah, and wraps her hands around Suffiyah's windpipe and squeezes.

"Sufee! Sufee!"

Lee Lee shakes her awake. It takes a moment for her to realize where she is.

"What's wrong Lee?"

"I don't know. You was the one screaming my name in your sleep. I thought somebody was breaking in. I was 'bout to jump out the window and leave you." Lee Lee smiles while reaching out to touch Suffiyah's sweat soaked forehead. "You wanna talk about it, Su?"

"No, don't worry I'm good. Go get some sleep. We'll talk in the morning, okay?"

"Kay, goodnight." Alicia turns out the living room light on her way back to her bedroom.

Riding the high from his last two successful murders, the killer feels he's entitled to a little celebration. But what? Nothing gives him greater elation than coupling with a woman and enticing her to suffer with him. But he's not naïve enough to believe that he can keep committing the crimes so closely together. If he's believed to be a serial killer too early, the heat will be turned up considerably. So maybe he'll just go on *BackPage* and find a companion for the night. For a couple of well-placed coins, there is nothing one of these women won't do. Isn't it funny how a flimsy green piece of paper can make most humans compromise their morals? Everyone has a price tag in his opinion, you just have to know where to look. Which lands him in *Wet*, a gentleman's club in Belleville. Standing against the wall he observes all the dancers prancing around in G-strings. He traded in his earlier dress clothes for a grittier, urban look. In his work clothes, he would have stood out like a sore thumb in this crowd. He swapped his dress shirt for a form fitting thermal shirt on top of which he wore a Pittsburg Pirates team jacket. His slacks exchanged for a pair of black *Robin* jeans and on his feet a pair of black and yellow Jordan 1's. The three day old stubble on his usually clean shaven face gives him an edgier look. He now resembles every other drug dealer who frequents this establishment.

"Can I get three hundred singles?" he says passing the bartender fifteen twenty dollar bills. He did it in a manner to allow the dancers to see the contents of his pockets. As if on cue, a pretty Spanish girl starts strutting in his direction. She wears a money green G-string with money green pastie stars over her nipples. Her body glistens in the low lights. Dressed up somewhere in the world, she'd be perfect for the title of wife. But in this den of sex and intoxication her title never exceeds prey.

"You watching me, Papi?" she ask sultrily as she pushes her breast into his lower chest.

Looking up in his face for any signs or desperation or thirst, she sees none. The stripper known as "Allure" is use to men openly drooling over her. Gawking at her model beauty and naturally toned thick body. In a world of plastic filled copies, she's an original. As he looks down at her face with an expression that says, "He can do with or without her company", her spider senses started to tingle. This is a man of some means, financially. Unlike most of the rest of the dudes in here with their last $300 and the pipe dream that it will land them a night with a world class vixen, such as herself. Turning her aggressiveness up ten notches, she pulls herself forward by grabbing his coat. With her lips pressed to his earlobe, she whispers.

"Damn Pa, I'm not pretty enough for you?" Her aroma is like fresh fruit and soap topped with the heady scent of sexuality. "Que pasa?" Allure asks nipping his ear erotically as she backs her face up, while allowing her thigh to brush his manhood. This pulls a smile from him as she feels his hands grip her waist. He was caught up in her "allure".

Allure tip toes through the hotel room collecting her clothes. She looks over the bed and considers straddling his naked body and giving him a freebie after last night's sexcapade. But she has to get home to her daughter. She's probably going to be hoarse in the morning from the way he was choking her, but for a thousand dollars for the night, she would have let him punch her in the eye.

"Somebody had a date last night, huh?" Suffiyah asks.

"If a date was work, then yeah. An all-nighter. You checkin' for me?" Benji asks her.

After their lunch date they've been speaking by phone regularly.

"Nah not *checkin'* for you, just checking on you. I called you like three times last night."

"I fell asleep on the sofa in my office. I apologize for missing your call. I saw it when I woke up at like 3:00am, but I would never intrude on your night like that, so I waited until now."

"I was up. I couldn't really sleep. You ever been to *Top Golf?*"

"No, where is it?"

"Edison. How would you like to meet me and Lee Lee, there?"

"Sounds cool. So that's why we haven't had a date, no chaperone?"

"Ha-ha, yeah something like that. But look call me later, okay?"

"Got 'chu. Later."

Suffiyah crisscrosses her toes over each other as she finally tinkles. She ended the call because she didn't want him to hear the toilet flush. That would have been embarrassing. What if he would have assumed she was defecating? Not really the vision of her that she wants in his head. She was so excited to see him call, she hurriedly pressed accept before realizing that she was on the toilet. She finishes her business and washes her hands before leaving the bathroom. The morning looks so beautiful and peaceful. Suffiyah lifts the blinds all the way up to enjoy the view. It's funny how detached a picture can be from the actual griminess that surrounds it. Looking at the world from a window makes you want to become part of the beauty and live the scene. Until you enter the portrait and experience all the unseen ills that inhabit it. Then the only thing you wish to do is run back to your looking glass and away from the actuality. It's so much easier to watch life then it is to live it. As Suffiyah comes out of her thoughts, she notices most of the passersby are looking in her direction. Some are smiling, a woman shakes her head, and an older man gives her the thumbs up. For about five seconds her face is a mask of confusion. She suddenly snatches at the blinds causing them to shut. Her morning routine is to go to the window and enjoy what the world could be and pretend that it is not what it truly is. But she lives on the 8th floor, Alicia doesn't. So from the 3rd floor apartment window, all the neighbors who were out had seen Suffiyah in nothing but a pair of lacy boy short panties.

Alicia keeps looking over at Suffiyah smirking.

"Lee Lee, if you laugh I'm going to punch you in your eye." Lee Lee bursts into laughter.

"How you mad at me 'cause you showed the neighbors those bullets you call nipples? Shit, I should be mad at you. You gonna have everyone walking pass looking at my window like one of those Red Light rooms in Amsterdam." She makes light of the situation as they drive to *Top Golf*. "Then to add insult to injury you get downright gorgeous for tonight. Jeans amplifying your booty, titties spilling out your shirt, hair on fleek. Did you shave? Never mind, ten times out of ten you did, so coochie on fleek. I just have one question. Are we hoeing or golfing? Let me know now so I can be prepared." Lee Lee's humor is contagious, Suffiyah can't help laughing.

"Lee Lee, I swear your mother birthed a whole clown."

Benji pulls into the parking lot of *Top Golf*, which is as big as a warehouse. He's nervous like a kid on his first date, maybe more so. The kid only has to impress and entertain one girl, he has to double that. He spots Suffiyah getting out of a Nissan Murano and finds a spot close to them. After spraying on his *Bvlgari* cologne, he takes a deep breath before getting out. He glances at his reflection in the car window. The green and yellow varsity jacket from *Who R U* fits as if it was custom made solely for him. Underneath he wears a yellow *Polo* rugby with green writing. Dark blue *Zara* jeans fall onto his crisp construction *Timberlands*. In *H&M* he happened upon a hunter green skullcap that matched his jacket perfectly. Dentyne is keeping his breath pleasant. His outfit is on point and thanks to *Bvlgari* he smells excellent. He walks towards the women who have their backs to him.

"Good evening, ladies?" They jump at the sound of his voice. "Sorry. I thought y'all saw me pull in."

"No, Lee Lee had me distracted," Suffiyah says leaning in for a hug. "Benjamin. Alicia." She makes the introductions formally. "Hurry up and shake hands before I freeze."

As they enter *Top Golf,* the ladies lead him straight to the bar. "Can we have two Apple Cirocs and apple juices?" Alicia orders. "And?" she adds while looking at Benji.

"A double shot of Grey Goose and a bottle of water," he replies. "Let me take y'all coats." As he helps Suffiyah out of her trench coat, his jaw almost drops. Next he helps Alicia. "Damn, y'all look gorgeous. I feel like I'm not dressed right."

"Nah, you pulled your little ensemble off, especially with the reading glasses. You don't smell too bad either," Suffiyah compliments. "I see you showered since we last saw one another."

"Jokes huh? Say no more. I appreciate the compliments even though they came with a dig." He pays for their drinks, and then two more rounds for the ladies.

As they prepare to play golf Lee Lee speaks, "I see you only had one drink while we had three. What you up to, Casanova?"

"Ha ha. Nothing at all. I just don't overindulge anymore. There was stint in my life when things were so real for me, that I damn near lived in a bottle. Drugs have never really been my twist, feel me? So I used the alcohol to cope with the everyday pain of reality."

"Oh okay. Understandable. What high school did you go to?"

"Westside."

"Did you love your school?"

"A little bit. Why you ask that?" He smiles.

"You must've really loved your school to tattoo it," Lee Lee says with suspicion in her eyes.

Damn. Who's the investigator me or her? Benji thinks. He can see in what direction her questioning is heading. He can either duck her inquisition now and be viewed as a liar later or tell the truth and see how it plays out.

Fuck it. "Aiight, check. We gonna do this two second style. I can see where your line of questioning is going, so let's get it over with. Any questions asked I'll answer, truthfully. Shoot."

"Why do I get the drug dealer vibe from you?"

"Because I'm a street dude and everybody who isn't from the streets think we all sell drugs. Have I ever? Yeah, when I was younger. But, I read a book called *African American Organized Crime* and it made me see drugs for the poison they are. Next?"

"Why you got Westside tattooed on you?"

"Because I'm a blood and—"

"Okay dates terminated. Let's go Suffiyah, you not fucking up your career over a gangbanger. I refuse..." Lee Lee says as she pulls Suffiyah.

"Suffiyah!" Benji says in an assertive way without yelling, causing both women to halt. "I gave y'all the opportunity to question me about anything and I would answer honestly. All I ask is that you afford me the opportunity to answer and hear me out." Seeing they were no longer moving, he continued. "Blood as y'all see it and Blood as it was created differ greatly. I was once ignorant enough to follow blood as y'all see it but through maturity and growth, I left it behind. I no longer identify with a set. I am Blood by essence, not affiliation. I told you I had another business, right? I run a magazine called *Why We Bang.*" Benji hesitated for a moment. He didn't want to tell them about the magazine. At least not yet. Both women gave him a peculiar look. For a moment they believed that Benji was lying. He continued to speak. "It touches on the roots of the atrocities being committed which first gave Blood necessity. Google it, then judge me. Machiavelli said, 'He who has not first laid his foundations may be able with great ability to lay them afterwards, but they will be laid with trouble to the architect and danger to the building.' Blood has a bad stigma behind it and I'm willing to fix it, even to my detriment. This is my dream. You became a cop to create a safer environment for our people, and I embrace Blood for the same reason. America and France both fought Hitler. I say that to say, just because we in two different armies doesn't mean we don't fight the same war. I'm gone though, enjoy the rest of y'all night."

How is it, that sometimes silence is louder than words? The quietness like a probe searching your conscience in search of guilt. Suffiyah sits and wonders as they drive home saying little. "Lee Lee? What did you think? Was he telling the truth?"

The look on Benji's face was heart wrenching. At first she wanted to see where Lee Lee's interrogation would lead, until she experienced the aftershock. So many emotions played on his façade. Embarrassment fused with anger which allowed a hint of sadness that transformed into contempt.

"I told you, eyes and posture—"

"Cut the psychological BS Alicia! Please? Just answer me," Suffiyah explodes with so much feeling in her voice it causes Lee Lee to pull over on the shoulder and look at her.

"Su, why are you crying?"

"That was messed up, Lee. Did you see his *face*? I have never seen a man that genuinely hurt because of me. It's like we dragged him out here to ambush him. Oh my God! Did we? We did, didn't we? That was so evil and I feel like a coward. I could have asked him when I saw his tattoo at lunch, but *nooo*," she says exaggerating the word, "I had to push my responsibility on you. Now what?" Lee Lee shifts her body in her seat to face Suffiyah.

"Now you stop beating yourself up. One, I believe he was 100% sincere in his answers and feelings toward you. But two, which is always the number of something stinky, for the better or worse of it, he admitted to being in a gang. He never downplayed his former ignorance, to his credibility. But, you do understand some of those unsolved cases you have sitting around can easily have his name on them? And if so, how do you separate emotions from business? Sweetie, you are a detective and he's a Blood. Your lifestyle can only increase his worth in the eyes of the world. But on the other hand, how does his lifestyle make you look? I'm sorry, but all I can see out of this union is pain and suffering."

CHAPTER 8

S PRING TIME IS OFFICIALLY HERE. The flowers are starting to bloom as lawns transform back to the full beauty that winter robbed it of. Everything is rejuvenated, given a renewed sense of life. Well almost everything. In two different parts of the city, two people have yet to overcome the effects of the cold winter. Detective Suffiyah Adams clawed her way back to active status. Working cases with a cold vehemence, foreign to her style. They say your job should be something you do, but your career should be something you love. For Suffiyah it was, now she loathes it. Love at first sight is a myth. A fairytale created for people to have faith in the imaginary thing called, a soul mate. These are things that Suffiyah tells herself, but the pain that reverberates through her chest with every heartbeat tells a different story. Her career deprived her of her myth. Of her fairytale. She had to choose, or better yet feared the outcome of not choosing, work over a man. A man she barely knew, who quite possibly would have rejected her, a blow her pride couldn't withstand. So she returned to work with no love and sheer determination. There was no "Sufee" in the office, just Suffiyah. No longer was this a place of family, just a place of business. On her lunch she sat at her desk and read. Printed in bold font, the title statement of the article screamed for attention.

Man sentenced to 85 years for vicious gangland murder.

This title is one that piques the interest of all who come across it. As humans, majority of us have a morbid infatuation with death and imprisonment. Regarding the names in the editorial as breathless characters in contrast to being sons or daughters. This perception allows us to detach ourselves from the aftermath of the incident, but that is not my perception. Dwayne Richards, a nineteen year old father of two, murdered Alfonso Jeffries, a twenty-two year old father of two. Two young men swayed into believing their only alternative to success in Cincinnati, Ohio was the business of the streets. Entrenched in strife, forgotten by the government and ensconced in poverty, these two fathers sought refuge in their only available resource. The streets. Fast forward to the day of the tragedy, in which we will see two "thugs" willing to die over the drug trade, instead of seeing two providers seeking to protect the only means of feeding their families. Until one laid in the throes of death as the other fled into the night. For those who only followed this story, it ended for you when Dwayne Richards was sentenced to 85 years. But to those of us who live this story with them, such as myself, it has only just begun. I went to visit both families and though there was only one casket, two men actually died. But only one was physical. Four children were orphaned. Two mothers were mugged of their hearts, yet we move on. How? Both men each had a son that may follow in their footsteps. Replaying the same chain of events that are concurrent worldwide. Not *only in the ghettoes of America, but the slums of Ireland, the tenements of Jerusalem and villages of Africa. Only thing which can change these events are the initial change of self. Then unifying as a race. Not a race as far as nationality, but as a race of human beings. Together we can persevere the ills of the world. Never give up. Never stop fighting. If success was a sprint, the world would be successful. But because it is a marathon, few remain to see the goal. I'm no terrorist. I'm not anti-government, I'm just pro-us. Let's save us. My words end here, but never the love. Peace!*

Just Benjamin

His words resound with the effects of a hammer. Suffiyah has ordered every issue of *Why We Bang* printed. Reading his words are like hearing him speak, so this is how she calls on him.

The teacher excuses himself from his class and leaves them with Benji. After the incident at *Top Golf,* he dug deeper into his work. Creating a mentoring nonprofit company called MISFITS. Part of that venture is going to high schools and speaking to the students. He always asks for the teachers to leave so he can have the youths comfortable enough to speak freely. Only way to amend faulty thinking is to get to the root of it. So the kids have to be able to express themselves without judgment.

"Good afternoon, young brothers and sisters. First and foremost, y'all see I got rid of the teacher so we can kick it and be a hundred with each other. No outsiders."

Twenty-two students and forty-four eyes watch him with suspicion as he rolls up his sleeves. Their eyes settle on the tattoos that adorn his forearms. This is the icebreaker to gain their trust. Anyone who is from the streets can read the story his arms tell.

"My name is Mr. Cooper. I represent Misfits." The kids laugh.

"What the fuck is Misfits? A clown school?" A young male asks causing the laughter to amplify. Bingo. He's exactly who Benji was looking for, the class spokesman.

"Me." Benji says. "And you. And her. And majority of the class. Misfits is an acronym which stands for Misguided Individuals Seeking Fortune in the Streets. I chose that name to represent us street individuals. A name that has no age, nor ethnicity, nor gender. A name that defines you..."

After class Benji sits in his van and processes his progression. Years ago you couldn't pay him to go to high school. Now he goes to multiple high schools, for free. His charisma and upfront demeanor wins over the most rambunctious teenagers. He gives them his whole life, in exchange for just a small glimpse of theirs. *Time to get back to work.*

CHAPTER 9

"DETECTIVE ADAMS, SINCE YOUR RETURN you seem..." He thinks for a second, "For lack of a better word perturbed. Your demeanor is standoffish and insulting to some of your co-workers. You once walked around with warmth emanating from you, which has been replaced with frigidness. These are just my observations. I would love to hear yours." Dr. Jackson turns the floor over as he crosses one leg over the other.

His waves are perfect as though he had them drawn in. Sitting with quiet arrogance in his gray slacks and powder blue dress shirt with suspenders. The gold *Oyster Perpetual Rolex* gleams in the office light. He looks like he's posing for a *GQ* magazine cover instead of working. Why couldn't she feel for him? It would be so easy. Their lives and work are so similar. How could it end badly? She remembers at the first lunch with Benji, he said, *"Everybody's regular around here. By regular I mean the same. Damn near every man and woman emulates the next until their like the same entity. Fad chasers. It's so easy to fit in and be invisible. Overlooked. But to stand out and be accounted for, that's hard. To put your flaws on the forefront and be judged by a condescending world. Anything easy is usually not worth having. But the thing that is hardest to attain and keep is usually worth more than we can imagine. That's why my realness is my greatest treasure. Because it's priceless and its nothing anyone could trade me for it."*

"I would say I'm bitter. But who wouldn't be? I returned to a job I almost died for, only to be a victim to gossip and suspicion. Given a shove out the door as if I was a panhandler. Defamed by my lieutenant, decried by my peers. Then cheated out of a life that would have been hard to live, but I know I would have loved. Only to crawl back here and swallow my dignity, my pride. Have I no right to be bitter?"

"What is the life you were cheated of?" Dr. Jackson, steeples his fingers together while looking at her quizzically.

"I met someone, but our occupations don't agree or complement each other. Or so I've been told. So to save this life, I traded that one. Did you ever hear that song when Alicia Keys asks, *'Have you ever tried sleeping with a broken heart?'*? Well my answer is yes. For many months now and I'm still trying."

Benji stands on the balcony of his hotel room. Never one to be particularly religious, he just stares at the sky. "If you exist, what's Your problem with me? Everything You place in my life for a moment, You snatch back. You aren't nothing but an Indian giver. I cry and cry, while You are up there laughing at me. What do I have?" Warm arms wrap around his waist as a feminine frame presses into his back and rests her head in the crevice between his shoulder blades. He instinctually goes to cover her hands with his own and just like that, the presence disappears. "Nothing." Benji answers himself.

Duty calls. There were two more murders in Essex County. In the first, a twenty-seven year old Hispanic man sat in his car as a masked assailant rapidly approached the driver's side window. Opening fire into the dark tinted window and striking the victim in the chest three times. He was rushed to the hospital and listed in critical condition. But his nine year old daughter, who was in the passenger's seat, was shot through the left eye and pronounced dead on arrival by EMT's. Every scene is depressing but a murdered child is Suffiyah's *Achilles Heel*. To see the innocence which is a child, displayed in such a macabre fashion is beyond too much for her. Which leads her here to the second scene. This seedy, drug infested hotel on Halsey Street is a hot bed for depraved crack whores, dealers, and all walks of the underworld. The tenants of the establishment peek out their rooms nosily, in an attempt to get a glimpse of the cause of the commotion. Suffiyah holds her breath in as she prepares herself for the image she's about to walk in to. The pent up breath escapes her lungs in relief. Instead of a nude "Suffiyah" look alike, with her card on their person, there is a gorgeous Spanish woman. She lies on the bed in a defensive position, which means she died fighting. She looks to be about 5'6 with a body worth millions. Her perfect nails and expensive clothes which are strewn over the floor, reveals her status is far above others who frequent here. Ronald Eastman walks beside her.

"Nice to see you, Detective."

"Morning, Ronnie. What could you tell me?"

"Facts. She definitely had consensual sex before whatever led to this." Motioning for her to follow him to the body. "Look at her neck. The marks are conducive of strangulation, which first led me to believe our perp had struck again. Though the physical description has changed, that isn't abnormal. But these," he points to her face. "Don't fit his modus operandi." Her face is bruised, the upper lip split, her eye shows a popped blood vessel. "The perp was angry. No control like at the previous scenes, Detective. Too much testosterone was in this room. Luckily, we were able to bottle some of it up. Our guy left some DNA."

"That's great! Hopefully it matches something in our database. Do we have identification?"

"Aaliyah Perez. A twenty-three year old from Harlem, New York."

"What is she doing in Newark?"

"If I could answer that question, then I'd be doing your job along with my own."

Suffiyah smiles. "Thanks Ronnie."

Marie Ciccio, is a thirty-something, history teacher. Equipped with all the traditional assets that give Italian women a classic beauty. Long hair, grace, a fiery attitude and a hint of her mother tongue fused with her English.

"Mr. Cooper, what is it you say that's so special or secret, that I can't hear it?" she asks Benji, as she sits on the edge of her desk with her arms crossed. Her knee length skirt shows off her muscular calves, accentuated by her high heels. He could tell that underneath the clothes lays a body of a Goddess.

"No secrets, Mrs. Ciccio-"

"Ms.," she says with emphasis while dramatically flashing her ring-less left hand.

"Pardon me, Ms. Ciccio. But it's really to create a less scrutinized environment for the students. Without fear of disciplinary consequences or judgment, they'll give you their hearts. They just need to know the person their passing it to will care for it and protect it. That's my burden and no disrespect to you or any other administrator, but I don't know you well enough to share the task."

"You speak of it with such romance and passion. I'm going to give you my students but they come with a price," she says staring. "...Lunch. You owe me lunch afterwards. And for the record I'm great with hearts. If I'm allowed to get my hands on one, I treat it as my own," she says as the bell sounds and the students start spilling in. In the blink of an eye the lust disappears from her gaze and is replaced with a more appropriate look, as she breaks her eye contact with Benji. "Settle down, my lovelies. Good morning, unfortunately I will not have the pleasure of your company this period," she explains with the flare of a drama major. "But I will be leaving you to this intriguing gentleman, Mr. Cooper. I ask you to please extend to him the same trust and respect you grant me. Ciao!" she says and sashays from the classroom with a little more twist for Benji's benefit. Benji faces the class and rolls up his sleeves.

Benji stirs the sugar into his Peppermint tea as he sits in the coffee shop. Across from him is Ms. Ciccio, who has shed her glasses and released her dark tresses from its ponytail.

"Not much of a coffee drinker, Mr. Cooper?"

"Nah, it ain't really my twist. Oh pardon me, I meant—"

"Perfectly fine. I understood. Talk as you feel comfortable, it's refreshing."

"Okay. By the way, call me Benji."

"Benji it is."

Over bagels and tea, their discussion touched on the intimate and personal aspects of their lives. Benji found out Ms. Ciccio was a divorced gym rat, who loves yoga and traveling. Only thing that she loves more are her students. Through teaching she's living out her childhood dream. She speaks of it with such fervor, that she creates an atmosphere that makes him want to spill his passions. He starts with MISFITS and goes into *Why We Bang* which, uncharacteristically for him, leads to Sakinah. Sakinah is a hand he keeps close to his chest and reveals to few. His sentiments show on his face as he tells his tale of lost love. Once he gets to her murder, he dances around the specifics to keep from tearing up. As they walk out of the coffee house, Ms. Ciccio slides her slight hand inside his.

"I asked you to speak comfortably," she begins. "So I'll do the same. But I want you to keep looking straight ahead, because I'm shy. If you disagree with what I say, you can let go off my hand and I'll drop the subject. But, if you agree, I will lead you. Okay?"

"Aiight."

"You suffer so much, that words can't begin to remedy your wounds. But I want to ease your pain, because I know I can't stop it. The strongest weapon against pain is love. Since I don't love you, I would like to fuck your pain away. If only for a moment. My home isn't far. Can you allow me to give you a reprieve from your burden?" Benji says nothing but continues to hold her hand. They continue walking with Ms. Ciccio leading.

Suffiyah sits at her desk with her face in her palms. She is extremely fatigued. Today has been an emotional rollercoaster in every sense of the term. First the crime scene pulled at her heart strings. The way these young women are being demoralized by these men. Giving away their virtue trustingly before they turn around and find their souls fleeing this world rapidly. It's beyond saddening. Then they found the victim's cellphone vibrating in her jeans pocket. The screen showed fifteen missed calls from *My World*. The person ended the call before she could pick up and the phone had a password. So there was no way to retrieve the number. Then, as if they could feel her willing them to call back, they did.

"Hello?"

"Mommy, where are you?" the little voice boomed through the phone.

"Your mommy lost her phone, Sweetie. Is there an adult there I can speak with?"

"Momma!" she yells.

After speaking briefly with the victim's mother and getting her address, Suffiyah made the trek to Harlem. The only thing worse than being at a murder scene, is having to relay the news to the family. Seeing the four year old miniature twin to the deceased only made it that much harder. The mother broke down and was inconsolable. She wept openly on the floor of her project apartment. Mucus leaked profusely from her nose and mingled with tears. Which caused the little girl to cry even harder than the grandmother, as she tried to help her up. The woman snatched her down in an embrace as if she would never release her. Tragically holding onto the smallest piece of her world she had left. When the heaviest of emotions finally subsided, Suffiyah was able to find out nothing from the mother. She had no explanation for her daughter being out of New York. As she left she saw a woman who could have only been the victim's sister. When Suffiyah approached her, she started crying before a word could be said. Sometimes the bond with family is so great, they can feel one another's pain. Suffiyah rode through the tunnel more distraught than she initially was. She left New York behind her, but not empty handed. The little sister knew exactly what she was doing in New Jersey. The mother only knew of her job at McDonalds. But according to the sister, she moonlighted as a stripper in Jersey. Her stage name, was "Allure".

CHAPTER 10

*S*AKINAH DISROBES SLOWLY. IN HER *mind she thinks of all kinds of ways around the worst outcome. As she unclasps her bra, she feels the release of her breast being freed. His eyes drop from hers onto her perfect bosom. Taking in the minutest of details. From the small beauty mark on her left breast, to the odd coloring of her areolas and the protruding stiffness of her nipples. Her black work pants are removed next. The roundness of her bottom making the action more taxing, but seductive, as her breast bounce and sway with each effort. Finally removing the dress pants, she stands in only a pair of baby blue thong panties. He motions for her to spin in a circle so he can admire her. If considered cute when dressed, she would have to be rated drop dead gorgeous in her naturalness. As she slowly spins, she can feel his eyes touch every inch of her exposed body. Upon finality of her 360, they are once again eye to eye.*

"Panties," he says low, but in a commanding manner. Placing a thumb on both side of her panty line, she gradually removes the only remaining article of clothing. He adjusts the hardness of his erection as he fantasizes about the taste of her jewel. Her love tunnel commandeers all his attention while he salivates over its beauty. The entire area cleanly shaved, showcasing the plumpness of her lips. The smallest amount of pinkness peeking from in between them, causing pre-cum to leak from his ever growing member. With one hand he pulls at his sweatpants, exposing himself. Removing them swiftly, her eyes drop to his manhood.

He proudly grants her a view of what her nakedness does to him, as he slowly strokes himself. She parts her lips to speak.

"Shh." He places a finger to her lips before a word could be said. "You used me. Now I use you," he whispers venomously. "You never speak of this and it will be as if it never happened. But if you make a noise now, you will cease speaking forever." The look in his eyes driving home the seriousness of his statement. "Lay down."

She complies to avoid further upsetting him. He produces a pair of handcuffs and cuffs her hands lightly to the radiator. Only then does he relinquish the knife he was wielding. Removing his hooded sweater, he gets on his knees and takes her sex in his mouth. She can't figure out why this is happening. Why a man, she so openly trusted, would do this to her? The madness in his eyes unlike any she ever witnessed. She silently prays for him to have a quick release, so she can run away from this situation and never look back. Her eyes open as she feels her body shift. He's no longer between her legs, but hovering over her with his face glistening from her juices. Strong hands grip her butt cheeks as he pushes inside her. In two minutes flat she feels his explosion and thanks God for His mercy. He dresses quickly and reaches for the cuffs. In mid-motion he pauses, her eyes on his hands the entire time. Before she can react, they grip her. Her eyes bulge instantly as she's denied breath. The cuffs bang noisily on the radiator as she squirms. Tears drop from his eyes as he watches her life dissipate at his command. With the last jerks of her being, he finally releases her. And with consistency to the psycho he's proved himself to be, he breaks down crying and professing his love. After his tirade ends, he un-cuffs Sakinah. He needs more than memories to remind him of his lost love, so he picks up her panties. Turning to leave, he's pulled back by temptation. He takes multiple photos of her. Now she will never be forgotten. Once back in the safety of his vehicle, he places a call after blocking his number.

"911, what's your emergency?"

"There's been a murder…"

"Let me hear about the dreams, Detective Adams?" Another session with Dr. Jackson finds Suffiyah in the ever present hot seat.

"I'm a little girl. Well, I'm assuming it's me. It looks like me, I think," she says, doing a good job of confusing herself. "Well anyway. The little girl is in an attic, surrounded by boxes. She can't be older than about three. But she's hiding behind these boxes. Not by choice though, someone directed her there. Then a monster comes. But it's really a man, though my dream tells me he's a monster. His voice causes me to almost wet myself whenever I hear it. Anyway, the dream grows in detail every time I have it. The last one, I wasn't alone in the attic. There was another kid, not my age though, older. The monster caught the boy or girl and they pointed to my hiding place. And then..." Suffiyah stops talking.

"And then what?" Dr. Jackson asks.

"I wake up."

She refuses to divulge to him about the caller in her dreams. Dr. Jackson looks at her like she's psychotic and he's trying to mentally compel her to reveal more of her lunacy.

"That's it?" Suffiyah nods in agreement. "Okay we're going to focus on this dream since it seems to be a derivative of your shooting. Next dream, you come straight to me?"

"Copy, Doc. I'm going to get back to work." He bops his head once in acknowledgement.

"Good day, Detective."

Today has been nonstop for Suffiyah since her arrival in the office. It began with a meeting with all the detectives and Lt. McFarland. Basically touching on how each case was progressing and what obstacles were in place causing them to remain unsolved. Suffiyah had been to almost every strip club in Newark and was yet to get anyone who knew Aaliyah Perez. She's put it on her schedule to stop by *Exotics* in Elizabeth. It's popular enough to be a place she might have worked at. After the meeting, she had to filter through all the calls from alleged witnesses to multiple crimes, which by chance have rewards offered. Charles Lewis walking into the office put her in a bad mood immediately. He is a prime example of why she became a cop. He cares for no one, even himself. He would put a murder on a Popsicle if he could make it stick. His tactics include bribing addicts for false statements. Exchanging low level drug bust releases, for them to point out pictures of suspects they have never seen before. Out of every ten of his cases, six will indict innocent people. His motto is, "When you're in the game, whether you ride the bench or shoot the winning shot, you're still part of the team." When he works a case, you won't be surprised to see a grandmother who peddles nickel bags of weed, being arraigned on triple murder charges. To him a criminal is a criminal. She practically runs to Dr. Jackson to get away from him. She feels guilty because no one rats him out, including herself, because nothing comes before blue. As she arrives to Lt. McFarland's office, she receives depressing news.

"This stripper murder is creating hysteria with the higher ups," he began. "This is the third victim by strangulation and the words serial killer are beginning to buzz around. This is a case that *has* to be solved, by any means."

"I'm going to *Exotics* as soon as I leave the office. I'm doing everything I can, Sir."

"I know you are. I wasn't implying that. We just have to even the odds on these bastards. They have anonymity over us, but we have experience over them. You're partnering with Detective Lewis for this case. He'll bring that experience and a fresh eye."

No matter how fast or far you run, when you look over your shoulder the devil's still standing there grinning.

Detective Charles Lewis is a fifty-two year old country boy. Born outside of Richmond in a town called Chase City, Virginia, he's the product of an alcoholic father and a prostituting mother. At the age of fifteen, he left Virginia and went to Maryland. His dark, pock marked skin and features were abhorrent to him. Leaving his self-esteem at an ultimate low. He was always the butt of everybody's joke or the target of a bully. At the age of eighteen when it seemed life could grow no more exciting for him in Maryland, he sought out a heroin dealer named, Curtis. Curtis was as tall as Charles but is the polar opposite in looks. His fair skin and curly hair, kept a lady around him. His cool demeanor kept him with plenty of friends and the revenue he created from heroin kept him in the latest threads. He was one of the few who showed young Charles love and took up for him. As they stood in the alley behind the Laundromat, he realized he envied Curtis for being everything he couldn't be. A smooth criminal. And in that instance he comprehended how much he hated him as he drove the knife into his chest repeatedly. He left Curtis' corpse in a heap in the alley and Maryland behind him in that same night. What better place to flee to then up North? And what better place could a killer hide than a police precinct?

"Detective Adams, I know I'm not the pretty boy type you usually partner up with," Lewis says as they drive to *Exotics*. "But you have a coldness coming off you that'll freeze a polar bear."

"I'm perfectly fine, Detective Lewis. Just focusing on all the pieces to the puzzle."

"Okay, well remember this. You have the law and you have civilians. As the law, we trump civilians. Which means we stand over them, but we must stand together as law or the civilians will overrun us. Because out of every ten civilians, seven of them are criminals. Whether petty thieves or sadistic killers, you'll never know 'til you catch them in the act. That's why you have to view a criminal as a criminal," he says as he leans back in his *K-Mart* suit and tie.

Suffiyah has never been happier to see a strip club. Upon entering, the owner dismisses the pictures and said he didn't know the girl. He gave his consent for them to speak with the dancers. A skinny dark skinned girl recognizes the picture.

"That's that bitch that be with Storm. What her conceited ass do?" she asks nosily.

"Who's Storm?" Suffiyah asks.

"She's in the back," the girl replies with major attitude over being ignored.

She turns rudely and walks away. In the back they await Storm to come out. She is expecting a person who resembles the woman off the *X-Men* movies. She's looking at the door waiting to see the beautiful brown skin woman with silver hair. Then a high yellow woman walks up to them with red hair and she's completely naked. Standing in front of a man old enough to be her father, with no shame. She's petite but thick, with the biggest, reddest nipples she had ever seen. The chain going from nipple ring to nipple ring, drawing her attention to them.

"Y'all holding me up, what's up?" she says feistily while she lotions her body.

Surprised, Suffiyah can't help asking. "Why do you call yourself Storm?"

The pretty girl smiles as she sways seductively to imaginary music. She runs her fingers all over her body as she gyrates her hips and butt. Stopping her fingers at the lips of her vagina.

"Because once this heavenly body blows through, it starts to rain money," she states staring at Detective Lewis, who's wearing the cheesiest smile. Suffiyah shakes her head and waves the picture at her.

"You know her?" Storm looks at the picture with distaste.

"That's the homegirl, Allure. I haven't heard from or seen her, so whatever she did, that's y'all problem." She turns to walk away, giving Detective Lewis the mooning of a lifetime.

"But she does owe me a coupla' dollars. When y'all catch up to her, ask her can I get that?"

"She's dead." Suffiyah says, stopping her in her tracks.

As she turns around the arrogant sneer is replaced with a more somber expression.

"Let me grab some clothes."

The trip to *Exotics* proved to be worth her while. Turns out Aaliyah was the best that *Wet* had to offer. She's their number one money maker and as Storm tells it, her after hour clientele was booming. Now it makes sense that she was in that hotel room. Given that she turned tricks after the club, only complicates the case that much more. Trying to find a john in Newark is like trying to find an ant at a picnic. To further complicate things, she rented the room herself and went in alone. No one remembers seeing anyone worth noticing coming in after her arrival. So either her killer was a magician or smarter than they thought.

A few days later, DNA analysis came back with a match. Not for a perpetrator but for a victim. The semen at the scene matched the semen found inside of another victim years earlier. Detective Lewis had been going through all old cases of relevance, he came back carrying a folder with a huge smile on his face.

"I've been doing some research." He says, "And out of everything I've seen, I really like him." He rifles through his folder and produces a picture. Tapping it with much enthusiasm and emphasis. "Boy, I really like him!"

CHAPTER 11

MUSIC IS LIKE A SOUNDTRACK to everyday life. People listen to what motivates or speaks to them on a personal level. Benji zones out to the hypnotizing voice of Jay-Z, as he does his last repetition of pull ups. He always tries to end his workout by pushing his body to its limit for the last set. He's on thirty-nine, but going for one hundred straight pull ups. Jay-Z is his personal trainer as he speaks solely to him, "*I had to hustle, my back to the wall ashy knuckles, pockets filled wit' a lotta lint, not a cent gotta vent, lotta innocent lives lost on that project bench, what they hollering, gotta pay rent bring dollars in, by the bodega iron under my coat feeling braver, doo-rag wrapping my waves up, pockets full of hope...*" Eighty-two. Benji lets go of the bar eighteen shy of his target number. No one came to pat him on his back or applaud his performance. That's the reason he attends the gym at six in the morning, there's hardly anyone there. Except for loners such as himself who don't do it for the accolades, they do it for themselves. His upper body is swollen from overexertion, making his tank top constrict tightly. You would never imagine all these muscles hiding beneath his shirts and jackets. Sakinah called them his "secret weapon" when she first saw him shirtless. He doesn't wish to be buff and draw attention. He loves when people underestimate him and think they have him figured out. He grabs his towel and heads for the shower. His target number has never exceeded seventy-five, but he was trying to shed some extra stress. After all these months, Suffiyah called him twice last night. It took every ounce of willpower he had to ignore her. He has yet to stop thinking about her, but he can never allow himself to be that vulnerable again. Rendering himself susceptible to the hurt he endured that night at *Top Golf.* The judgment, the rejection.

It was a beautiful day out. *What can make this day more beautiful?* Detective Lewis asks himself as he stands on his front steps. *An Arrest. One more criminal gone.* Is his response and with determination in his gait, he begins his hunt.

Benji sits behind his desk putting together everything he has on this kidnapping case he's working. A theory begins to take form in his mind when a knock at the door breaks his concentration. The janitor can't grab his garbage can because the door is locked. He gets up to let him in.

"Tone—" To his shock, it's a tall, ugly guy who resembles Lurch from "The Addams Family".

"Can I help you?"

"Benjamin Cooper?" asks the ugly mug.

"Yeah. Who's asking?"

"Pardon me." He smiles, which looks like a butt cracking. "I'm Detective Lewis. I was hoping to impose on you for just a few minutes, if possible," he requests politely.

Benji looks him over and can't help but notice even minus the scales, he still sees a snake. "I'm kind of busy."

"It won't be long, I promise. It's regarding Sakinah Rogers."

Just hearing her name said out loud almost floored him. "Come in," he beckons.

Detective Lewis walks in and plops down on Benji's sofa uninvited, showing his lack of manners. Benji overlooked the small disrespect to hear about Sakinah.

"Mr. Cooper. Well, Benji. Can I call you Benji?"

"Mr. Cooper is fine," Benji says extending no pleasantries.

"Ah, Mr. Cooper it is. Any who. I've been going over Ms. Rogers' file. It broke my heart to see that beautiful young woman in that way. The more I looked at her, the more her face spoke to me. Do you know what her face said? *Help*. I couldn't live with myself if I didn't attempt to answer her plea. So, here I am," he says crossing his legs and looking at Benji as if saying, your turn. But Benji returns the look with impatience. "Mr. Cooper, what can you tell me about that day to contribute to my investigation?"

"Nothing more than I told the police at the hospital. I was in school. From there I went home and fell asleep waiting on Sakinah to arrive. I called her as soon as I awoke and her father relayed the news to me."

"That's it?"

"That's it."

"It's mighty peculiar that every day prior to her murder, phone logs show your number *consistently*. But on that day? *Nothing*. Until well after midnight. Strange right?" the detective asks smiling his ugly smile.

"If you say so." Benji crosses his arms.

"Did you love Ms. Rogers? I mean truly love her, Mr. Cooper?" Benji looks at the floor to avoid the detective seeing his face.

"I still do. With everything inside of me."

"I thought so. And it's for that reason. For this girl that you love so dearly, that I ask this. Son," he says with pleading eyes. "We need a sample of your DNA." The sadness that was so evident on Benji's face is converted to uncontrollable fury, as he realizes Lewis' implication.

"What?" he hisses.

"For Sakinah, Mr. Cooper."

"Get the fuck outta my office. Next time you decide to knock, bring a warrant."

Detective Lewis stands smiling as if everything is going swell. "You have a lot of prior infractions, Mr. Cooper, but no convictions. So you're either always in the wrong place at the wrong time. Or you're very, very elusive."

"Are you getting out or do I have to show you out? Please choose the second."

"Temper, temper. See you around, Benji." Lewis walks out the office baiting him.

Benji slams the door in his wake. Two seconds later a card slides under the door. He leaves it there and sits on the sofa. Crossing his arms on his knees, he lays his head on his forearms. A knock on the door jars him. He looks at his watch and can't believe he's been in that position for over a half an hour, it only felt like seconds. He gets up and opens the door. To his surprise Suffiyah stands on the other side this time.

"Hello Benji," she speaks awkwardly.

"Good morning, Detective?" he replies with little feeling.

"May I come in?" Saying nothing, he stands aside.

"I attempted to call you last night."

"I know."

"Oh? I guess I deserve this treatment. So, I'm going to say what I came for and get out your way."

"Cool." His nonchalant disposition was killing her.

"You got it. Well for some reason a detective is looking into your direction in a case we're working. I asked him what links you to anything, but he's being very secretive. So what I'm asking is if there is anything I should know?"

"Ha ha. So I'm guessing you're the good cop to Detective Lewis' bad cop?"

"Wait. How do you know Lewis?" she inquires genuinely confused.

He indicates the card on the floor, which she picks up still looking lost.

"You didn't know he came here?"

She shakes her head.

"Okay, I'm gonna play your game. What do you know about Sakinah?"

"I'm sorry?"

"You're serious aren't you?"

"I truly don't know what's going on."

"Okay. I'm going to tell you about Sakinah and you can judge me how you judge me."

With that Benji spoke his story. Stopping at the most intimate moments and reflecting.

"Now you know why he came. Do what you need with it." He opens his door signifying her time was up.

Suffiyah looked heartbroken at the gesture. "I apologize for that night. I was wrong and I have to live with that daily. But, I'm sincerely sorry for your loss." She rests her palm over his heart and kisses his cheek. As she turns to walk out, he sees how watery her eyes are. He quickly grabs her hand and pulls her to him. She wraps her arms around his neck and really cries. Her feelings are crushed and she can't help it. Benji massages her back consoling her. He's never felt like more of a prick in his entire life.

"I'm sorry, gorgeous. Please don't cry because of me?" he pleads.

This only causes her to cry harder. He kisses her eyelids, her cheeks and her top lip as he holds both sides of her face. He doesn't know what he did to hurt her so badly, but he'll kill himself before he does it again. She pushes off from him embarrassed and flees his office.

"Stupid, stupid, stupid." Suffiyah reprimands herself.

She can't believe she just performed like that in front of Benji. Between the ways he was treating her, her guilt and his story, her sentiments were on the brink and spilled over.

"Boy I need you bad as my heartbeat, bad as the food I eat, bad as the air I breathe... boy I need you bad I can't take the pain, boy I'm 'bout to go insane..."

Jasmine Sullivan's voice picks at her raw emotions. It's like the radio was attached to her feelings and played the song that perfectly spoke her passions. How could Lewis visit him without mentioning it to her? What was he up to that needed to be kept top secret? What does Sakinah have to do with this case? Could Benji actually have played a part in all of this insanity or is he just a target of Lewis' fishing expedition?

CHAPTER 12

B ENJI STANDS IN FRONT OF a row of houses on a one way block keeping a close eye on oncoming traffic. His footing feels foreign even though this is his homeland. The drug transaction are coming in such a rapid succession, it's unnerving. The block is South 11th street, between 13th Avenue and 12th Avenue in Newark. But through the love of their Westside ties, he and his cohorts named their strip, *Cali Block*. He is one of the originators of the drugs infested, dismal area. A burgundy Chrysler 300, with limo tint pulls up, all eyes are glued to it. Out jumped another originator of *Cali Block*. This man is the closest semblance Benji has to a brother. His day one friend, Lay Low.

"My guy!" Lay Low greets with sincere joy. "What brings you out here to these corners of the Wild West? This don't even fit you no more."

When Benji severed ties with the streets, it broke Lay Low's heart. Not only did he lose his right hand man but he lost the architect, the blueprint was in Benji's head and he built their territory up from basically nothing. In his absence Lay Low had to alter his brain to emulate Benji's. To his success, because Cali is a thriving business.

"I'm just trying to spot the lost souls and give them light, Lay. I don't want *no* smoke." Benji raises his hands in mock surrender.

The two men embrace momentarily giving onlookers a glimpse of their unspoken love.

"Come on, Ru. First you leave, now you trying to take the little bros from me? You gotta leave me a little sumthin." Benji looks at all the action surrounding him.

"Shit, it looks like you have a lot of something to me. Enough to pack up and end the show."

Lay Low looks at his main man as he ties his dreadlocks in a bun.

"Bro, this all us right here, we run this show. If I end it now, what the little homies got in me except a deserter?"

"Lay, we was shown the life by the same man. So as far as you running this show, you're delusional. What was Bruh's golden rule?"

Lay smiles. "Blood don't run nothing, if Blood don't own nothing."

"Exactly, the more we own, positively, the more we give them." He points at the young bloods. "The more we give them, the less we deprive them off." He now points at the addicts and neighborhood.

"Ru, so you woke up off your Geronimo Pratt wave and couldn't think of nobody to make feel like shit but me?"

"Ha-ha. Nah never, my guy. You know I'm a firm believer in 'sometimes you gotta do bad to do good.', but only as a means to an end. We supposed to use a negative situation to create a positive one for us, our families and our communities. Not increase the degree of negativity. To the point a five year-old is the caretaker of his three year-old brother, because his mother's addicted to pills and his father's dead from bangin'. You know I ain't here to judge you, Lay. I just want better for all of us. But the real reason I'm here, is because I needed to be around genuine love. And if nobody else got it for me, I know Lay do." Benji smiles and daps Lay Low. Both their eyes spot the charcoal gray Chevy Trailblazer at the same time. It slow rolls as Benji attempts to see through the impenetrable darkness of the tints. He's just waiting for the doors to bust open and the shots to start flying.

"Ru, stop staring. That's that work. We out."

It's funny how you search high and low for a rabbit and can't find it in the field. Just when you give up searching, you spot it in the one place you neglected to look. Inside the rabbit hole.

This isn't just coincidental, Detective Lewis thinks. According to Benjamin Cooper's rap sheet, his first arrest was on this block. "I found your hole, Benji Rabbit." Lewis says with excitement. This is even better than he believed. Everybody and their grandmother gangbangs on this block. "Birds of a feather flock together, Mr. Rabbit."

The initial reaction to Sakinah Rogers' case was sadness. Suffiyah didn't see the pictures until last. Once she did, she was immediately transported back to the scene on Ridgewood. Minus the card, this was the scene. Only difference was the date. Sakinah could have passed for Suffiyah herself or a sister. What connected these four murders besides strangulation? Sakinah was murdered while Suffiyah was still a patrol officer. There was no card, call or mention of her name. Next, Marissa Cooke. She was the victim on Ridgewood and the first time the caller reached out. Then came Alyssa James on the picnic table. Three women who were either in school and working or just working. Who, just by chance, all look very much like herself. Which brings on the final case of Aaliyah Perez. Besides being strangled in Newark, she had nothing in common with the other girls. They were black, she was Spanish. They were career women, she was a stripper and prostitute. How did her case point at Sakinah, which in turn pointed Lewis at Benji? Then something she read reminded her of a piece of evidence she had forgotten until now. The semen matched DNA left in another victim. That victim was Sakinah Rogers.

"But she's a DT."

"And I'm a private investigator."

"Let me see your badge." Lay Low holds his hand out and pulls it back empty. "Exactly. Big difference. If you was saying you wanted to get some and go your separate ways, then that would be cool. But you all googily eyed over there. It ain't gon' work."

They sit in *The Office*, a restaurant/bar in Montclair, New Jersey, picking at their food. The conversation is like a wrestling match fueled by Sangria.

"Please explain ya logic, Lay. I gotta hear this."

"Okay, Mr. Ru. Take me and you for instance. I'm dark skinned and cute, but you, you brown skinned and ugly. Total opposites." Lay blocks the playful jab thrown by Benji. "Nah for real though. As street dudes we deal off facts and actualities. We gather information correctly before passing judgment. But they judge us geographically and off of opinion and hearsay. If you from here or there, you're automatically a suspect. If you're a minority it's impossible that you've never committed a crime in your life, even if you were never caught. They get three different stories about a gun from three different people. One says you were wearing a red hoodie and had a nine. Another says you had on a black jacket and brandished a revolver. The last witness says you had a AK-47, but you were wearing a skirt and eating a ham sandwich. Three months later you and the ham sandwich both getting indicted."

Benji laughs so hard Sangria comes out of his nose and chokes him.

"Ha ha. I'm for real, Ru. They don't care what things really are, they just care how they seem. From the three witnesses' perception you're a gun slinger. So in the law's eyes, that's what you are."

Elsewhere

Lee Lee brings dinner plates in the living room for her and Suffiyah. Work has been hectic for the both of them, they hardly see each other. As she takes her seat she gives Suffiyah her undivided attention.

"Okay. Now go 'head."

"Before you say I told you so, just listen." Suffiyah forewarns Alicia.

Lee Lee makes a motion as if zipping her lips. Suffiyah tells her story in its entirety, ending with the file on Sakinah.

"Now go 'head and run ya mouth. I know it's killing you," Suffiyah says.

"I told you so. But…" Lee Lee nods her head while holding up one finger at Suffiyah's expression, "I don't believe he's capable of those crimes. Wait, this is important. When you were crying, how did it feel when he kissed your face? Like it was rehearsed or fake?"

Suffiyah sits her plate down and tucks her feet under her thighs and smiles. "Like heaven. It was so romantic and thoughtful. It wasn't like trying to put the moves on me, he was tryna take care of me. The best way I could describe it is, I could feel how it pained him to see me hurt and that meant everything."

"Oh my Lord. I can't wait to get you to Cancun next week. I'm gonna find you a Mexican man that God blessed with a nice taco and I'm gonna hold you down while he feeds it to you. My baby is probably in love with Michael Myers."

CHAPTER 13

A LITTLE GIRL COWERS IN THE *corner of the attic, as the monster frantically searches for her. She silently prays to God that he doesn't look behind the boxes of clothes stacked in front of her. "Suffer! Suffer!" He screams as he flings objects out of his path. "Here you are!" But his voice is coming from across the room, directed at someone unseen. "Now you must suffer with me." The girl peeks from behind the boxes as the monster lifts someone by the collar. "Where is she?" The monster barks. She sees a little finger point in her direction. The monster turns towards her with eyes the color of heated coal. The scrawny boy, in his massive hands, squeezes his eyes shut tightly. "You..."*

Suffiyah's eyes pop open and take in the strange room. Alicia's silhouette can be seen in the light of the moon, as she rests peacefully. Her dreams or nightmares have followed her to Cancun. Refusing to let them ruin her vacation, she turns over and forces sleep to take over.

"You have too much on top," Lee Lee comments.

"I just have a few things on my mind, that's all." Suffiyah replies, using her hand to block the sun as she looks over to Lee Lee.

"I mean your bikini top. You doing too much. Free your titties, free your mind."

Alicia lays on the beach towel with her 34D breast on full display. The layers of sunblock causing them to shimmer in the sunshine.

"No thank you. Maybe you don't see all these men." Suffiyah looks around. "And women staring at your hooters, but I do."

Using her pointer finger, Lee Lee lifts up her dark shades to look at her friend. "You see these people, Su? How many of them have you seen before? How many will you see again, after we leave?"

"None. But—"

"Exactly!" Lee Lee interjects. "None. So they are invisible to me. No one matters, but me. If you were at home and had a backyard with a fence, knowing no one could see you, would you lay by your pool with your top on or off?"

"Off, but—"

"Well this is as close as you're getting to that setting right now. So put your shades on, pop your boobs out and let ya mind go. That's an order," Lee Lee says pulling her shades back down.

Suffiyah sits up smirking at her friend, who just dismissed her. Intent on proving she could live, she pulls the string of her bikini top. Letting her golden peaks improve the view of the beach. She sees the grin sneaking on Lee Lee's face as she lays back. Pulling her own shades down, she imagines every person ogling her goods, is invisible. She's never felt freer.

"Excuse me, Mr. Cooper, but what kind of private investigator *are you*?" The older man asks sarcastically, as him and his wife sit in Benji's office. His anger is apparent in his tone and movements.

"One with morals, Mr. Porter. Also, one with a conscience. While some people can compromise their integrity in the name of business, I can't."

"But you're paid to *investigate*. So what's stopping you from *investigating* my son's murder, if I'm willing to pay for it?"

Benji is sympathetic with their loss, so he's answering politely. "As I told you when you first entered my office, I don't handle murders. I can give you the number to several homicide detectives, who can be more helpful than me."

"But *why* don't *you* handle murders?" the man persist.

"Murders are a sensitive subject. I pay attention to the circumstances behind the matter, not just the fact that someone died," Benji says, intentionally directing the speech towards Mrs. Porter. "Sometimes, the deceased was the actual aggressor and his murderer was only protecting the only life he has. How could I find that man and send him to prison? Especially, when his only crime was not wanting to die? So, I couldn't in my better judgment take your money knowing, if I found that the misfortune occurred in that or a similar manner that I would never reveal that man."

"You lazy, hypocritical bastard!" Mr. Porter says rising from his seat, spittle flying with each syllable.

"Mrs. Porter." Benji ignores his insults. "How many mothers have *your* son caused this same grief?" Unable to maintain eye contact because of guilt, Mrs. Porter stares at the handbag she clutches in her lap. "Why didn't you come here to get justice for their families, when your son was the culprit?"

"Elliot, I'm ready to leave," she mumbles.

"You worthless rental cop! I should break your nose, you son of a bitch! How dare you—"

"Elliot!"

With a huff he snatches his wife from the chair and storms from the office. Benji stares at the door that stands wide open. Instead of going to shut it, he stays seated, quietly seething. Being from the streets, he has the advantage of getting his intel directly from the streets. The Porter's baby boy was an oppressive bully. He murdered, robbed, hustled and lived lavishly at the expense of the community. But when arrested, he turned everyone in for doing exactly what he does, in exchange for being released to recommit the same debaucheries. Sometimes street justice is more honorable than judicial justice.

"How long have you been purchasing narcotics in this neighborhood?" Detective Lewis asks the small addict in the backseat.

Her body is in such poor condition, it's impossible to calculate her age by sight. She could be anywhere from thirty to seventy-five years old. The scent coming from her is unbearable, but Lewis is so focused on the task at hand that he doesn't notice it.

"Maybe two, like two years," admits the skunk lady.

"Okay. During the course of those two years, you have never laid eyes on the gentleman in that picture?"

"No sir, and I know all 'em 'round here." She says confidently.

Feeling his opportunity slipping away, he decides on another approach.

"If I gave you $50 to buy some crack for me, would you? We can split it. Five and five."

Skunk lady looks at him greedily while trying to determine if this is a ruse.

After a long day of swimming, zip lining and riding four-wheelers, Suffiyah and Alicia sit in the fancy Mexican nightclub in dresses that mention all of their unmentionables. The tequila shots they down in unison, loosen them up nicely. No problems can reach them here, the only problem is they can't stay here forever. Two men from Detroit have been vying with other men for their attention all night.

"Su, you take the cute one and I'm gonna get the cuter one. You ready?"

"Girl, I ain't come here for no men." Suffiyah brushes her off.

"Me either, but they come with the drinks. Listen you can act like a nun and get none. But I'm her to enjoy my freedom and my life. And if that comes with one of those cuties and an orgasm, I'm in!"

Suffiyah laughs. "Pervert."

"Hoe."

"It's too hard living... but I'm afraid to die..." The killer belts out along with Sam Cooke.

This statement is beyond true for him. Majority of his life he has contemplated suicide as a way out of his suffering. Drunk out of his mind with a loaded pistol in mouth, he always chickens out. Why? He's too afraid of what comes after the grave. Is there really a hell? Because if there is, he's confident he'll be attending. So why rush? And if not, then only thing after death is an eternity of nothing. That's truly hell. An eternity stuck with himself is more terrifying than any story of fire and brimstone he's ever heard. To have to live with the demons in his mind, would break him. This is why he decides to live and alleviate his sickness by bringing death and suffering to others. Which is why again, he finds himself entering *Wet*. As security stops him to ask for identification, he looks around at the action. Suddenly he begins patting his pocket in search of his wallet. He seems to have misplaced it. Signaling to security to give him a second, he backs out of the doorway. Once outside, he sprints to his van while pressing unlock on the keypad. Sweat trickles down his brow as he gets in the vehicle. He exhales loudly. The look of fear he sees staring at him through the rearview mirror causes him to laugh. Now that he's behind the safety of the tinted windows, his near brush with imprisonment seems humorous. Amongst all those beautiful faces, Detective Lewis stood out like a toenail fungus on a foot model.

"Not today, Detective. Not today."

CHAPTER 14

THE HEAVY RAIN PELTS OFF of the building's façade in a rhythmic manner, creating a soundtrack to today's session. Suffiyah lays back on the chair in a dark gray, pinstriped pantsuit. The pink blouse rises with each breath, the space between her buttons displaying a peek of the flesh beneath it. Her caramel complexion is a little darker from her vacation, which somehow makes her prettier than she already was. With her eyes closed, she appears as you would imagine Sleeping Beauty.

"Describe the child for me."

"He's tiny, for his height. Like he was malnourished. Maybe five or six years-old. Very fair skinned and his eyes," she becomes quiet as she struggles to remember her nightmare. "I remember they were shut so tight that I felt he was either hurt or frightened to death."

"Did you recognize him? Was he a sibling?" Dr. Jackson asks.

"No."

The fact that she's a foster child was never discussed in her sessions. That's more embarrassing to her than anything else in her life. When things go wrong in other's lives, they have a parent waiting with open arms. Waiting to shoulder the pains of a world that their children are ailed with.

"Dr. Jackson, can I ask you something?"

"Of course, Detective."

"What was your favorite cartoon?"

Dr. Jackson leans back in his chair. He's looking at the ceiling as if the answer is written on it. When he looks back at Suffiyah, the professional sternness has dissolved from his face. His eyes smile at the memory his mind holds.

"I don't know honestly. Cartoons were my own world, so I loved them all. I was the Roadrunner, fast enough to escape any harm. I was a Power Ranger, able to combat any evil. I was…"

He looks so human right now, his words faded and Suffiyah could only focus on his face. His words were like ointment soothing her.

"What about you, Detective?" Suffiyah just stares. "Detective?" He says snapping his fingers, causing her to jump.

"Huh?" She catches herself.

"Did I bore you?" he asks.

"No, I'm sorry. What did you ask me?"

"You're favorite cartoon, what is it?"

"Doc, don't judge me or feel pity for what I tell you, okay?" He nods. "I am a foster child. So the love and simplicity of home life that others treat as mundane, is exotic to me. Which is why Peter Pan was always my favorite. He and the Lost Boys are a *real* family. With no parents around to love them, they managed to love each other. But, no matter what they still craved a mother. Do you remember when Peter Pan asked Wendy what a mother was and how was it to have one? I felt he spoke just for me. I listened because I needed to know. What did I do to become a Lost Boy? I'm smart, ambitious and caring. Maybe nobody could see it or acknowledge it, except Lee Lee. That's when it all made sense. I'm Peter Pan and Alicia's my Wendy." His eyes mist as he watches tears spill from hers. "Why didn't I deserve a mother? A *real* mother, who wanted *me!*"

Suffiyah feels so empty right now, she is her fourteen year old self all over again. Instead of being surprised at the feel of his lips, she welcomes the sensation. Hungrily pulling him forward as he kisses her neck. A moan escapes her lips as his hands brush her mounds beneath her blouse. She tugs her shirt free from her pants, yearning to feel his hands on her bare breasts. Reaching down she caresses his growing bulge as he undoes her buttons. Euphoria envelopes her as she feels his mouth suckle her breasts. She needs her emptiness filled immediately. As his hands cup her firm cheeks, her panties moisten more. Her vulnerability is so evident. It's now or never. She pushes back looking at the floor. Turning her back in humiliation.

"I'm so sorry, Dr. Jackson. I can't... not like this," she says while fixing herself.

Never looking back or awaiting a response, she leaves. She would not succumb to finding a temporary filling for her permanent void. It only ended in more heartbreak, for her.

"As misfits, most of our wrong moves come from fear," Benji explains.

"I ain't scared of nobody," declares a young girl of about sixteen.

She's not as well dressed as some of the other students and seems more withdrawn. She probably only spoke up because his attention was directed at her when he made the statement. He fancies himself a rare jeweler or an appraiser. He'll pick through a handful of rocks and find the gem that's been overlooked a million times. He's here looking for his diamonds in the rough.

"What's your name, sister?"

"Lenae."

"That's a beautiful name. Very unique and special." Her cheeks crimson immediately. "Now, when I say fear, Lenae, I'm not only speaking of people. It can be fear of a place, a situation, a thought, a perception or a fear of standing out. In my opinion, the worst fear is the fear of reality. The things we have to deal with on a regular basis, is sometimes scarier than any monster Hollywood can dream up."

A kid in the corner with a tattoo under his right eye, watches him intently. He's been staring out the window refusing to participate or interact. Something Benji said grasped his attention.

"Bruh, if you don't mind, can I ask your name?" Benji asks the kid with the tattoo.

"Drama." The kids laugh.

"Okay, Drama." Benji concedes to his moniker. "Do you agree with me?"

"Moreless, I can't say. I don't know if you chattin' for a check like these teachers or you rockin' wit' real," Drama says.

"First, I do this for free. To help people like me see the flaws in our ways, before they're forced to hurt as I hurt. Second, I ain't wit' 'chattin'. Real recognizes real. Do I look familiar?"

Drama smiles before answering. "I agree that wrong moves come from fear. I fear starving so I hustle. I fear being hurt, so I hurt first. I want to be different so my Moms can be proud of me, but I fear that if I change an opp might off me," Drama says, referring to the opposition. "Then all she can do is cry over me. See all that talkin' 'bout change sound good when you don't have to deal wit' reality. When you do it's a whole different ball game. What you fear?"

The question and admission catches Benji by surprise. "Fear?" He shakes thoughts from his head. "Too much. I fear not living up to the person I wish for y'all to be or exceed. I fear not saying what needs to be said and seeing one of y'all on the news or in the obituaries. You mean more personal?" Benji asks seeing the scowl on Drama's face. He nods his head. "I fear falling short and reverting back to being a corrupter. Or all my past wrongdoings coming back and causing me to spend the rest of my life in confinement. I fear dealing with the conflict of who I was and who I want to be. I fear reality. And reality is, I fear love the most. I lost my girlfriend, well she was murdered. It hurt me so bad that I know if I was to find love and lose it, life would end for me as I know it now and I would once again be that corrupter. Is that real enough?"

Drama stands ups and walks to the front of the class. He puts his fist out for a fist bump, Benji obliges. Then he walks out the class with twenty minutes left. Benji stares at his back, feeling like a failure.

"He never stayed in class longer than five minutes or spoke. You kept him here for forty minutes and got him to contribute. That's success," Lenae says, reading his face. Benji smiles at her.

Suffiyah enters her apartment feeling abandoned. She allowed Dr. Jackson to regress her back to the needy girl who settled for any inkling of affection. The turmoil in her soul stirs and can't be quelled. As she undresses and slides under her sheets, she just cries. Lewis is trying to provoke her, Benji and Dr. Jackson are trying to take her, the world continues to treat her unfairly and it seems as if God is still trying to break her. She made up her mind that she will no longer be taking sessions with Dr. Jackson.

CHAPTER 15

THE SCENT OF THE TULIPS are intoxicating and soothing. Thick cranberry carpet covers the floor of the suite as natural sunlight bounced of the white walls. Dr. O'Malley is a squat, Caucasian woman in her fifties. Gray streaks are starting to show in the roots of her red hair. Her round, dimpled face is as pleasant and welcoming as her office. Shoeless, her pudgy pedicured toes are absorbed in the plushness of the carpeting. She bites down on her bottom lip as she thinks before speaking.

"Repressed memories are memories that have been unconsciously blocked due to said memory being associated with a high level of stress or trauma," she explains of the prior diagnosis by Dr. Jackson.

Unlike Dr. Jackson, Dr. O'Malley has no ties to the police department or law enforcement. So Suffiyah can speak liberally about her dreams, the caller and everything else which stresses her.

"There are multiple ways in which we can attack this, some practical while others are experimental. The former consisting of traditional doctor-patient dialogue until we start to make headway. The latter being hypnosis, if all else fails. The route we pursue is totally your decision. My office is a place of comfort and trust." Dr. O'Malley gives a motherly smile. "No pressure. Now, let's begin." She sits back in her chair and crosses her feet, attentive to Suffiyah.

"So, repressed memories are real?" Suffiyah asks.

Dr. O'Malley makes a face which says 'sort of, kind of'.

"Studies show, that the first documented stories of repressed memories started dating back to the nineteenth century," she replies while biting on her pen. "The clinical terminology is *Dissociative Amnesia.* Charles Dickens' character, Dr. Manette, suffers from it in *'A Tale of Two Cities',* that was in 1859. But deeper investigation turned up an opera, *Nina,* by Dalayrac and Marsollier from 1786. Before that, the subject was never broached. So some say it's just a creation of the imagination of the therapist. While others believe it to be a legitimate ailment. I, being of the latter. So don't fret, I shan't judge you a lunatic," she says playfully.

Suffiyah tells of the shooting, her dreams, the murders, the calls before the murder and her job.

"Interesting." Silence. "What makes you believe all of these events intertwine?" O'Malley inquires while still scribbling in her pad.

"The timing. It all coincided with each other. Not natural like a snow storm, but overwhelmingly unnatural, like an avalanche. That's the best way I can explain it."

"Well, that's only speculation, my dear. Now the caller says…" she refers to her pad. "He'll make you suffer as you've made him suffer. The monster in the dream says for you to suffer with him. That's what stuck out to me, Suffiyah."

Suffiyah sits there and ponders the relevance of the statement. Until Dr. O'Malley said it she never gave much thought on the actual wording. But the caller does say suffer repetitively. That's very peculiar to say the least.

"Let's backtrack. Which was first, the call or the dream?"

"The dreams. They started after the shooting. While the first murder didn't take place until almost ten months later."

"Okay. So the word suffer wasn't a product of the fear of the caller entering your subconscious, sleeping mind. The dreams were brought on by the trauma of the shooting. Whether it was you being shot or you taking a life, is what we need to establish. Everything has a root. I believe if we get to the root of one problem, the answers will be obtainable to the rest. What is it that you believe the caller wants?"

"I feel he wants me and is using my work to bring me to him."

"But why?"

"If I knew that, Doc, I could save myself some money and you and I wouldn't know each other." Suffiyah smiles.

"Very clever observation. Maybe we should switch seats." Dr. O'Malley returns the smile. "But I asked what you *believed*, not what you *knew*."

"I wish I did know something. It's beyond puzzling, like he's trying to keep me rattled. I walk into my apartment as if I'm entering a hostile area, every time. Maybe I'm just paranoid, but I've found a motive in almost everyone in the precinct."

"I disagree. What if you're looking too close? Expand your view. Think back on what began all of these events transpiring."

"You mean me being shot?"

"Is that all that occurred that day?"

"All that I remember."

"No, all that you want to remember."

"What's that supposed to mean?"

"You were not the only person hurt that day or don't you recollect?"

"You mean?"

"Tyler Scott."

The name smacked Suffiyah like a ton of bricks. Before the name was said it was nonexistent. Not thinking about Tyler in the least helped her sidestep being the one who removed the light from his eyes. Giving a name to his corpse forces her to have to see him as more than a junkie, robber. It made him a son, student, boyfriend, a friend and a kid. But moreover, it made him human and just as deserving of life as she is.

"What does he have to do with this?"

"He also died that day you sustained your injuries. You told me you've never discharged your weapon at an actual individual prior to that day. In the first time you have to, it results in the target's demise. That's traumatic enough alone, so pair it with you being shot. It's easier to forget it even happened as you try to do. But you have to face the truth to get an honest answer. The media had a field day with the story I imagine. I know your face would have been front page worthy. Granting the entire country a glimpse at the face that ended this young, promising life. Including?"

Now it hits Suffiyah what she's implying.

"His family," she mumbles.

Tyler Scott was a twenty-one year-old financial whiz. His career on Wall Street was already predetermined after college. His presence was sought in multiple firms. With only one school semester left, he was on his way to unimaginable riches. How ironic is it that he was planning to make his life off other's money and instead he ended up dying for the same reason. He was from a very prominent family. His mother was a doctor, father a surgeon and three brothers of various ages. All of whom viewed his dying and her surviving as catastrophes. A fact that they didn't attempt to sugar coat or disguise.

"Don't you believe that they suffer, also? Can you think of anybody else who you could have caused more suffering?"

"Here you go," skunk lady says excitedly.

She dumps five vials of cocaine in Detective Lewis' hand. Unconcerned with his intentions for the narcotic, she on the other hand, can already taste the drug. Her leg shakes in anticipation as she waits to be dismissed by the detective. Addicts will sell their own soul for one dollar. So how much can anyone else's be worth?

"Sonya?" Suffiyah calls before entering her cubicle. Sonya swivels her chair around to face her.

"Hey, Missy. How can I help you?"

"I need to ask you a few questions about the Tyler Scott case."

"Honey, why would you step back in that mess?"

"I think I overlooked something substantial while out there. Did any of his siblings have a record?"

"No, they was as clean as the Brady Bunch. No records, perfect attendance, honor roll students. You name it, they was it. He became the black sheep after meeting a girl named Cynthia Rocelli. According to his brothers, she was the source of his addiction."

Sonya goes on filling her in on all she knew. Giving Suffiyah plenty to think about on her way back to her cubicle. She would put the number for Cynthia to use later on. First she has to do a little digging on her own.

It only took five long strides to cover the distance from the front entrance to the man placing the beers in the refrigeration units. Soon as he was secured the other two gunmen entered immediately. There was no opportunity for a reaction between the first man's entrance to the last two. Shock and fear covered the owners face as he watched the first assailant wrap his arm around the workers neck and shove the gun in his temple. Menacing eyes stared at him through the slits of the ski mask. He had thick plexi-glass put up around the entire counter of the liquor store to withstand an assault such as this. Although he is in the safe zone, his brother wasn't so lucky. One of the other masked men shoved the only two customers face down on the floor, after he caught the lady staring too hard.

"You know what it is, Pa! Don't be stupid."

The last of the trio commands as he aims his pistol at the glass. The owner still stands stunned, frozen. One hundred and fifty percent of his faith went into the glass, so he became arrogant. Antagonizing consumers who he felt were beneath him. He would curse them out, throw their change or just blatantly disrespect them. Knowing something like this would happen, he was just waiting for it. He imagined himself laughing at the exercise in futility as he and his family watched from behind the safety glass. But in none of his visions were one of them *out* of the safe zone, like now.

"Pop that shit now, Poppi!"

The words snatching him from his thoughts. A little pee trickled down his leg as he stared down the barrel of the 44. Desert

Eagle. The hole in its nose and the size of the seven bullets that he knew filled its magazine, erased the surety of the safety glass.

"I want all the scratch offs, the money, ya watch, whatever's in your pockets and anything of value, Pussy!"

The first gunman rifles through the brother's pocket as the directives are issued. Popping the gold cross from his neck, he then instructs him to remove the bracelet and watch from his wrist, before violently striking him with the gun. Causing him to babble in Spanish as he removes his jewelry expeditiously. Seeing his brother suffer caused the owner to place everything in the bags more swiftly. When he was done, all the booty was shoved through the rotating door in the glass.

"For now on watch ya mouth and know who 'hood you in. This personal." He says.

The desert Eagle roars to life. The owner hit the floor as soon as he saw the flare from the giant cannon. Gunfire exploded rapidly filling the silence with terror. Hot piss escapes the lady's bladder as she reflects on her last moments.

"It all happened so fast there was nothing I could do. By time I looked up they already had my brother."

"How many of them were there?"

"Three morenos. Motherfuckers killed my brother. Diablo!" the owner states crying.

"Mr. Arocho, it's important we get a description from you to get the suspects. Every second counts."

"You don't think I want to help? Please," He places both hands out, palms up. "Please tell me how do I give a description of a face mask? Or should I let you show me a line up of face masks to see which is the closest color? Hmm? *Stupido*." he mumbles but Suffiyah still hears the insult. The muggers told him it was personal. Judging from his attitude, she finds it hard to believe the situation has took this long to escalate.

93

"Let's take this from the top, Mr. Arocho. And one more thing. If you ever insult me again, you'll be down here pressing charges for police brutality also."

The two customers are being held in separate rooms. This is to keep them from comparing what they know and altering their version of the incident based on the others recollection. Suffiyah will take Ray Brown after she finishes with the store owner and Detective Lewis will focus on...

"Olivia Watkins," Detective Lewis says in a spirited manner. "What age are you?"

"I'm twenty-nine years old. I'm from around there, I see a lot!" she replies with emphasis.

"Is that right Ms. Watkins?" he asks skeptically, trying to understand how a twenty-nine year old could pass for fifty so easily.

"That's right," she affirms.

He hasn't started recording their conversation. It's procedure to find out what a witness has to say before going on the record. So he skips the formalities and speaks plainly.

"Stinkin' Lincoln, what you know good?"

The woman he dubbed "Skunk Lady" smiles her rotten toothed smile. "Lots, Detective. Didn't I tell you I know all them around there? From they walks, how they dress, down to their tattoos. I know that what Stinkin' Lincoln know is worth more than five shitty dimes."

"Give it to me. Let me judge."

You can tell from her facial expression that she's deciding which factors of the story she's willing to pass on for free.

"Wayne-Wayne came in first and grabbed the young poppi by the collar."

"Wait. How do you know that if he had on a mask?"

"He wear those same *Robin* jeans 'til the rhinestones fall off and those Jordan's with the pink shoestrings."

"Okay. What happened next?"

"One of the other boys came in. I don't know who he was, but Munch came in last."

"How do you know it was Munch? Does he wear the same outfit too or was it his cologne?" Lewis asks sarcastically.

"Naw. Munch different. He keeps a low profile but he's dangerous as shit. A real cowboy. So I gotta be John Doe if I tell you anything."

"You mean Jane."

"Huh?"

"Jane Doe. You would have to be Jane Doe."

"Well her too. As long as I ain't me."

Detective Lewis rubs his face in frustration, "If you can't tell from his outfit, which wouldn't be worth shit anyway, how would you possibly know it was him?"

Skunk Lady sits quietly, smirking, baiting him deliberately. This tad bit of information would keep her floating on cloud nine for a week easy.

"What's it worth, Lewis?"

CHAPTER 16

GRUNTS OF PLEASURE ECHO OFF the walls of the bedroom. The smell of sex lingers in the air and coats their perspiring bodies. His fingertips push through her hair gently and massage her scalp. A guttural moan leaves Suffiyah's lips as the motion between her thighs intensifies. One hand remains in her hair while she lays on her back, the other travels her figure and rests on her bottom. The warmth of his hand couple with the soft roughness of his calluses and makes her moisture overflow. He grips her right cheek emphatically and pulls her into his thrusts. She runs her hand down his back. The crevices feeling like little canyons as she senses his muscles flex under her fingertips. Her legs spread wider as she places her hands on Benji's butt and forces him deeper in her tunnel and herself deeper into delight. Wetness drips from one orifice and soaks the other, which he immediately slides his finger into. Her pleasure upsurges at the alien feeling invading her as his finger nestles in her back entrance. Benji kisses her face tenderly with each stroke.

Forehead.
Left eye.
Right eye.
Cheek.
Other cheek.
Nose.
Top lip.

Bottom lip.

Suffiyah locks onto his aperture as if it's her only source of oxygen and she's close to her demise. The sweet heat of her breaths as beautiful and inviting as the passionate whimpers laced in between them. Increasing his hardness as he guides his vessel into the depths of her flooded river. His pace quickens. Her legs wrap around his waist, arms around his neck. Her swollen entrance trapping his girth. Suffiyah's body tenses signaling her imminent eruption.

"Harder. Deeper. Ohhhh…"

The sound of her voice pushes Benji over the edge as he attempts to fuck her worries into nonexistence.

"I'm, I'm, I'm, ummm!" She explodes.

Pulling the sheets between her clenched thighs against her throbbing femininity as she grinds her mattress. The orgasm drenching her sheets as she awakens. The moonlight kissing off her bare posterior as she pants heavily into her pillow. Never in her thirty-three years has she had a wet dream. But if they all feel like this, she can't wait to fall back asleep.

"A German astronomer once said, 'I much prefer the sharpest criticism from a single intelligent man to the thoughtless approval of the masses.'. Feel me?" Benji allows the depth of the statement to permeate the mental. He rarely has time to do this part of his job, except on this day. The three family home houses MISFITS. This is where his most intimate and critical counseling takes place. The red *Nike* jogger he wears allows him to feel more akin to the youths that surround him this Saturday morning.

"That's a powerful spill. Especially in today's world where the consensus is if you aren't doing what everybody else is, than you're nobody. The question we have to ask ourselves is, 'How can a somebody be a nobody?' The answer to that is, as long as you be you, you're somebody. But the moment you feel you have to maneuver like everybody else, you become nobody. Why? Because to become someone else means you must first lose yourself. So you bartered what made you special. What made you unique. To appease the thoughtless masses." he states while staring at Drama.

After their first introduction, Benji canvassed the area around the school daily until he found him. Inside Drama's eyes he sees himself and the tumultuous path he was tossed down. If he can be the voice that persuades him away from that road, he'd give every Saturday up for the rest of his life.

The room light twinkles off of the silver heart nipple rings as they bounce up and down vigorously. Storm is "rolling". The gram of *Molly* which she mixed into her drink increases her sexual appetite and decreases her grip on reality. This makes her job easier to deal with and to stomach. Money has no gender or nationality. It isn't judged by its looks, only its worth. A hundred dollar bill can be wrinkled, dirty, written on, stinky or torn, but it still spends like a hundred dollars. So that's the same manner in which she conducts her clientele. Her eyes are glazed over as she performs the reverse cowgirl better than any porn star she has ever watched. He's mesmerized by the way her small waist moves her jiggly bottom. Waves flow across the surface of her derriere as she slams on his pelvis. His eyes lock onto the tattoo of the handprint on each butt cheek. Her beauty is a rarity foreign to this bedroom. She looks over her shoulder to see if she's earning her keep. It takes all her willpower not to laugh as Lewis sits with the goofiest look on his face she can remember ever seeing. He's been paying for this joyride since he saw her at *Exotics*. His mouth is wide open, his eyes shut. He looks like a chocolate crocodile. This causes her to bounce harder, it's now a game to her. How much uglier can she make this ugly face? To him this is an experience but for her, it's just another day of work.

Cynthia Rocelli was nothing like the image Suffiyah had envisioned. Her mind's eye was seeing a well-dressed, beautiful Italian woman. Maybe a little nerdy but exuding femininity. Instead she was being inspected by a portly female with multiple facial piercings. Clad in black from head to toe, resembling a neo-Nazi from the streets of London, she stares at Suffiyah with disgust. Giving her little more respect than she would dog feces.

"License, registration and insurance, please?" Suffiyah asks from the driver's side window.

"Why?"

"Because I'm an officer of the law and I'm requesting your credentials."

"But why are you stopping me?" the pincushion asks defiantly.

She's been driving properly, not exceeding the speed limit and signaling when necessary. This is a blatant violation of her rights and she refuses to stand for it.

"I'm stopping you because you just purchased narcotics at the corner of South Orange Avenue and Smith Street. I can both search you and call the K-9 Unit to find the drugs or we can have a conversation and I may go away alone. But if you decide you don't wish to speak to me, then we'll be leaving together."

The arrogance melts away and is replaced with fear. The twenty-two bags of heroin in Cynthia's bra have her looking at jail. Not only will her parents kill her but she can kiss her scholarship goodbye. As she eyes the plainclothes officer only two words play in her mind. *I'm telling.* This has to be about the dealer and she's willing to give him up with no problem. If it is one thing Newark has in excess, it is dealers. So she can always find another source.

"Do I need a lawyer, Ma'am?" she asks respectfully for the first time.

"You come answer my questions and then you decide. Deal?" Cynthia nods her assent. "Okay, then follow me."

The cops hastily exit the car before anyone has a chance to run. The group of young men sit on the steps of the abandoned house. Guilt or nervousness etched into each of their faces. They were so focused on their phones they didn't notice the lone patrol car creeping through the intersection.

"You fellas live here?" The officer points at the boarded up door. "If not, you're loitering."

Silence.

"Okay. Let's see some ID guys?"

Realizing this is just a regular case of the heat hassling them and nothing more, the men relax. Everyone is clean so they allow the police to search them.

"He just searched me," the man says.

"Thanks for telling me," the other officer says smirking. "What's your name big homie?"

"Marshon Welch. I ain't no big nothing either."

"Sure, sure. The rest of you get the fuck outta here." He demands while frisking Marshon. "Look back if you want and see if I can't find a gun for y'all to share." Prior incidents convince them that his threat is legitimate. They leave their comrade behind with very little fuss or concern.

The bare room is sparsely furnished. Three chairs and a table are the only items occupying the windowless space. The architect must have structured this room to induce extreme discomfort. He overdid his job from the look of Cynthia. Sweat soaks her to the underclothes as she sits in the lone chair on her side of the table. A part of her is angry. After sitting in the room alone for the past half hour, she has finally figured out the officer's face. Like a bad dream, it all comes back to her. Tyler's death, the officer being shot, her being alone and no one around to take the ridicule but her. The door to her little box opens, interrupting her thoughts. All business is the expression worn by Suffiyah as she enters wielding a thick manila folder. Cynthia's eye bounce back and forth from the folder to Suffiyah face. Anger has taken a backseat and anxiety is driving.

"Ms. Rocelli, I'm Detective Adams. This is regarding an issue with your vehicle. First, are you the only person who drives your car?" Cynthia thinks for a second.

"Yes."

"Even while Tyler was alive?"

"Yes."

"Are you positive?"

"I think. No, I know no one else drove my car."

Suffiyah opens the folder and shuffles through the papers. The thing that was nagging at her memory finally surfaced.

"It's strange you say that. I didn't peg you as a suspect, but it's no other possibility. You just confirmed that you don't let anyone drive your car. This is video surveillance from the bank." She slides the picture over for Cynthia to see. When she pulled Cynthia's 1999 Pontiac Bonneville over, she couldn't help but notice that although the car was navy blue, the driver's door was white.

"Is that your car, Ms. Rocelli? Because if so, then you are a co-conspirer to robbery in the first degree. Oh and felony murder, because the robbery resulted in the death of Tyler Scott."

The car that backfired was Cynthia Rocelli's. Suffiyah misunderstood. Tyler wasn't surprised by the car backfiring, but more at seeing his getaway car getting away from him. Her defiant streak once cracked, is now broken as she stares at her car. The water pours from her tear ducts like it's a faucet. Suffiyah's face remains stoic. The seconds of silence become insufferable.

"I wasn't there, I swear to Christ!"

"So that's not your car?"

"Yes."

"But you don't let anyone drive your car, remember?"

"Yes, but no. Geez, this is so un-fucking-fair. I don't want any trouble. Why are you doing this to me?" Cynthia transforms into a helpless child.

"You're doing this to you. When you decided to play the transporter to your boyfriend. I'm tired of this." Suffiyah waves her hand in exasperation. "I'm going to read you your rights so you can officially be charged."

"No! Please, Miss? I wasn't there. I swear to Christ I wasn't there!"

A puddle of snot takes form over top of her duck lips. She weeps and kicks at the table legs.

"So who was?"

"Not me! I was going through heroin withdrawals, my bones ached. I could hardly walk, let alone drive. But that's my car so—"

Cynthia expression changes as if she's been smacked mid-sentence.

"Mally! Fucking A-right, it could have only been Mally." She smiles at something in her head, brightening up her pug like face.

The bare room is sparsely furnished. Three chairs and a table are the only items occupying the windowless space. The depiction of this room seems redundant to say the least. But in the lifestyle of the average criminal, what we call redundancy they interpret as living. Some spend more time in these little rooms then they do at home. Some against their will, but many by choice. The code of the streets are like fairytales in today's society. Standup men in the underbelly are like dinosaurs, once believed in but now extinct. If you were to see one you would believe yourself to be hallucinating. But Marshon Welch prides himself on being raised by dinosaurs and the prehistoric code is embedded in his DNA. The unbothered look showcases his sentiments towards his current dilemma. Detective Lewis walks into the room with a single photo in hand.

"Good afternoon, Mr. Welch? How's it going?"

Marshon stares at him as if he's of no more importance than the chair in which he sits.

"That good? Okay well I only have one question." Lewis places the photo in the center of table. "What can you tell me about him? I can make the fifty bags of heroin you were caught with go away."

It never ceases to amaze Marshon how many law officers are willing to break the laws. He was searched thoroughly by the first officer and he came out clean. The second officer sends everyone else away as he checks him and a brick magically appears in his pants pocket. He smiles smugly at Detective Lewis. They've done this dance on an occasion or two, mostly to Lewis' disappointment.

"This conversation appears one sided, don't you think?" Marshon spits on the floor. This is usually around the time when Lewis gets physical. His interrogations are very hands on.

"Well since you can't tell me about him, let me tell you about you. Three nights ago, three masked men entered a liquor store. The first one in was Wayne-Wayne. He grabbed Victor Arocho at gunpoint. Sound familiar? No? I'll continue. The last of the gunmen had a tattoo on each wrist. The right wrist says, *Cali* and the left says *Boy*." Lewis makes himself comfortable in the chair. "I'm willing to bet, Mr. Munch, that under those sleeves I can find those words."

"I-"

"No, don't speak. You've been so quiet thus far. But hear this. Forget the brick, it's gone. That was just the price of conversation. But in three days, I will have a murder warrant for you. I could care less about a dead spic." He taps the picture. "Get me him or I get you. Your choice." Munch is speechless. "You're losing your smug expression, Mr. Welch. Go get you some air for a couple of days. I'll see you in seventy-two hours."

"You've broken my heart," the caller claims. "It's as if I don't even exist to you anymore. After all I've done to catch your attention?"

"Why are you doing this? What did I do to you?" Suffiyah asks.

She looks under the doors in the bathroom to make sure none of the stalls were occupied.

"But I blame myself," he continues as if she's said nothing. "I guess my best wasn't good enough for you, so I apparently have to do better. Expect a gift in a few days." The call ends.

Suffiyah stares at her phone. This is like an episode of the *Twilight Zone*, only question is—when does it end?

CHAPTER 17

T HE STACCATO RHYTHM OF THE assault rifle mugs the night of its peace. Sixty-two year old Emma Wise immediately rolls from her bed to the floor and covers her head with her arms. As a lifelong resident of Newark, she knows the necessary precautions to take in these events. The gunshots are so close they sound as if it's being fired in her living room. Thunder. That's the most accurate way to describe the sound. Just as actual thunder announces the impending rain, so does the gun. When the thunder subsides it will rain tears, hearts will flood with pain and hope will be washed away. Ms. Emma lifts her body from the floor as the noise ceases. Silently she thanks God for His protection. The rapid patter of bare feet causes her heartbeat to skip as she visualizes one of the stray bullets implanted in her granddaughter. Instead of the footsteps coming closer, they seem to be going in the opposite direction. She hears the front door jerked open.

"Nooooo!"

On her front porch lays a body that will never lift on its own again. Blood leaks profusely from the many exit wounds and paint the steps crimson. His baby face can be seen partially beneath his hood. His lips frozen in a permanent smirk. The phone by his hand showing his last conversation via text.

"Open the door in one minute"
"Say please"
"Gtfoh!"

"Closed door means closed legs :p"
"LOL please"
"LOL coming"

Zzzz Zzzz. The phone vibrates nonstop. Benji's hand drunkenly slaps the nightstand in search of his phone. Sleep blurs his vision as he attempts to make out the name on his screen. He blinks repeatedly until he can clearly read the name. His eyes go from her name to the time. *What the fuck?* It's 12:43 in the morning.

"Hello... Yeah... Breathe... I can't understand... Just calm down... I'm on my way..."

Benji awakens fully but is now further out of touch of what's going on. The incoherent call might as well have been in a foreign tongue. Very little of what she said was comprehendible but the urgency was evident.

"Have you ever seen A Bronx Tale?"

"Why? You think your one of the great ones?"

"Okay, I'm going to take that as a yes. Don't be an ass, Benjamin." Sakinah plucks him.

"Anyway. Lorenzo the bus driver says the worst thing in life is wasted talent. Do you agree?"

Benji smiles at her question. She comes out of the clear blue with these questions. You never know where they came from or where they're headed. Only thing for certain is there's a purpose to whatever she's saying.

"I guess I do somewhat. I never really gave it thought."

"So, think now. Yes or no?"

"Yes."

"I'm glad you said that." Sakinah gets up from the couch and walks out the room.

When she returns, her hands contain notebooks and pens.

"Every day you always have these handwritten letters for me. The way you're able to communicate through written word weakens me. I'm addicted to it. I think if you neglected writing me for just one day,

I'd be physically ill. Your words are so powerful and real, but secretive and unheard. Baby, just imagine the affect you can have on the world."

"Nobody's interested in what I got to say."

"Maybe, maybe not. But I am. So I want you to write me a story."

"About what?"

"Anything."

"You think I could do that?"

"No, not really."

"So why—"

"But, I know you can do anything." She smiles, passing him the notebooks. "You're my superhero."

"My girl usta say the worst thing in life is wasted talent. What you think?"

"No disrespect but I think it's stupid. Some people don't have talent. So how do you waste what you don't have?"

"This just it though. Everybody has a talent, you just have to identify it. You ever wanted to do something in life, but it seemed farfetched?" Drama opens his mouth but it shuts automatically.

"What?" Benji asks.

"Nuthin."

"You was 'bout to say something, Playboy."

"What so you could jail off of me? Nah, I'm good."

"For real bruh you could holla at me."

"My G cuz," he apologizes, "if it seem like I'm playin' you, but I ain't 'bout to be out here daydreaming. Too much real shit be goin' on to be fantasizing."

"Understandable. But its only fantasy if you choose not to make it reality. Just trust that I'm being a hunnid, aiight?"

Drama tosses this around mentally, after a few moments he mumbles, "Acting." He does so while staring out the window.

"Why acting? Have you ever done it?"

"Nah. But if given the chance to be someone other than a baby loc from down bottom, if only for a half hour a day, would be a relief. It feel crazy waking up every day wondering if you gonna see tonight. Or coming out at night and wondering if you will see the sunrise. So I envy these clown ass actors. They make a living being a different dude than the one they were cursed to be."

"If you had the opportunity to pursue acting, what would you do?"

"Leave all the drama behind me." He says still staring out the window.

Death is so common an occurrence around these parts, even this sixteen year old boy is planning ways to evade it. Benji is saddened by his admittance. Silence joins them on this journey as each entertains his own thoughts. They eventually pull in front of a house in Montclair. After Benji places a call, an older woman comes outside. He goes over to her and they speak briefly before both walk to the car. Drama rolls down his window as they approach his side.

"Hello, Draymon. My name is Mrs. Burnett. How can I assist you?"

"I don't know. I ain't know I was in need of help," he replies with much attitude.

"Everyone does, my love. Everyone does."

"You said you had a dream. Well, Mrs. Burnett is your genie," Benji interjects.

"My what?"

"You said you wish you could act. Well, Mrs. Burnett is an acting coach. She's going to grant your wish."

"I can't afford that and my words wasn't for everybody," Drama responds more riled up.

"Calm down, Draymon. This is my pleasure. There will be no charge except that beautiful smile," Mrs. Burnett butts in now.

No matter the age of a woman, their charm is ever present. Drama smiles and blushes like a school girl.

"See? You just paid me. Now I owe you my services."

~~~

Moisture seeps into the denim pants' seat as Benji sits on the curb in the rain. He rubs his palms roughly into his eyes as he tries to get some type of understanding on everything or better yet, anything. This day started off so promising as he cruised the city with Drama. He can't bring himself to look over at the white sheet. This morning he was given an opportunity to uncover his dream and tonight he's covered in his nightmare.

"Over twenty shots. It had to be like a choppa," the young man says enthusiastically.

Suffiyah writes his words, all while staring down the street. She watches as Lewis walks away from a father and daughter on the other side of the yellow tape. Something about the smile on his face makes her uneasy.

…I heard the body fall and I knew it was over."

"Did you see the shooter?"

"Huh?"

"Did you see the shooter?"

"Oh nah. I ain't here for all that."

"Mr. Cooper?" Benji looks up with bloodshot eyes.

"I don't know if you remember me, but I'm Detective Lewis."

He extends his hand towards Benji to be shaken. Benji looks from his hand back to his face before turning his head.

"So you do remember me? Well what brings you here to *my* scene at this time of night?"

His statement and presence reverts Benji back to his former goon at this point in time.

"You pigs fuck me up! It's a little homie under that sheet gone forever and your crab ass over here chattin'. He don't mean nuthin' to you but more paperwork. We don't mean nuthin' to you, so you give us nuthin'. No love, no options. You view him as one less gangbanger and you don't even know him, pussy!"

"Mr. Cooper!"

Lenae flies into his arms stopping his verbal tirade. The heat from her tears burn through his shirt as his embrace muffles her cries. Her little hands clench the back of his jacket desperately. She holds on as if her grip is the only thing keeping him from disappearing, while his hold reassures her he'll never leave. If looks could kill, Lewis would drop dead right now. He doesn't even have the decency to grant them a moment. He just stands there smirking while Benji eye fucks him.

"How do you measure failure?" Benji asks from the pulpit. "Because as I stand here, I can't help feeling like I failed. Draymon was me at a bad point in my life. His anger, his pain, his despair. Most of all his courage, his heart. As much as he feared the world he faced it. But as tough as his exterior was, if he loved you it was real and evident. And even without him saying it, you knew the love was eternal. There was no bounds to what he would risk for what he loved, even his life. Sad to say, but that was the same love he had for the streets because he had nothing else to consider his own. To feel like he belonged there, until I found him and he found MISFITS. Every Saturday he would wow me with his perception of the world. Under his eye he tattooed 'Why?'. So I asked him what made him do it and what it meant. He said *'What it say?'*"

Benji laughs at the memory as he looks at the ceiling. He figures keeping his eyes off the crowd will keep the tears in his eyes.

"*'It means why.'* That's what he said, so I just gave up. Five minutes later he picked up as if we never left the subject. *'Why we poor? Why we starve? Why we hate each other? Why I gotta hide my tears? Why do I gotta be scared? Why this only life for us, bruh? Why are people so judgmental that they write my tattoo off as a stupid mistake, instead of calculated thoughts? They say that we don't think and this tattoo is a reminder to the world that I'm always thinking.'* Those were his words to me. Now I look at his casket and then up to God and ask why?"

Benji used money from his grant for MISFITS to pay for Drama's funeral service. His mother was an addict and she could only afford to cremate him at best. Not while Benji was still breathing.

Suffiyah sat in the back row of Perry's Funeral Home, as Benji gave the eulogy. His words brought back the image of the baby faced boy with the mutilated torso slain under a sheet. He provided a soundtrack to the silent movie playing in her mind as she found herself crying. The repass will be held at *MISFITS Inc.*, which is her next stop. She looked to her left and Detective Lewis eyed her with disgust. She rolled her eyes. Just because she was here at a professional capacity, doesn't mean she wasn't entitled to have feelings. Being a cop doesn't erase her humanity.

Benji walks to his van. His body sags from the weight of the world he's carrying. The repass was more depressing than the funeral. Holding Lenae together was a task he was ill prepared for. Her heart was left in the cemetery and it was no changing that. As he held her, he remembered himself when his heart was left in the cemetery. There were no words anyone could offer to console him. So he wouldn't insult her with worthless words, he just gives her his shoulder. How he kept a dry eye through all this is blowing his mind. Instinct causes him to turn around abruptly. The Honda Accord is only about two feet away and creeping. He places his back to his van and stares at the oncoming car. Why couldn't this car have come five minutes earlier, before Lay Low pulled off? Through the window he can make out a feminine silhouette, which eases his tension some. She puts her hazards on and steps out. Seeing Suffiyah here is the last thing he needs. His emotions are so discombobulated, he can't control them.

"Sorry to hear about your student."

In the life he once led you were either friend or foe. For the life of him he can't figure where to place Suffiyah.

"You don't have to be so cold around me. I didn't come to be a cop. I'm here as a friend. I know how strong you are." She steps into his personal space. "But that doesn't mean I can't be strength for you too."

"Why?"

"Because it feels right." She shrugs. "Follow me." Benji frowns. "Please?"

They both get in their vehicles.

Suffiyah walks through her home barefoot in sweatpants and a t-shirt. But she feels nervous as if she's uncovered.

What is making me this bold and reckless? Loneliness?

She takes the cup of tea in her bedroom. The portable Bluetooth speaker bedside plays music from her phone. Benji sits on the edge of the bed with his face in his palms.

Uhm Uhm, she clears her throat. He looks up and accepts the mug of tea.

"It's peppermint. When I'm going through a lot, it soothes me."

"Thank you."

"Can I take your coat?"

After hanging his blazer, she walks around the bed. Placing herself behind him, she massages his shoulders.

"When you were giving the eulogy, I cried. He was truly a baby. I overlooked it at the scene. As an officer we're taught to detach ourselves from our emotions. But at the funeral, through your eyes, I saw him for what he was. I saw him for everything you knew he could be. I saw beyond what other people perceived from face value. I saw his promise, his ambition, his worth, his fear. I saw the love that the girl lost, so I cried. Then I realized I was crying for you. I could see the torment in your face, but not a tear. So strong or so stubborn. You were fighting your emotions and you still are. So I came to be your peace. Your strength. It's okay to cry for him. Look at me?" Benji maintains his focus on the floor. "Benjamin?" She pulls his face and sees the tears restlessly pooling inside of his eyelids. "Aww. It's okay, Baby, cry." She hurries in front of him and hugs him.

With his face pulled to her stomach he finds solace. As he links his arms around her waist, he releases thirty-one years of pain and hurt. Suffiyah lays her cheek on his head and does the same.

CHAPTER 18

Dreams and nightmares.

Today is a day in which I was forced to reevaluate my dreams. I was under the impression that chasing your dreams was a means of outrunning your nightmares. Each running concurrent to one another, but on parallel planes. But what if your dreams and nightmares originate from the same place? Originate from the same pain? Are they not congruent? To fully grasp or appreciate joy, do you not need to experience its opposite? Today I buried sanity. Today I buried hope. Today I buried tomorrow. We proceed throughout life anticipating these definite tomorrows. But what if today is it? The day that the parallel plane ceases to exist and dreams and nightmares collide. Only one will survive the collision. I promised a young man that if he pursued his dreams, I'd protect him from his nightmares. And he believed in me. So, today I also buried my word. Because today I buried that young man. A young man whom I never told I love him and he was more precious than any jewel unearthed. That the world was undeserving of the treasure that was his presence.

The city too small and envious to be considered his home. His body unable of containing his prodigious soul. And I unentitled to the honor of his loyalty or friendship. In this endeavor we call life, what makes it easier to cope with and special is having someone to share it with. A strength to your weakness. A hope to your despair. A calm to your storm. In you someone had that and today she lost it. As we buried the frame that housed your greatness, I dug up the truth. Though alive, few of us barely live. Though walking, few of us rarely move. Though talking, few of us ever say something worth hearing. Though we have eyes, many of us lack vision. Even given slumber, so few of us ever dream. And that's the nightmare. From my mouth to your ears, Drama, I love you. For being the boy who was man enough to say something worth hearing and dream. I am eternally grateful to have been blessed with your acquaintance.

Just Benjamin

S UFFIYAH READS THE ARTICLE FOR the tenth time. Each time her pillow absorbed more moisture as she stared at a still sleeping Benji. Here he was in her house when the whole department had him as the prime suspect, thanks to Lewis. But not in her eyes. Last night he shared so much that she felt privileged. With the skill of a seasoned cat burglar, he stole her heart while disrupting nothing. After he cried into her t-shirt, she removed and used it to erase any remnants of his agony.

> *"You're just too good to be true, can't take my eyes off of you, you'd be like heaven to touch, I want to hold you so much, at long last love has arrived*

and I thank God I'm alive..." Lauryn Hill's voice caters to the mood perfectly.

"Every time that I hear this song, your face appears in my mind."

Suffiyah confesses as Benji's eyes rise from her stomach, where his head just rested, to her bare breast where they linger momentarily. Next to the bullet scar in her shoulder. Then finally up to her eyes. She still saw the sorrow but it was now coupled with longing.

"Since the first day in the mall, I knew I needed to see your smile every day."

Securing both his hands, she places them on her waistline.

"I blew that opportunity and paid with my heart. Did you know that?"

She cups his face as he slides her sweatpants down slowly.

"So I started reading every article you've ever written. Just to be close to you. Just to hear you."

Her hands drop to the buttons of his shirt as she unfastens them methodically. Seductively.

"They touched me emotionally, like I wanted you to do physically."

She stepped out of the sweatpants which now were around her ankles.

"I could see your face, taste your lips, smell your cologne, hear your voice, but," Placing her thumbs in the black lace boy short panties, she wiggles out of them. "I couldn't feel *you*."

Gently, she pushes him back on her bed and unbuckles his belt.

"So every time I hear Lauryn's voice on this song. I crave the feel of you."

Her mouth waters at the sight of his chiseled frame and the tent created in his boxers.

"Now I can." She straddles his waist and kisses him passionately, as they lay chest to chest.

With her feet, she pushes his boxers down. As his hard key grazes her lock, a shiver shoots through her body. *"I need you bae-beee if it's quite all-right, I need you bae-beee to warm the lone-lee nights, I love you bae-beee trust in me when I say, okay?"*

"Heaven."

That's the best way to describe it. Benji has never experienced a feeling like that. As he lays with his eyes closed reminiscing on the nights events, he feels Suffiyah's eyes on him. He doesn't need to open his to recognize the angel lying next to him. If this is a dream, he isn't allowing it to end anytime soon. Her body was perfection. Plain and simple. When she placed him inside of her, the wet warmth of her tunnel fit him like a glove. And acted as a conduit for his frustration to pass through.

How could this get any better? Then he feels her lips touch his.

Zzzz Zzzz

Of course the phone would interrupt her moment. Her sixth sense is telling her not to answer or risk being whisked away from all this. But the continuous buzzing is hard to ignore in the quiet room.

"If you need to take that call, I'll be quiet," Benji offers, picking up on her hesitation.

He isn't asleep? Only now does she think how she must appear to him. Lying in bed naked with him after one lunch and what can only be rated as the worst date in history. Now her phone rings nonstop in the wee hours of the morning. Only two words can be going through his mind right now. *Booty call.* She suddenly feels the necessity to defend her honor.

"It can only be work. No one calls me. Not at night, not like this. I don't date or have male friends on that accord."

Her explanation seeming as futile as swinging at shadows. Abandoning explaining, she grabs for the phone to prove herself.

"Excuse me? Hello, Detective Adams…Where?... Now?... Does it matter that I'm off?... Be there in ten minutes."

She didn't hear Benji get up, but he stands there dressing silently.

"Stay, please?"

"It's okay, you have to work. I do too."

"At 3:30 in the morning?" she asks in disbelief.

The jealous undertone of the question doesn't go over Benji's head. He chuckles. "Yes. I have to finish the article you were reading. But…"

He extends his hand towards the bed and she grasps it limply. He pulls her from the bed and embraces her naked body.

"I appreciate what you've done for me." She frowns. "Not the sex. Just simply gracing me with your company. You said you'd be my strength and you kept your word."

The experience of being in Benji's embrace was debilitating. Which made her appreciative of his strength, because right now it was the only thing holding her up.

Zzzz Zzzz

"Detective Adams." Suffiyah initiates the Bluetooth feature as she drives.

"I told you I had a gift for you," the unmistakable voice says.

"You know I won't rest 'til I catch you, right?" Unwilling to be further bullied by the bodiless voice, Suffiyah stands her ground.

"Seeing as you and your friend are just splitting ways a few moments ago, I don't believe you were getting much rest anyway."

This causes Suffiyah to shudder. He's watching her.

"Suddenly it's so *quiet.* Ungrateful whore. Where'd the brave detective go? All that I do for your attention and you fuck Benjamin. Now you'll really suffer. Meet you at the scene."

"Perfect," Detective Lewis says under his breath.

Eying the curves of her breast and contour of her hips, her beauty is undeniable. The woman lays on full display for Lewis. Is it weird that he's lusting over a corpse? He's human. He has the right to admire beauty, even if it's no longer breathing. It's like looking at a nude sculpture. If he's weird, than so are the billions of museum attendees. He mentally defends his inappropriate erection. Jumping from the tap on his shoulder, he turns to face Suffiyah.

"Detective Adams, I didn't hear you coming."

"I just arrived. What do we have?"

"Apparently Mr. Benjamin Cooper has given us another beautiful cadaver. She's a replica to Sakinah Rogers and the other two women." Reading Suffiyah's expression, he says, "You disagree? They're like identical quadruplets."

"No. You're right, it's uncanny. But how can you be sure it's Mr. Cooper?"

"Well I can't physically prove it, but I only need a few more weeks and he'll never see the light of day again."

It's slightly after eight in the morning and Suffiyah's just leaving the scene. Before pulling off two calls are placed. The first to Dr. O'Malley, procuring an immediate session. The second to her rock.

"Hey, Sugar! Who do I have to blow for this early morning surprise?"

"You are so raunchy it's sad, Alicia." Suffiyah enjoys the much needed laugh.

"Sad for who? Shit, I'm smiling. But how may I help you Suffiyah?" Lee Lee says.

"Is your shoulder preoccupied or is it available for little ol' me?"

Turning serious at the tone of Suffiyah's voice, Lee Lee responds, "Always. As soon as I get off work I'm going to go to your house."

"Okay. I have to see my therapist and then I'll meet you there."

"Su, are you going to be okay or should I call out?"

"I'm good, Lee. It's a lot but we'll get through it. See you later, babes."

"Kay."

The tiny Mexican woman smiles up with her discolored teeth as she clips his toenails. He places his foot between her breasts with little subtlety. Using his foot to fondle the woman at his behest. The large tip that they're accustomed to when he frequents this establishment affords him more advantages than they extend to the typical customer. He views them as vassal. Put here to carry out the orders of the breadwinner. If Suffiyah could only switch roles with these women and understand her position. The feel of her mouth and breast as unforgettable as her smile and walk. He could feel her nipple budding under the expertise of his thumb.

"Poppi?" the woman says hesitantly.

As he's snatched from his reveries, his eyes land on the discomposed look on the woman's face. The smile remains but it lacks sincerity and her eyes are downturned. Now he realizes he was openly groping her. His hand cups her bosom as his fingers roamed. He snatches away abruptly.

"Done, Poppi?" she inquires, eager to get him out of her area.

"Okay so I brought wine and wine. It seemed like it was going to be that kind of night. I ordered us pizza, too. It should be here in a few minutes. Now what's bothering you?"

Suffiyah relays everything to Lee Lee in totality. From the first murder to all the calls before this morning's incident. Only stopping to get the pizza.

"I hope you forgive me, Lee. I couldn't tell you about the tire without risking placing you in further danger."

"Yeah, I forgive you. But that bastard owes me a new tire." Depend on Lee Lee to bring sunshine after the rain. "Where do we stand on suspects?"

Suffiyah shuffles closer to Alicia on the couch as she goes to the *Notes* app on her IPhone.

"Dr. O'Malley told me to look into Tyler Scott's background, so I did. Nobody on his side is a big fan of mines. After pulling over his girlfriend, I found out about his partner in crime. Jamal Wright. He was my first suspect. I pulled up his profile and I can honestly say, I've never seen him before."

"That doesn't discredit him because you don't know him. Lots of people are harmed by crazy strangers daily."

"You're right. But everything about these crimes have a personal feel. You don't think?"

"A little, keep going."

"Suspect two, Lieutenant McFarland. The cards at the scene scream 'insider'. Who else besides a cop could grab them so freely? Remember how upset he was at me when he suspended me? Prior to that, there were whispers about him being envious of my exposure with the shooting at the bank. Somehow he felt overshadowed. Then, I return and he places me with Charles Lewis?" She sips her wine. "Definitely suspect number three. He's crooked as the letter S. I always, I mean always catch him staring at me with perversion. Then girl get this, I'm at the scene this morning and I swear to God he's staring at the dead woman like he wants to have sex. I figured I was bugging. But he turns around and really has the nerve to be hard. It took everything in me to remain professional. It just strikes me as funny that McFarland would pair me with him. Maybe they're in cahoots." She rolls her eyes in exasperation.

"Those are your only suspects?"

Suffiyah stares at a spot on the wall for what seems like an eternity before speaking.

"Lee, I slept with Benji last night."

"Whoa! What?"

"Before all this happened, I was going to tell you. I met him and invited him back here. We talked, he cried. No, we cried. Together. Then I knew I wanted him and I can't explain it but I knew beyond a doubt that I loved him. So, I gave him the greatest gift I could give. Me."

"That's so sweet, Honey. I'm happy for you, but why do you look so sad?"

Suffiyah looks at Alicia now instead of the wall.

"Because, he's my fourth suspect."

CHAPTER 19

"A PRINCE, THEREFORE, BEING COMPELLED KNOWINGLY to adopt the beast, ought to choose the fox and the lion; because the lion cannot defend himself against the snares and the fox cannot defend himself against the wolves. Therefore, it's necessary to be a fox to discover the snares and a lion to terrify the wolves. Those who rely simply on the lion do not understand what they are about." After reading this passage out of *The Prince* by Niccolo Machiavelli, Benji pauses to gauge the affect it has on his pupils. When first taught this lesson by the man who introduced him to the Blood lifestyle, it was like receiving a new set of eyes. He viewed everything differently after that.

~~~

Lay Low and Benji sat in the living room of the shabby apartment. The smell from back to back Newports being smoked by their OG, Do Rite, was suffocating the little fresh air in the room. At this point Cali Block wasn't in existence, it was hardly an aspiration. Merely a plan on a sheet of paper. This meeting was the first brick laid to the foundation of that plan.

"Here's the problem." Do Rite pauses to take another drag of his cigarette.

He was a man of few words, but the ones he said held the weight of mountains. The cigarette smoke pirouetted in front of his face. He was a dark skinned man in his mid-thirties. Patches of hair were growing back onto his almost always freshly shaved baldhead. His slightly cocked left eye and the jagged scar running across his face only adds to his menace and heightens his disreputable reputation. Some people look like gangsters but act as gentlemen. Then there are those who look like gentlemen but are truly gangsters. Do Rite is of the small party who actually have the look that fits his persona. And as the smoke gathers and billows in front of him, Benji can't help but thinking of being at a meeting with the devil.

"The money all goes to the house. They got cameras all 'round the house, so they're always aware of the surroundings. All the fee-l's know to go there and whenever we post in front of there the heat burns down. How we get the win? Where do the team get in at?" Do Rite poses the question to his protégés.

Lay Low speaks first, "We mask up and hit the house. Lay everybody down and get the work. Kill two birds with one stone."

"What you say, Benj?"

"I'm saying, I'm with Lay. Or either we hit a fiend on their porch and shut they shit down," Benji responds.

"Now y'all thinking like lions, Blood!" Do Rite says with enthusiasm.

Earning a smile from the duo. Compliments from Do Rite are given sparingly, so when extended they should be received with pride.

"What 'bout the cameras though, Lay? Or I guess they can't see you coming for them? Givin' them enough time to strap up and wait for us to blitz. Then they turn the tables on us. How smart is that?" Do Rite assassinates Lay Low's suggestion while Benji shakes his head. "That was stupid right, Benji Ru?" He now turns his attention to Benji.

"Where you hustle at?"

"On 11*th*."

"Where they got the apartment at?"

"On 11*th*."

"Trillz, so you're standing outside hustlin' while they're in the house. When you kill the fiend on they steps and the heat start runnin' down every day, they gonna bypass you standin' on that corner all day?"

"Nah."

"Aiight, so nobody gonna be able to eat, right? How that benefit us?" Lay Low and Benji remain quiet after the berating of their ideas. *"Bein' a lion is cool, because it shows strength. But bein' a fox is necessity, because a fox is clever. A thinker. A lion knocks down the unlocked door, where the fox would have just turned the knob. What's a muscle wit'out the brains or brains wit'out the muscle? A waste. In every situation we gotta be the lion and the fox."*

~~~

"I was taught the value of being a dual beast many years ago. Throughout the time, I've applied that mentality to every situation. At first I believed it was only a tool to physically conquer a goal. But now I understand it to be a means to conquer life. Society throws so many obstacles in our way to impede our progress," He walks over and takes hold of Lenae's hand. "So we have to be smart enough to duck the ones we can, but strong enough to overcome the ones we can't."

CHAPTER 20

THE DINGY BUILDING LOOMS OVER Detective Adams as she stares up at it. It stands just pass the intersection of Washington Street and W. Kinney Streets, on the W. Kinney side. Across from it is the 440 Washington Street Apartments. This area is a drug addict's paradise. Every strain of drugs can be found here, ranging from Viagra to Heroin. Another addiction brings Suffiyah here though. As she climbs the stairs and presses the intercom to be buzzed, the door is flung open forcefully. A shabby looking couple barrels through, arguing and brushes right pass her as if she doesn't exist, never breaking their stride. The wind created from the door carries the pungent smell of urine and body odor, causing her to scrunch her nose. The door jamb is blocked with all types of foreign objects, enabling anyone to come in unannounced. Taking this as a sign, she proceeds inside. The smell intensifies once the door closes behind her.

Boom! WOOF! WOOF!

She jumps at the sound of a large dog slamming into one of the apartment doors. Dogs terrify her, even poodles. This one though, sounds like a monster. In her mind she pictures a cross breed of a Pit-bull and a real bull. Fear that its owner might open the door causes her to scurry up three flights of stairs hastily. Her destination is in the front of her behind a once beige door, which is now several variations of browns. KNOCK! KNOCK! A TV can be heard in the background but no answer. KNOCK! KNOCK!

"Yoo! What the fuck!" comes the voice from inside of the apartment.

"Who the fuck is it?"

"Ranesha, its Detective Adams. May I come in for a moment?"

After what seems like an eternity, the door finally swings open. Suffiyah sees a naked woman walking away from the door and she enters. The living room wouldn't make a home designer magazine but it's tidier than she expected. The young woman lays back on the couch and lights up a Newport 100.

"You want me to step out so you can get dressed?" Suffiyah asks. The woman cocks her legs and gets comfortable, further exposing herself.

"No, I'm cool," she replies. "Ranee—"

"S-T-O-R-M. You call me Ranesha like we fly. You don't know me. We ain't that! So miss me with that Ranesha shit!"

Feeling herself getting aggravated, Suffiyah breathes deeply before continuing. "Storm, I need help finding Aaliyah's killer. So many pieces are missing that I don't understand and I need to in order to bring this man to justice."

Storm looks her up and down and then down and up. Making sure she is looking Suffiyah directly in the eyes before replying, "You don't think you too cute for all this police shit?" But she pronounced it like po-lease.

"No. I never knew it was a beauty standard for the job."

"Well. Storm smacks her lips loudly. "Have you ever been tasted by a girl before?"

"Been what?"

Storm shakes her head annoyed

"Have you ever let a bitch eat your pussy? Is that clear enough?"

"No! Where did that come from?"

"I been up all night rollin' off these mollies and I'm horny. I could see your coochie print through ya workpants and I wanna kiss it. That's that," she says with the ease which with someone asks for a piece of candy.

"No thank you," Suffiyah says while allowing her hand to cover her private area.

"Well, I guess we don't have nothing for each other then. Lock my door when you leave, Miss?" Storm says as she starts to massage her own private area. Suffiyah looks on in disgust before turning to leave.

"Umm, ass fat too." Suffiyah slams the door to Storms laughter.

Detective Adams couldn't have been in the building for more than ten minutes at the most. The man thinks as he watches her start her car up. He watches through his driver's side mirror and waits until she turns the corner to perform a u-turn. In a matter of seconds he's parking in the spot Suffiyah just vacated. Adrenaline pulses through his body at the thought of his brass movement. Every move made thus far has been premeditated. This plan differs in the sense that it is all improvised. His hands begin to perspire as he knocks at the apartment door. Everything is happening so fast. It's as if he transported himself from the car to the third floor of this building. Nervousness sets in as he realizes he doesn't know what he's going to say when she asks "Who is it?" He doesn't want the neighbors overhearing him. As his mind races, he can clearly hear her approaching steps. His mouth dries out as he prepares to respond. Surprisingly, the door swings open. He's greeted by the rear view of a nude body retreating further into the apartment. Her hips sway in a hypnotizing manner as she pushes her fingers through her hair.

"I knew you would be back. Go in the living room and lose those pants. I bet you won't be coming here to question me next time. This tongue is heaven, Detective Adams. You ready to be an Angel or naw?"

Dr. O'Malley's office has become a sanctuary of sorts or better a war room. Suffiyah's brain seems to function at a higher frequency with the assistance of Dr. O'Malley. The puzzle pieces come together more clearly in here.

"Okay. So the Tyler Scott angle isn't written off but it needs more digging. I've been thinking, maybe we have to go back further, because we're missing a vital piece." Dr. O'Malley says, "Do you think you can get your entire foster history from child services? If so I believe we can tie your dreams and these crimes together. There is no way that these dreams are of zero relevance."

The relationship between the two of them has exceeded the doctor/patient stage and graduated to a friendship. Since a little girl, Dr. O'Malley has been intrigued by mysteries. Which led to her occupation presently. The mystery of the human mind is far more complex then crimes. Because it's the mind which shapes the necessity to commit the crimes. In language arts class, you're taught about cause and effect. Crime is only the effect, but the mind is the cause. Breaking into the psyche and establishing the when, where, who, whys and how's, is what drives her. Her nature is what first excited her about these sessions. Her woman's intuition though, is what led her into befriending Suffiyah. She sympathizes with the situation Suffiyah is in and the fear she is tortured by. She sees the hand of death closing in on her and would do anything to keep her out of its grasp.

"I believe I can. I just have to find the time between all of these cases."

"You have to, honey. The victims are all you in the killers mind. Which suggests to me that it's only a matter of time before he becomes disinterested in these stand-ins'. I believe he's using them for practice and once he's confident enough he'll go for his real target. Time is not your friend this go around. We don't have the luxury."

The man looked at the reflection of himself in his rear view mirror. A glint of satisfaction and accomplishment showed in his eyes. His aggravated notions of retribution left him unperturbed by his cravenly acts. The evidence of his encounter stains the front of his pants. He gropes himself as he plays it back in his memory. The look of shock on their faces is almost as great as the release. He didn't even have to strip her of her clothes. How befitting of the moment.

CHAPTER 21

6:00AM

THE SMELL OF COFFEE IS ingrained in the meeting room as the officers drained the brew. Coffee and adrenaline courses through their veins as they prepare for this morning's activities. Tactical gear and vests are strewn all over the room as the men and woman stare forward attentively.

"This man is a murderer, comrades. Don't allow yourselves to be lulled into complacency by his calm demeanor. Inside his mind cold, calculated thoughts are running rampant. We have time on our side, he knew we'd be coming, he just didn't know when."

Detective Lewis incites his charges. While the others are shaking the remnants of sleep from their bones, Lewis is fully charged. He's been awake since three this morning, awaiting this moment in his day. The raid should go off without a hitch, but spooking his colleagues into over aggression is his intention. This way they would be zero tolerant when approaching the suspect. In turn treating him coldly and in a threatening manner, which should have him running into Lewis' open arms. Anything to get away from a swarm of trigger happy cops.

"From my investigation, I've learned he's the shoot first ask questions later type. So let's not grant him the opportunity to shoot, huh?"

"You're such a thug when you want to be. Why you make that face?"

Benji looks at Suffiyah on face time, not realizing his features are easily read. Her smile shows her confusion.

"Nah, just something 'bout that word. To me words have a definition that add up to character."

Benji lays back in his bed as he considers how to word his thoughts. "I feel in life you have thugs and gangsters. A thug is belligerent and impulsive. Capable of thinking but never doing it at the appropriate time. The proper reaction is usually an afterthought with them. Gaining them notoriety from the wrong eyes too early. While a gangster is a visionary, intuitive, attentive, mannerly always. Sensitive but aggressive. Able to fit in and standout simultaneously. This is just my opinion though, but let me give you an example. When they were doing the RICO sweeps on the Italian Mafia, you had John Gotti running the Gambino Family. He ordered all the made members to come to his social club to pay homage. This was his way of exerting his superiority over other members of his family. A pure ego move. Majority of the made members were unknown to federal agents until Gotti paraded them in front of them. He never thought that far. I view him as a thug. Then you have *Vincent 'Chin' Gigante*," Benji says the name with such reverence it was apparent he held him in high esteem.

"They charged 'Fat Tony' Salerno for running the Genovese Family. The whole time he never was. Chin was running the family for numerous years. He usta walk his neighborhood babbling to himself in pajamas and a bathrobe. His social club was where he spent his days but nothing was said in there pertaining illegal acts. He was diagnosed as schizophrenic and overlooked. But he took to the streets after midnight and resumed his role as boss every night. Showing law enforcement what he wished for them to see, he forbade everyone from mentioning his name out loud to keep him safe from any future wiretaps. He never took any out of country trips exposing his wealth. By the time fingers pointed his way his family was good. Why? 'Cause his moves were premeditated.

Thought out, he was a gangster to me. I feel thugs live for today and gangsters prepare for what's coming tomorrow."

"You always got a philosophy on something, even this early. I think it's more to you than you're showing me, Mr. Cooper."

"What you see is me. The gangster is extinct so I could forever be the gentleman."

Meanwhile....

Car after car spills into the block as quietly as possible. On the block behind this one, the same scene is transpiring. All chatter is quieted behind the dark windows as the troops of police in each car mentally prepare for what's next. They've received confirmation that the suspect is in the house. All that's left is to apprehend him as swiftly as possible while minimizing the possibility of endangering any of the officers. Their faces were fearless but in the silent cars you can hear the butterflies fluttering in their bellies. Giving away the nervousness the masks hide.

"On my mark, exit the cruisers and surround the house."

Lewis' voice comes through the radios in each car, each breath is held as they await his go ahead.

"Car two, rear door. Car three, take the left side. Car four, take the right side. Cars five through eight, stay alert and watch for movement. Let's go!"

"I gotta get ready for work. I'm going to call you back when I finish getting dressed. You're not leaving the house no time soon right?" Suffiyah asks.

Benji places his arm behind his head relaxing more. "Not for another hour or two. My schedule isn't that crazy today. I'm going to be just laying here waiting on you." He smiles. His smile is so sincere it makes her hate herself.

"See you soon, Benji."

"Later, beautiful." Benji has no intentions of rushing out the house. For some reason he can't shake this ominous feeling. This gets under his skin because he can't pinpoint the source. His bad feeling must be contagious, because Suffiyah has been smiling all morning. But her smile never seemed to reach her eyes.

BOOM!

The burly officer almost puts his big foot through the door as he kicks it open. Wasting no time, the rest of the team follow his lead and sweep the house. Guns held out at arm's length as they rapidly approach the bedroom. Picking up pace when they see the still dark room. The beams of the flashlights show the surprise and fear on his face.

"Don't you move! Hands up!"

"Let me—"

"Shut the fuck up! Show me your hands!"

"Please move so I can decorate your wall with your brain," an officer begs.

The way the pistols are aimed steadily at his face lets him know that this isn't an empty threat. A black cop rushes out the background and pushes him from the bed. By the time his body touches the floor, the cop's knee is in his neck as his arms are yanked behind his back. The way he aggressively pulls his arm feels like his shoulder is being dislocated.

"Uggh!"

The cuffs are cinched as tight as possible.

"Secured sir."

The suspect lifts his face out of the carpet. He sees a kneeling figure in front of him and struggles to make out the face. A smile plays on his lips. "Easy gentlemen. This is a friend of mines." Detective Lewis stares down at him. "Son, I told you we'd speak again."

Knock! Knock! Knock!

"Who is it?"

"Detective Sonya Fields, Essex County Homicide. May I speak with you for a moment?"

Sonya can see the shift of light behind the peephole. She imagined herself being inspected with skepticism by the floating eye behind the door. She is just hoping the inspection process was a short one, because after spending her morning in this rank hallway she knew the odor was embedding itself in her clothes. She imagined that after standing in this stink hole knocking on every door in the corridor, the fabric softener smell has been eradicated from her clothes. Now she is the walking embodiment of the rancid stench which is this building. The slight creaking of the door brings her focus back to the task at hand. An older woman wearing a bonnet stands in the cracked door clutching her housecoat at the chest. The remnants of sleep are still evident in her age creased face as she eyes Sonya suspiciously.

"Yes?"

"Good Morning, ma'am excuse me for knocking on your door at this hour, but I'm investigating a murder in this building. So I'm going door to door to see if anyone has saw or heard anything. As of right now I have absolutely nothing to build off, so any information that you can provide me with would be appreciated."

"May I see your badge, Detective?"

The woman peers through the chained door still treating her dubiously. Sonya fished her shield from beneath the blazer of her pants suit and holds it up for examination. The lady wasn't an expert on badges but it looked real enough to her. "And I.D?" she persists. All Sonya can do is smirk. She now realizes how frustrating a traffic stop could be. Going in her handbag and retrieving her wallet, she holds it close enough to be viewed.

Click!

The door closes on her face. Her mouth stands open as realization registers. Suddenly the soft clang of the end of the chain being removed precedes the door being open.

"Come in officer."

"Thank you." Sonya passes her threshold and it smells of baked goods and fresh laundry. Compared to the hallway this was heaven.

"You can't be too careful in this building alone. Mr. Franklin downstairs, thought he let the exterminator in his apartment and them mens beat him upside his head and took what they could grab. Mrs. Reyes grandbaby got stabbed at the front door. I even heard—"

"Excuse me Ms. ? " Sonya interrupts knowing if she didn't the whole buildings problems would be laid out.

"Adams."

"Adams?"

"Adams," The woman says definitively.

"Okay, Ms. Adams. I know you're aware your neighbor across the hall was murdered. I was hoping you maybe could provide some insight into what might have happened. Did you know Ranesha Felder?"

"I was getting there when you interrupted me," Ms. Adams responds impatiently. "But she was so sweet. I mean precious. The heart of an angel, but that old devil never quits. She kept plenty folk in there. Men folk and womens. Sometimes two at a time, you know what I mean?" She asks tossing a sideways glance toward the door. Sonya just nods encouragingly. "It was sad. So beautiful a girl, but God bless the dead, she couldn't close her legs to save her life. I even heard she'd have sex for the medicines. The blue ones!"

"What do you mean?"

Ms. Adams held up a finger excusing herself and went to the bathroom. She came back carrying a small medicine bottle emptying the contents in her palm. "Medicines!" She holds the thirty milligram Oxycodone's out for Sonya's inspection. "I don't take them. Doctors gave em' to me after my hip replacement. Made me feel sluggish. I'm already old, I'm sluggish enough. So I give her, my 'scription so she don't have to sex for them. The day she passed I was about to take her these, but police was knocking at her door. A woman dressed like you. I saw her from behind through the peep in the door."

"How do you know it was a cop if you only saw her back?"

"She said it, I remember because we have the same name. That's why I looked out the door hole."

"What's the name?"

"My name?"

"No, ma'am, the officers name."

"Oh, Sophia Adams."

"Shit!" The drops of hot coffee splash Lee Lee's wrist as she slams on the brakes. She was so caught up in her thoughts that she almost ran the traffic signal. The old woman on the corner, with the poodle in her arms, glares at her with repugnance as she steps into the crosswalk. "Old Bitty," she mouths looking back at the woman. She's now more aware of everything going on around her. Ever since her and Suffiyah's conversation she's been spooked beyond explanation. Though she would never reveal this skittish movement to Suffiyah. For as long as she can remember, she's been Suffiyah's rock. To turn into a pillow in the period of her life when she needed the strength of that rock to keep her anchored, would be disadvantageous to her best friend. She needs as much support as possible right now. So if that means acting like a lion for her friend, when she truly feels as helpless as a mouse, then so be it. It's so easy to put this all off on Benjamin Cooper. His eyes ooze in infatuation for Suffiyah whenever she's in front of him. Whoever is doing the murders can only be described as obsessed. Now is that look in his eyes infatuation or obsession?

"L.T., I'm not saying she's doing the murders, especially given the sperm in the last victims. But it's suspicious, to say the least." Sonya confides to McFarland. He steeples his fingers, listening. "Before, it was just the cards and the resemblance. Now her card was at the scene and we have a witness placing her there the same day as the murder. I don't have that much faith in coincidences. If I'm evenly partially right, that's a situation we want no association with. Me as a colleague and especially you as our superior. Didn't you suspend her for this same case already?" Her last statement made him aware of the severity of these implications. Not for Suffiyah but for himself. A mark like that on his record would guarantee a cease in his career growth. Maybe even a demotion. Nobody on this force was more important to him, than himself. "I also took it upon myself to show her picture around the building. A couple was able to identify her as the woman who was walking in the building as they were exiting. How many more warnings do we need before we acknowledge the emergency? It's mighty funny after five murders that we know of, we're no closer to a killer or a concrete suspect. Feels like he's getting an inside hand to me." Sonya's mind has been focused on the aspects of this case. The career launcher that landed in her lap with this last murder, is phenomenal. A serial killer arrested with the dirty cop who assisted him? She can see herself in McFarland's chair. Either he's going to aid her progression or be stepped on as she climbs the ranks. She's been ignored and looked over in this office long enough. It's time for new leadership.

"I'm partnering you with Lewis. This is your case now," he replies calmly.

"Got you, Lieutenant," Sonya says rising from her seat.

"Detective Fields," he calls as she reaches for the door.

"Yes, Loo?"

"I hope you solve this case, for your sake. I'd hate to lose two good women. Meeting over."

"Ah-ah." Detective Lewis silences him before he can speak. "The options are sparse in here. Two doors. One has an exit and the other is a trap. For you I'm going to label these doors. As a favor. Door one, we're going to call the smart door and the second one is the dumb door. I can tell by your face that you were headed to the dumb door. Your tongue is the key to both. The combination of words you use is what unlocks each doors. You were going to say 'I want my lawyer' right? I know. And the dumb door would have swung open and you would have walked in. My favor to you is guiding you away from that trap. You're welcome. Now there's only one door left. The smart money is on this door. With multiple murder charges against you. The smartest thing you can do is look for the exit. So how smart are you?"

Knock! Knock!

"Hold that thought," Lewis says as he leaves the interrogation room. He's had him isolated in that room for five hours, stewing. A couple of extra minutes could only break him some more. Detective Field stands on the other side of the door.

"Charles, after you finish up McFarland wants to see you."

"Copy."

"One more thing. Did you question Ranesha Felder with Suffiyah?" Lewis stares at her with a blank face.

"The name sounds familiar. Only vaguely though."

"The young girl who was murdered in the apartment on West Kinney. Her stripper name was 'Storm'?"

"Oh, yes. We questioned her once at Exotics but it wasn't leading anywhere. Outside of giving us insight into Aaliyah Perez's lifestyle. Why are you smiling?"

"No reason. Just crossing my t's and dotting my i's."

The waiting area of the Internal Affairs office is off putting. What the interrogation room is to a suspect, this office is to officers. She was sent here almost an hour ago by McFarland. No smiles and no explanation. Just an order to report here. So here she sits finding it difficult to steady her hands. Nervousness has her twiddling them one second and sitting on them the next. She feels out of the loop. This morning's raid was her first sign, because she was asked to sit out. Then ostracized from any participation afterwards and restricted to the proximity of her office space until the directive was given that landed her here. For the life of her she can't figure out what has landed her in the office of the police who police the police. Someone must have been reading her mind because the inner door opened as soon as she finished her thought. A skinny Caucasian woman stands there with her blond hair pulled back tightly in a bun. Not a strand of her blond hair is out of place. She removes her glasses and fixes Suffiyah with a stare which stirred consternation in her immediately. One thought passed through her mind involuntarily. *I'm going to jail.* Why she comes to this assumption is unclear but it doesn't abate the shivering fits that are overtaking her spontaneously. She attempts to tame them to no avail. "Cold, Detective Adams?"

"Just a little under the weather," she lies, because it feels like the proper thing to do. The way she's being scrutinized she refuses to make any statement that can be perverted and tossed back at her. She's seen firsthand how a simple statement could be distorted and the stator of those words vilified. Still allowing her un-blinking gaze to linger on Suffiyah, the woman speaks again.

"Let's continue in my office. I'm Detective Paula McNeil," she says in a voice which was all business. There would be no camaraderie in here. Once again the ephemeral thought comes. *I'm going to jail.* "Detective Adams," she says as she sits behind her desk. "I understand you were placed on a paid leave from work not too long ago. Can you explain to me the conditions warranting this leave?" *About not too long ago?* It seemed like another lifetime to someone wishing to place that blemish in their past. So much has transpired since that time. Still Suffiyah attempts to give words to the circumstances.

"As you know, there were two women strangled and raped. My business card was placed on their persons by whom so ever is committing these acts. The two victims bore a striking resemblance to myself and I assume that became a red flag to my superiors, as well as your office. I believe they felt I had a more personal stake in this case then I was revealing. Being that I wasn't forthcoming with this nonexistent information, I assume I was deemed unsuitable to continue to work."

"What is this information they wanted?"

"If I knew that, Detective McNeil, we wouldn't be speaking on my leave of absence, would we?" *Smart ass.*

"Aaliyah Perez." Detective McNeil said while shifting the files in her hands. "She was also on your caseload from my understanding.

There was a woman questioned in context to that case. A Ranesha Felder." Suffiyah nods her head in agreement. She shifts more files. "So you remember her?" She tosses four photos to Suffiyah. Her eyes stretch as she looks at Storm's crime scene pictures. While her eyes view them, Detective McNeil's eyes are glued to her. Watching for the slightest hint of anything telling. "Wh—when did this happen?"

"Saturday."

"But…" *I just saw her Saturday.* Though the words were said in her head, Detective McNeil might as well have been clairvoyant because she read them as if written on paper. "I didn't know."

"After your card was found *yet again*, it was decided to keep you out of this. May I ask when the last time you saw Ms. Felder was?"

Fighting nausea Suffiyah says, "Saturday morning."

"So that would be the day of her death. Can you tell me the purpose of your visit?" Detective McNeil said.

"I had additional questions for her concerning Aaliyah Perez's case, so I stopped by her residence to seek her assistance." Suffiyah says.

"I have it from neighbors in the building that outside of stripping, she also prostituted herself. Detective Adams, who did you partner with on this case?"

"Charles Lewis."

"Yes. I have from Detective Charles Lewis that the first time you happened upon Ms. Felder at her place of employment, she attempted to entice the two of you with her nudity. Would you agree?" Suffiyah replayed their first run in and given their last encounter, Lewis statement seems feasible. "Maybe. It could be possible."

"How did Detective Lewis interact with her during Saturday's questioning?"

So this was her trap. "He wasn't there on Saturday."

"So you have a witness who is of a shady disposition to say the least and you choose to consort with her alone? Given her character, why wouldn't you want your partner there to corroborate anything that took place?"

"I didn't look at it in that manner, honestly."

"Furthermore, Detective Lewis says he had no knowledge prior to, during or after your inquisition of Ms. Felder. What was so confidential about this meeting that you felt it appropriate to keep it from your partner?"

"She wasn't willing to cooperate, so I ended up leaving. I had no further information to improve our case. I didn't consider it vital to relay the outcome." *Not to mention I don't trust Lewis but saying that will make me seem more suspicious.* Paula McNeil was staring through her and straight to her soul. She placed her glasses back on and asked a final question, "Detective, what was Ms. Felder wearing when you last saw her?" *I'm going to jail.*

Three Days Later

As the afternoon sun shines beautifully. Lay Low can't escape the cloud of gloom following his car. *"You know I'm a firm believer in 'sometimes you gotta do bad to do good', but only as a means to an end. We supposed to use a negative situation to create a positive one for us, our families and our communities. Not increase the degree of negativity. To the point a five-year old is the caretaker of his three-year old brother, because his mother's addiction to pills and his father's dead from bangin'. You know I aint here to judge you, Lay. I just want better for all of us."* Benji's voice and words replay to him as clearly as if they were just said. Maybe it was his ego which kept him from understanding the depth of the statement then. Or maybe he blocked it intentionally. But since that day it's been apparent that more truth resided in those words then he gave credit. It's been a domino effect of calamity around here. Every bad action is followed by a worse reaction. Its days like this where he misses Benji's presence the most. This recent raid and arrest has him out at this moment searching. Only one person has the answers, he needs and he intends to get them. He's so engulfed in his thoughts as he parks on Cali Block, that he doesn't notice the white Hyundai Sonata. It's been no more than a block behind him this entire time. As he places one booted foot on the pavement, it pulls adjacent to him. "Yo," his words catch in his throat as multiple arms are raised at him.

CHAPTER 22

"*In Newark, New Jersey on a city street in the West Ward. A suspected Bloods gang leader was savagely gunned down as he exited this burgundy Chrysler. Over thirty spent shell casings were found on the scene. Apparently nineteen found there target. Any information from...*" Benji tunes out the rest of the report as he looks up at the ceiling.

"You know what your problem is?"

Benji looks to his right and Sakinah lays facing him. "You take things too personally. Anything that happens is a direct affront to you. Like God is trying to break you. It began with me, then Drama and now Lay Low. But did you know God gives his hardest battles to his strongest soldiers?" Benji stares at her with dry eyes. "You started drinking again? I thought we made it pass that? You once told me pain was like magic, it's only as real as you believe it is. Do you believe in the way you view life now? Because if you do, that gun won't make you anything but a hypocrite."

"But it hurt, Kee."

"I know. But it's growth in pain. How can you be the man God wants you to be if you don't grow?"

"If I was on the news, Lay would paint the streets red in my memory."

"So now you embolden negativity?"

"No, but I miss him. I miss you."

"Why? I'm here," She touches his heart. "Always. How can you miss what's always with you? I'm hurting for you, but don't let this revert you. Bang better. For us. Bodies die, baby, but legacies live forever." She kisses his forehead. In a blink of an eye he's alone again.

"The chief and Administration has deemed you unfit of the badge," McFarland says coldly as he holds Suffiyah's shield. "Your service weapon is needed and clear your cube. I.A is looking into charges of misconduct on your end. On behalf of the department, you're a disgrace. I personally wish that the South Orange cop would have done us a favor and saved us this humiliation." His insinuation is not lost on her. Suffiyah just smiles. She knows the reaction he wants and refuses to grant him the pleasure.

"Understood, Sir."

Is killing to live a contradiction or a survival instinct? In the circle of life something has to be sacrificed for something else to survive. Even outside of death the strong preys on the weak and the weak prey on the weaker. So the weaker man must become stronger. He can only attain this by adapting to his environment and hiding from his aggressor. Or becoming more aggressive than his aggressor. If not in strength then in cunning. In this state of aggression the lines tend to blur in some individuals. What they view as justifiable is seen from the outside as murder. This new found ability of being able to kill is like a drug. Taking the user to higher heights. At this height is where the killer stops killing to live and starts killing to feel alive. Not too long ago this was Benji's problem. This drug coupled with ignorance is a dangerous combination. As a young man he wasn't as aware of the world as he is today. Which is ignorance at its purest form. Killing someone for wearing a blue bandanna was a priority. Never considering that under that bandana is a person. A son who will never see his mother again or make his brother smile. Karma is a subject he never truly considered until now. Maybe his evils come back in the form of losing what he holds dearest and he's left to witness its absence.

The saying goes something to the effect of, what takes years to build only take seconds to destroy. All the time and dedication and hard work Suffiyah put into her career and it's over. She never imagined herself at this junction in life. Her heart hurts like a woman who's sacrificed her dreams and world for a man who just wakes up one day and decides to walkout. In some way this analogy is almost completely accurate. Her life revolved around her work. In the beginning she doubted herself. As a rookie fresh out of the academy, she was placed on foot patrol around Pennington Courts projects. She was so small that she felt like a child in a Halloween costume and that's how the dealers treated her. They were more amused by her then weary. One said, "They better not leave your lil' ass out here by yourself or truancy gonna think you one of the kids. Then I'm gonna have to come sign you out." Then there was the night she heard all the shots and realized that she was running *away* from them instead of towards them. "Look at 'Little Shoes' she hauling ass."

"You a cop, go that way!" Another laughs. She was so embarrassed, but after seeing the sixteen year-old boy twisted on the ground her resolve was strengthened. She needed to be in this world to stop things like this from transpiring. This was the kid who said he'd have to sign her out of truancy. They say when you're about to die your life plays before your eyes. So it seems it's safe to say they killed a part of her. Tears of anger or sadness stain her blouse as she aimlessly wanders the streets, no destination in mind except away from the pain.

In Greek folklore there is a tale of a wise demigod by the name of Silenus, a companion of Dionysus a Greek God. King Midas hunted the forest a long time for the wise Silenus without capturing him. When Silenus finally fell into his hands, the King asked what was the best and most desirable of all things for man. The demigod wouldn't reply. But after much urging from the king, he gave a shrill laugh and broke out into these words; "*Oh, wretched ephemeral race, children of chance and misery. Why do you compel me to tell you what it would be most expedient for you not to hear? What is best of all is utterly beyond your reach. Not to be born, not to be, to be nothing. But the second best for you is--to die soon."*

Our killer first came upon this story while reading 'The Birth of Tragedy' by Nietzsche. He believes Silenus' statement to be one of the truest ever spoken. How many women and men are murdered daily? Children kidnapped or molested? Or consider the homeless situation? Why are we living? Isn't it a blessing to these women that he's ending their suffering? But the cops call him a killer. Have they no idea how much energy they exert trying to put a negative twist on his positive actions? Even though his actions weren't born of good intentions, they are no less therapeutic. Vengeance is driving on this road that he travels but right has always been his passenger. The pain that Suffiyah created in his life can never be erased. So his goal is to recreate it in her life so she can live with it. Or she can do the admirable thing and die from it. Take her service pistol and blow all her wrongs into the atmosphere where they can finally be righted. He is no killer, he realizes. He's no more than a leech. Leeches attach themselves to their host for purely selfish reasons, but end up being a remedy to that body. But leech is an ugly word, he prefers remedy, yes he's a remedy. The cure for a very ill world.

T.H Huxley said, *"The consequences of our actions are the scarecrows of fools and the beacons of wise men."* So it's okay to be stumbled by your short comings, just never let them floor you. They should guide you through the worst of circumstances. Men gravitate towards what easiest for them even if it comes with the harshest conditions. When they should lean towards what's hardest because the outcome is usually more gratifying. As Benji reads, *Warrior of The Light* by Paulo Coelho, he gets to a page that intrigues him. Paulo says, *"A Warrior of the Light knows that certain moments repeat themselves. He often finds himself faced by the same problems and situations, and seeing these difficult situations return, he grows depressed, thinking that he is incapable of making any progress in life. "I've been through all this before," he says to his heart. "Yes, you have been through all this before," replies his heart. 'But you have never been beyond it.' Then the Warrior realizes that these repeated experience have but one aim: to teach him what he does not want to learn."* Reading this passage out the book, just confirmed what Sakinah told him in his dream. He didn't want to wake up, it's been so long since he's been next to her. It's depressing when you can only find solace in your dreams. As he reads Lay Lows last text message from the morning he died, Sakinah's sentiments were almost identical to his friends.

"Ru, Gm bruh. I don't wanna hear no funny shit about me being soft lol. But I'm proud of you and envious of you at the same time. You packed up and left this nonsense behind you without a fear. Not fear of consequences, but fear of how you would be viewed, by Blood, by the streets or by me. That took a strength I could never have. I finally became somebody to someone when we became what we was. What I am. Even then I don't think you ever needed this gang shit to be you. So that could only mean you loved me enough to follow my lead. I appreciate it Ru. Even tho I'm older, you might not have recognized it but I always needed to know you approved and that's what motivated me. To be honest at one point it felt like you left me. I was bitter. Now, I ride around in my g-ride solo and realize I left you. My passenger seat empty because everything else was more important then my brother. I say all that to say, it's about to be us again. Let me tie up these loose ends and they could have the streets after that. I was wrong too. Maybe ol'girl can be your peace in this crazy world. Hold on to her, only an idiot denies peace. Dont reply I just wanted to get my thoughts out. Meet me at The Office later, Sangria on me, Dubs!" Who on earth could have guessed that this would be their last correspondence? After all Benji's preaching, Lay Low finally saw the light, and in a matter of minutes someone turned it out.

In a place only a half hour away from Newark but a whole other world away stood a city called Livingston. Many influential people reside in this town. The peace and calm that overtakes a person as they enter this city is a feeling a dweller of Newark would die for.

What type of person would trade the environment, great schools and opportunities, only offered to the elitist, for shoot outs and prison sentences? You can smell the money before you even see it. In Newark, the acidic smell of gun powder is so strong it singes the nose hairs and a blind man could see how poor it is. What type of person would trade that? This question is the one most repetitive in Myyonna's mind as she sits on the outrageously hard bench in the Essex County Courthouse. She prays the scent of the previous occupants doesn't settle into her designer jeans. She removed herself from this city over ten years ago, turning her back to her past and those who were once a part of it, including her son's father. Who's influence, she's sure, is the reason why she is sitting at this arraignment. At forty-four she is still as beautiful as the young woman she was when she fell I love with Stephon. He was the thug everyone wanted to bed for the rest of their lives. She was the one he chose, unfortunately. She at one time was unrelentingly chasing college to pursue a career in the medical field. Stephon on the other hand was chasing street fame. The simplest things about him created a moisture in her pants. His stance, the way he smoked, his attire, his demeanor. But the way he looked at her, like if given the chance he would suck her soul through her vagina, melted her. So one day when she was feeling brave enough, or through the pressure of her peers, she gave him that chance. This was the most thrilling experience of her life, but quite possibly the worst decision she ever made. She was hooked. He was so submerged in the street culture that he failed to see how a beautiful woman hidden in the hospital all day could raise his worth in the street's eyes. He wasn't searching for stability only credibility. What was the purpose of winning a trophy if you weren't going to put it on display? He convinced Myyonna that her dreams were for average people and wasn't equivalent to their lifestyle. By this time he already turned her against her entire family, so he was all she had. Her mind was clay which he molded to his liking. This love she held for him eventually had her on stage dancing for dollars to put him back on his feet. Every night he sat back in the strip club watching men drool over his greatest asset. He began to view her as a cash cow instead of his other half. When she found out she was four weeks pregnant he tried to convince her to abort it. All they used to talk about was kids, now it was reality. He couldn't imagine going nine months without the nightly income he'd become accustomed to. With nowhere else to turn she continued dancing for another month. Her feelings for Stephon waning daily created an emptiness in her. Stephon didn't feel it necessary to watch over her anymore. His absence left room for the young business man, who saw her worth, to talk to her. He eventually saved her from the unhealthy relationship and lifestyle. He promised to accept her and her unborn child as if it were his own. He never broke his promise. They created a transportation company and never looked back. Her son was raised in Newark until they were able to be well off enough financially to move away. Once in Livingston, they found the best school for him. He ran back to Newark every moment he could over the past ten years. Begging to move in with his father, he was denied. He despised his mother for this. Now as he stands in front of the judge with his attorney, paid for by his mother, she's the only one there. "Your honor his charges are first degree murder, first degree robbery, first degree felony murder, second degree weapon possession. I mean the list goes on. I can't understand how the defense can ask for a more lenient bail when he shouldn't even be allowed a bail," the red faced prosecutor states.

"Duly noted," says the judge. "However, I will set bail for $750,000 cash only. Marshon Welch you are to return back in front of this court should you be indicted. Next case." Munch looks into his mother's face and watches the tears fall freely as she shakes her head in dismay. Guilt grips his heart.

"God blessed you," the man said. "Where ever you go people just follow you. They gravitate towards your swagger, adopt you ideology, emulate you character and admire your stance. They treat your words as if they're water and the world's a desert. Nine out of every ten people around you will die for you, including me. I don't even know why. But,

I do know wherever you are taking us is where we need to be. So I'm not complaining. That's a gift."

Benji remembers these words that were spoken to him and weighs their value. He sits quietly and looks at his Misfits. All which are staring at him with the zeal of cult follower. Is he the leader they deserve or the stand in they're grasping onto while they await something greater? If he is the something greater, where is he taking them? Lenae smiles at him with certainty radiating from her. This breaks him and strengthens him at the same time. Though he feels unworthy of being their leader, he understands leaving them to fend for self in this world is a travesty.

"If I seem distant this weekend, I apologize. I lost a close friend, more like a brother. We always rap with each other on a straight up level and I would never disrespect you by being coy with my thoughts or feelings. I feel like y'all look to me for guidance. The unwavering faith I see in y'all eyes hurts my heart because I don't have that faith in me. The questions you ask, I don't have all the answers for. How do y'all feel so comfortable with that? How do you follow somebody who can't be certain of their own way?"

The group of teens look around at each other for the proper answer. Searching one another's faces for a hint of what should be said. Their unshakable faith in Benji was beginning to tremble after his questions. No one had an answer. After all that Mr. Cooper showed them they went quiet. Lenae never abhorred this group more than she did at this moment. He was practically begging them for a reason to go on. A stronghold for him to place his footing. He showed them through their darkest moments and they're not even willing to grab his hand to pull him up. "I follow you for that exact reason," she says. "Every other adult wants us to believe they know so much more than we do. But you make us equal. We all learn from each other. It's like everything was dark for us, well me. I'm gonna keep this on the 'I', because apparently I'm the only one who's benefitting from your presence. Everything was dark for me and you brought a much needed light to my life. Before I felt like it wasn't much I could do, now I feel as if it's nothing I can't do. So your question shouldn't be why are we following you, it should be why wouldn't we follow you?"

"You never lie to us," someone else says.

"We can relate to you," comes another.

"You make me want more when I used to want nothing at all."

Once Lenae responded it was like setting a match to a gasoline-soaked rag. She set the class ablaze. The state of elation Benji felt exiting Misfits Inc. was indescribable. To know he was having an effect on his group that equaled up to half of the affect they're having on him was more than enough to assure he was on the right path. No one outside of Sakinah ever believed he could change. This positive twist he was on was just a ruse to mislead the authorities, to outsiders looking in. Now here he was really making a difference even it was so small. As he walked to his van, he paid little attention to the occupied unmarked car parked across the street. Their presence was just a passing acknowledgement. The thoughts in his mind made the drive home relatively short. Routine navigated him to his house because his brain was elsewhere. Pulling into his driveway his smile never faded. That was until he got out his car and set his eyes on a sight that barely gained a glance from him twenty minutes ago. The navy blue Chevrolet Impala that was sitting in front of *Misfits Inc.* moments ago was now parking across the street from his place of rest. He's being shown none to subtly that he's on their radar. Nervousness settles into his bones. At this point in time he's a law abiding citizen. But the law's memory goes back further than "this point", so fear is the only suitable thing to feel right now.

CHAPTER 23

TIME PASSES AT A SNAIL'S pace as Suffiyah and Lee Lee sit in the waiting room of Child Services. Once called DYFS, the department of youth and family services, this place should hold some of the answers she's in need of.

"Suffiyah Adams?" the receptionist calls out. She and Lee Lee stand and approach the desk.

"Good Morning?"

"Good Morning. Mrs. Walters will see you now. Straight through that door." They pass through the hallway until they come upon an open door. A woman with agitation written on her face sits behind the cheap desk shuffling mounds of paper. Suffiyah knocks softly on the open door. She barely glances up from the paperwork.

"What can I do for you?"

"My name is Suffiyah Adams. I'm trying to obtain a copy of my file from foster care."

"How old are you, Ms. Adams?"

"Thirty three." Mrs. Walters now looks fully in her direction for the first time. She has the appearance of a person running off of very more than fumes. Frown lines crease her face. Suffiyah's only known her for a few seconds but she doesn't think this is a woman who smiles often.

"Thirty-three years?" Sarcasm is dripping from the question. "Ms. Adams, do you see this desk full of papers?" Suffiyah now looks at the multiple folders on her desk. Some are inches thick and they spread from one end to the other. "These are files from the past few months. If I had to pull files from thirty-three years ago there would be no room for me in this office. I get very little rest worrying over recent cases. To jump back thirty years would be to swear off sleep altogether. Leave your number with reception and we'll get in touch with you in a few weeks with any results," her tone says 'dismissed.'

"Thank you," Suffiyah replies with all the manners she can muster. Mrs. Walters eyes her back as she exits.

Sonya looks at her screen in disbelief at what its showing. This has to be an omen from a higher power. She was on the brink of calling it quits on this case. As much ambition as she has, her energy doesn't match. She's running around searching for invisible clues and nothing appears. Her feet are swollen two times their normal size. The worst part of this case is sitting on her left side.

"You going to answer that phone or keep staring at it like it's a unicorn?" Detective Lewis asks as if he sensed her thoughts of him. Instant aggravation plasters her mug as it does whenever he speaks. His presence irks her soul to no end. But he's just an impediment placed on her road to greatness. Fate wants to test her determination to reach her goal.

"It's not an important call," she snaps.

Her face heats up as she feels him eye balling her. It's unnecessary looking over to see the ugly smirk that she knows is present. She refuses to let his aura rob her of this small victory. Her only chance of getting anywhere on this case was Suffiyah. So her number popping up across the screen was a godsend. Her fingers text quickly in reply to the missed call. *Can't talk right now, Sufee. I'll return your call when I'm alone.*

What is she up to?

With all of this police training under her belt, Suffiyah hasn't once noticed the car that's been tailing her for days. The killer watched her and her friend disappear into the building which houses many state jobs. His first guess was she was seeking employment. But she isn't dressed for an interview, nor would she be accompanied by Alicia. She has to have an appointment in there somewhere. But where? Patience is a virtue and he has an abundance of it. He reclines his chair and awaits his quarry. Fear of being sighted by her is the only thing that keeps him inside the car. How would he explain his presence? Only thing that would do is cause suspicion. After about an hour they finally exit the building. Neither woman looking too enthused. He looks at the cameras on his passenger seat and wishes it was an eavesdropping device instead. He would give his right eye to hear their current conversation. Realization covers his face suddenly. He might not be able to hear their conversation but he could find out why they were there. He allows them to pull off before exiting the van. There's a desk in the middle of the lobby upon entering. A woman stands behind it doing check-ins on visitors. Any nervousness he felt recedes upon seeing a female. God hasn't created the woman who can resist him.

"Good Morning?" He smiles flirtatiously. The woman's hands automatically adjust her hair as she takes in the treat in front of her.

"Good Morning, Sir. How may I help you?" she asks in her sweetest voice. He just stares at her in open lust. Her face flushes from embarrassment. "Sir?" she says snatching him from the hypnosis she has him under.

"Uh, excuse me. I just…You have beautiful eyes."

"Thank you, but don't get lost in them you might not come back."

"You're right, I almost forgot why I came here. Can you direct me to Child Services?" he says. It's the only office he knows of in this building to ask for and not look weird. "You looking to adopt?" she asks nosily as she grabs the sign in book to pass him. He allows his fingers to linger on hers as he grabs the book while looking in her face.

"No, I'm more of a traditionalist. I want my first baby the old fashioned way." Her mouth opens wide but words fail her. "Can I have a pen please?"

"Oh, sorry," she replies momentarily discombobulated. "I need your I.D, Mr.?"

"Brown," he says reaching for his wallet. He taps his empty pockets in search of his wallet. "Pardon me, beautiful. I seem to have left my wallet in the car. Let me grab it and I'll be right back." he says backing from the desk. Luck was on his side. Her name was on the first page of the sign in sheet that was passed to him. But why in the hell was she seeing child services?

"Hey Momma!" Sonya hugs Suffiyah as soon as she walks through the doors of Applebee's. She texted Suffiyah to meet her here after work. All roads to solving this case lead back to Suffiyah. "This is my friend Alicia that I always talk about." Lee Lee extends her hand out of courtesy, but it's something about this cop that rubs her wrong.

"All I ever heard is 'Lee Lee this' and 'Lee Lee that'. I feel like I've known you forever." The statement comes across as phony as the smile on her face. "Table for three, please?"

"Right this way." The hostess leads them to a booth.

After she walks off, Suffiyah speaks, "Thanks for meeting me, Sonya. I had no one else to turn to that I could trust. So much has transpired over the past year it's weighing me down."

"Sufee, you know I've always been in your corner. Whatever you need me for, I'm here."

"Thanks, Sonya. Do you remember the murder on Ridgewood Avenue?" Lee Lee watches Sonya perched on the end of her seat like a cat about to pounce on a mouse. Her expression is that of a predator. Lee Lee looks at Sufee to see if she notices it. It was obvious from the hope in her eyes that she didn't. She decides right then to pay close attention to this woman.

"Of course. The first victim with your card. What about her?"

"It's going to sound crazy but you know me so you should believe me. Twenty minutes before the call came in, I already knew about the murder."

"Whoa, whoa, whoa, Sweetie. Slow down and take it from the top. How could you?"

"Someone called my extension and told me a woman was suffering on Ridgewood and I should hurry. I asked who was calling and he said 'the murderer'. I thought it was a prank and dismissed it. So when I heard it was a murder on Ridgewood I rushed out. After my card was found on the scene how could I explain the call and why I was just reporting it?"

"What happened after that?" Sonya hopes she doesn't sound as anxious as she feels. Her heart is beating so fast she's surprised they can't see the vibrations through her blouse.

"He called me before every murder except the stripper and also threatened to kill Lee Lee if I sought help. He even stabbed her tire to convince me. I know this is a tough pill to swallow but I swear it's the truth. Being that you took over the case I was wondering if you could review the evidence and see if I missed something? Whoever is behind it is closer than I wished to believe."

"Are you saying a cop?"

"I don't know but I wouldn't write it off."

"Okay. I'm with you. We're going to figure it out. Trust me."

Essex County Correctional Facility

The dayroom of the maximum pod is alive with activity. A mischievous energy fills the air as a room full of young men suffering from a mixture of stress and boredom search for an outlet. No news is being watched. One TV shows reruns of reality shows, while the other shows music videos. At a table sits a group of four men playing dominos. Insults are hurled across the table in good nature, for now.

"Marshon Welch!" the C.O. yells from the desk. Munch stops playing dominos and approaches the officer.

"Waddup?"

"Put your greens on. You have an attorney visit."

"Aight." He returns to the domino table and tells them to get a replacement. He had no idea his lawyer was coming down today. He's praying for good news, hopefully it's the bail reduction. He shimmies into the green jumpsuit and grabs his I.D. band. As he sits in the sally port awaiting floor control to open the door, thoughts of freedom dance around his mind. The door opens and he walks down the corridor to the room used for attorney visits. To his disappointment it isn't his lawyer after all. His face hardens immediately as Detective Lewis stands to greet him.

"Hey, Mr. Munch." So much enthusiasm lays within the greeting that it sends a shiver through Munch. He can't imagine any good coming out of this encounter. "That's no way to look at a man bearing gifts. Makes you seem downright unappreciative." Munch says nothing, so Lewis continues, "You're always so silent around me that it's hurtful. I think if I was a female you'd speak to me. You talk to a lot of girls on these phones. *A lot of girls*. But it's one that it seems you paid little attention to. When you first place the calls a female voice says 'All calls are subject to monitoring and recording'." Lewis' smile disappears. "By the time you leave this room, you're going to wish you heeded to that woman's warning."

CHAPTER 24

A LITTLE GIRL COWERS IN THE *corner of the attic, as the monster
frantically searches for her. She silently prays to God that he doesn't
look behind the boxes of clothes stacked in front of her. 'Suffer! Suffer!"
He screams as he flings objects out of his path. "Here you are!" But
his voice is coming from across the room, directed at someone unseen.
"Now you must suffer with me." The girl peeks from behind the boxes
as the monster lifts someone by the collar. "Where is she?" the monster
barks. She sees a little finger point I her direction. The monster turns
towards her with eyes the color of heated coal. The scrawny boy, in his
massive hands, squeezes his eyes shut tightly. "You ruined a beautiful
home, a beautiful family." Tears drip from his eyes and enhances the
madness within them. His lips curl into a sinister grin. "So much pain,
I suffer. Honest I do." He practically drags the boy behind him as he
comes towards the girl. His grin disappears. "But I won't suffer alone,"
he growls as he reaches for her hand.*

"Suffiyah, Suffiyah!" Suffiyah blinks multiple times as she hears
a snapping sound. Dr. O'Malley's face is only inches from hers as
her eyes adjust to her surroundings. "Are you okay?" Dr. O'Malley
asks her.

"Yes. Why did you bring me out of hypnosis?"

"Sweetie, you're drenched like you've just finished swimming,
and if the perspiration wasn't enough, you look like you were about
to go into a seizure. I thought you were going to crap your pants on
my sofa. You don't pay me enough for that." Dr. O'Malley smiles.

"Did you get anything from me while I was under?"

"Actually I did. Up until the point when the man reached for you, you were calm. I don't believe this is a dream at all." After running into a dead end at Child Services, Suffiyah decided to try her hand at being hypnotized. It couldn't hurt.

"So put me back under," she insists.

"No, that's not healthy. I don't have a machine to monitor them, but from your facial expression I can only tell your stress levels were dangerously high. Just rest for a minute."

Irate. That's the only word that fits the killer's mood as he follows his next intended target from one pointless destination to the next. His movements are so erratic now it brings a new excitement to the hunt. Right from the beginning he assumed he'd be caught for the murders, so he prepared for it. Carefully plotting out his every step in each crime was his way of staying under the radar for as long as possible. But after Storm's murder, which was done in broad daylight, he tossed caution into the wind. They are no closer to him after her death than they were after the multitude of premeditated acts he committed. His target number was three deaths before his face was plastered to every paper and local news station. Yet here he stands today, untouched. He feels the hand of God guiding him through this insanity. There is no need to plan when the plotter of all plotters is using him as a vessel. This is the closest any man can come to invincibility. He could jump out right now and kidnap her, and no one would look twice. But he won't do that. God always hid his miracles under the guise of secrecy and he won't be the one to do otherwise. In the movie "The Terminal", Tom Hank's character coined phrase was "I wait." And so will he. Slow and steady wins the race.

Since leaving Dr. O'Malley's office, Suffiyah has been in the house in heavy contemplation. All her gut is telling her to do is trust Benji. Out of all her suspects he's the weakest. He's only really a suspect because the other Detectives placed him there. A fat lot of good their opinions have brought thus far. Her phone ring breaking her train of thought.

"Detective Adams?" the voice spills through the earpiece. She hasn't heard this voice in so long it pauses her. "Hello?"

"Oh, sorry. Hello."

He laughs. "For a moment I thought I had the wrong number. I was going to be beyond upset. It took me eons to build up the heart to finally use your number and to have it changed on me would have been tragic. But here you are. How are you?" She ponders that. How is she? Is she fine? Is she distraught? If she isn't fine does she tell him that or does she lie?

"I'm making it," is what she manages to put together.

"Do you need to talk? I can arrange something for you, Detective." Images of their run-in flash through her mind.

"No, I'm fine Dr. Jackson and please call me Suffiyah. I believe my Detective days are behind me."

"You will always be my favorite Detective." She can hear the smile in his voice. "However, I understand how idiotic this system is and the peons they strategically place in the positions of power. Teetering between success and homelessness. Their next move dictating the final outcome. So everyone is expendable to them, especially a bright, beautiful, ambitious, black sister such as you. You're an unknown factor with so many capabilities it's scary to them. You are a representation of everything they fear, competition."

"You have me in here blushing. I can't say I agree with everything you said, but they felt good while you were saying them. They should bottle your voice up and sell it, everyone can us a little bit of Dr. Jackson. You'd be a millionaire," she jests.

"Thanks for your vote of confidence. I'll keep that in mind. Don't worry your dose will always be free of charge. Also, it's Shawn. You fired Dr. Jackson apparently. So If I can't be your therapist then I'd love to be your friend."

"Check out who has a human side." She laughs. "But I would love to be your friend, Shawn. I'm glad that you decided to call."

"No problem. But I have appointments coming up. Try not to lose my number and I'd appreciate if you use it."

"Okay, I will. Later."

"Good bye." Her smile right now can illuminate an entire housing project. She feels reassured in all her beliefs. Most importantly, speaking to him only reaffirmed her feelings for Benji. She missed him now more than ever. Scrolling through her phone she goes to his name and calls.

"You've reached Benjamin Cooper. Sorry I've missed your call. If you…" the answering service carries on but she just listens to his voice.

Smack!

Lee Lee's head is still buzzing and her tongue feels thick as she pushes it against the gag. You couldn't have convinced her in a million years that she'd be tazed. The acrid taste of bile fills her mouth, she wonders if she vomited? All these thoughts passing through her head doesn't diminish the pain from where she was just slapped. She can still feel the imprint of his fingers on her face. After her normal Saturday morning stops, she decided to grab something from her mother's garage. This turned out to be a bad decision. As soon as she entered all she remembers is intense pain and flopping like a fish. What makes matters worse is being blind folded, she has no idea what's going to happen until it happens. So she can't even prepare for the hurt. The cool air on her body tells her she is nude. If not for that, then the feel of his hands fondling her bare breast or his fingers grazing her stomach were a clear indication. Mentally she kicks herself for wearing a sweat suit with no underwear. Her destination was the spa so she chose the easiest outfit to slip off. Never thinking, until now, how easy it would also make it for someone else to slip off her. Like this lunatic. She doesn't know what she's handcuffed to but it isn't budging. Her legs are free, but after the force of that slap, she's second guessing kicking out at him again. Fear grips her as she awaits feeling his penis being forced into her. Not many rapist use condoms so her brain keeps screaming "AIDS!", making her heart race.

"I wish you wouldn't make this so hard." He whispers as he rubs her thigh. She cringes under his touch. He's told her every stop she's made over the past few days and outfits she's worn at exact times those days. When she added a stalker to her catalogue baffles her, but here he is. Suddenly something cold is placed on her vulva. "This was the sharpest knife I could find." He claims while turning it on her flesh methodically. "What do you feel about a hysterectomy?" A whimper escapes her gag. "Good girl." He's sure he'll get answers now. "I think we understand each other now. So I'm gonna remove the gag. Don't scream. There, isn't that better." The gag is tossed aside. "You and Suffiyah went to Child Services, why? Before you answer that. I believe you now know who I am and what I'm capable of. Now determine if you wish to be a victim or a conspirator. You have three seconds."

"Hurry up and come get me from my mother's house. I'm hiding in the garage, please hurry!" The text message flashes across Suffiyah's screen. Hiding from what? She thinks as she scrambles to get into her jacket."

"You could have been anything you wanted to be right? Aint that what you preach?" asks Drama.

"Yeah that's what I preach." Benji agrees.

"So you telling me everything you've been in life is what you wanted to be?"

"You always tryna finagle the bagel," Benji replies laughing. "But the answer is no. I was too weak to be what I wanted to be, especially where we're from. So I became everything I needed to be to survive. You get the difference?"

"Yeah, but I just can't see you as weak. It don't fit you."

"Maybe not physically, but I was spiritually weak. I couldn't be a sellout. What would my peers think? But eventually my spirit was strengthened and I discovered that the only person I needed to be was this dude you look up to. Every time I get around y'all I realize this

is who I should have wanted to be the whole time." Drama nods his head understanding.

"Wait. Hold up, Coop. So if this isn't what you always wanted to be, what was it?" Benji looks forward smiling.

"You ready for this? No bs though. I wanted to be a cop." They burst into laughter.

"You aint no cop J. Reed!" Drama mimics LL Cool J's character off In Too Deep. "That don't even fit you."

"I know. They never had to live our lives, I did. I just understand that it's more help in knowledge than incarceration. That's not going to fix our neighborhoods, it will only continue to be the divisive factor it's been. I believe keeping you with me every day is more beneficial than sticking you in the youth house. So I count that as a win. This way when you marry Lenae and build y'all family it will be strong. Because it's a strong man there to lead them."

"What made you say Lenae of all people?"

"I know how love looks, kid. What you thought y'all was a secret?"

"Yup." He laughs. "But you right. That's baby squirrel. She make me want that life."

Benji laughs at the memory as he walks back to his car. These young boys call they female "baby squirrel" as a term of endearment instead of "baby girl". This is a crazy generation. He grabs his phone from the armrest and sees a missed call from Suffiyah. *Baby squirrel.* This made his day.

The color drains from Suffiyah's face as she runs over to Lee Lee's limp body. This was her nightmare all over again. The rise and fall of her chest brings relief. "Lee, wake up baby." She smacks her face while removing the blind fold. Lee Lee begins to come around. Her eyes flutter open and land on Suffiyah, tears instantly fill her eyes. She wraps her arms around Suffiyah and sobs incessantly.

"I'm sorry," she whines.

"Shh. It's okay, Lee." The two lay on the ground rocking back and forth latched to one another. After consoling her and finding her clothes they go inside the house so they can talk.

"How'd you know to come here?" Lee Lee asks, the mug of tea trembling in her hand. She gained her composure for the most part but is unable to steady her nerves.

"You texted me, sweetie."

Lee shake her head. "I was handcuffed," she tells her tale as she remembers it.

"...he placed the knife to me and I had to tell him or I think he would have killed me."

"It's okay. I understand." Suffiyah sits in disbelief. Could he have been parked somewhere watching her arrival? Or was this his way of getting her where he wanted her? What's to stop him from coming in right now and killing them both? Nothing. She gets a hold of her senses and calls Sonya.

CHAPTER 25

"**H**E'S ONE OF THE FOUNDING fathers of Cali Block," Munch says as Lewis points at the picture. "But he squared up to my knowledge."

"We're speaking of this man, Benjamin Cooper?"

"I guess."

"What do you mean you guess?"

"I'm saying I don't know bruh government."

"So what did you call him?"

"Benji Ru." Lewis jots the name down before continuing.

"What is his status under your set? Wait, what set are you?"

"Piru."

"Okay and his rank?"

"He got double OG."

"I thought he squared up?"

"I'm saying Lay Low said they was in control and they both held the double. Maybe he was just allowing Lay Low to be the face." More writing.

"So you carried out the orders of your superiors, correct?"

"Yeah."

"Mr. Cooper and Lay Low, correct?"

"Yeah."

In his stack of paper he finds a picture of Lay Low. "This man Laywan Thomas is who you call Lay Low?"

"Yeah."

"He was recently murdered, correct?"

"Yeah," Munch replies guilty. He feels like a traitor at this moment.

"So with Laywan dead, who are your superiors?" Munch looks in Lewis face. His eyes dance in delight in anticipation of the answer he knows is soon to part Munch's lips.

"Benji Ru."

Excited, ecstatic, elated and any other word which is synonymous to these three words combined, couldn't describe the feeling coursing through Detective Sonya Fields right now. When she received Suffiyah's call she immediately dispatched a marked car to the residence until she arrived. When she walked in she found Suffiyah and her sneaky friend in the sitting room giving a report to the uniformed officer. She waved him off to take a look in the garage and patrol the area. It's very coincidental that after being released from the force, Adams has all this information on a case where she was clueless while working it. Now this invisible murderer magically appears and abducts her best friend? Amazing. Then of all people he texts Suffiyah to come rescue her. No other witnesses? If they were selling this story for one cent and an all-expense paid trip to Dubai, she wasn't buying it. They can go to all the extremes they want. Upgrade from the taser and use a handgun, but they won't convince her they're innocent. The way she has it figured, Lewis is smitten by Suffiyah and is leaking information to her about Sonya's investigation. So Suffiyah sought her assistance in an attempt to allay suspicion. But little does she know that no one cons Detective Sonya Fields. To catch a dummy you have to act like a dummy and Sonya can be as dumb as they come. While they think they're playing on her intelligence she's just collecting evidence to strengthen her case.

"Tell me about the liquor store murder."

"Me, Wayne-Wayne, and Turn-up got the call from up top to send a message to the Poppis in the liquor store. They were passing out samples to people. The big bruh's wasn't feeling that. So they sent us to express their feelings."

"Samples of what?" Lewis asks.

"Dope."

"Okay, so heroin? By 'big bros' you mean your superiors, correct?"

"Yeah."

"Laywan and Benjamin, correct?"

"Yeah."

"Okay, continue."

"Poppi got that bulletproof glass up, so we waited to catch one of them in the open so we could rob them. When Wayne-Wayne grabbed the brother we set the robbery off. The plan was to shake the store and shoot one of the poppis in the leg. Then shoot the freezers and shit to add to the damage. Wayne-Wayne shot poppi and I shot the glass. We aint know Turn-up was frying off the sticks which is another way of saying high off Xanax, while we was sticking to the plan he stood over poppi and did him." Munch says shaking his head.

"So Benji Ru sent you three in to leave a message?"

"Yeah." This couldn't have went more perfect. Breaking Munch was the best thing that could have happened to Lewis' case. Dwayne Tillman aka Wayne-Wayne, has been an informant since fourteen. His story started spilling as soon as the cuffs left the officers waist. But without a stronger witnesses' corroborating story it would make his claim probable at best. But with two of the three participants to the crime pointing at Benji as the button pusher, he's sure to get a warrant signed for his arrest. I know you are trying to figure out what this crime has to do with the strangling? Once convicted of a violent crime, the convict is mandated to submit a DNA sample. Once his DNA sample enters the database he can compare it to Sakinah Rogers and Aaliyah Perez's assailants DNA. "You just might get home before you lose all your teeth, Mr. Munch."

Suffiyah has never felt this safe in her life. She snuggles her body closer into Benji's sleeping frame and his arm automatically pulls her in tighter. Secure. Sick and tired of feeling like she was fighting this battle alone caused her to run to Benji. His response was everything she needed it to be. He practically forced her to come stay with him. Lee Lee fought him when he tried to make her stay, also. Ever the gentleman, he even still called and checked on her every hour on the hour. First thing this morning he's going to use the connections he's obtained through his private investigation service to try to get her foster care files. She almost told Dr. Jackson when he called her again last night. But it felt like a wrong move. Why would she need to confide in him when she's creating a trust bond with Benji? He twitches again. She didn't notice the first time they were together but he jumps in his sleep. It helps her to know that he is afflicted, too. Now they can fix each other. She rests her eyes for a second. When she opens them back sunlight spills into the bedroom. Cinnamon and grease aromas waft through the cracked door. Seconds later Benji walks through the door carrying a plate of french toast, scrambled eggs and turkey bacon with a glass of orange juice on the side.

"Good Morning. It was either orange juice or apple juice. I didn't have any Ciroc to put in the apple, so I went with the orange." He smiles. He's apparently a morning person.

"I thought all clowns have red noses?" she shoots back.

"Nice, but you got a little dry spit—" He uses his finger to point out the area. She covers her face and turns her head in embarrassment. "Sike! But if I wasn't joking I already saw it."

"If you didn't have that food in your hand I would've threw this pillow at you."

Benji passes her the plate and sits on the edge of the bed. "Out of all the days of the week, I value this one the most. Today I want to introduce you to the most important part of my life. You can bring Lee Lee with you. This way I won't have to be distracted by worrying over the two of you. I'm 'bout to grab a shower."

Lewis sits in the chair in McFarland's office relaxing with his hands folded above his gut. He observes McFarland's reviewing of his report with glee. Not only has he successfully resolved the liquor store robbery/murder, but also found an organized crime tie to reel in the main suspect of the next biggest serial murder scandal. All he has to do is prove they were all committed by the same perpetrator. A little more evidence to collect and he would have a judge sign off on an airtight warrant for Mr. Benjamin 'Benji Ru' Cooper.

As soon as Suffiyah and Alicia walk in the sitting space, all eyes lock in on the outsiders. The predominantly teenage boy filled room bursts into hurried whispers as lust fills their young eyes. The few females roll their eyes at the uninvited competition. Suffiyah wasn't expecting this when he said "the most important part of my life". The room is full of young thugs and ghetto girls. All of them in her previous occupation would have been prime suspects for questioning. A dark skinned fellow with a burgundy bandanna tying his dreadlocks into a ponytail, has a blatant bulge protruding from his pocket. She knows if she sees the gun Benji has to have noticed it. Anger creeps in as she naively perceives this to be a gang meeting. Benji stands center stage in an all-black jogger exuding joy at being the uncontested general of this dysfunctional army. One look at Lee Lee and she can tell she concurrs with her assessment. "Attention young perverts." This causes snickers throughout the room. "These two beautiful sisters are our guest and will be observing our little pow wow. The little one's spoken for but y'all can fight for the other one after class. Winner gets a date." Then he smiles and any negative thoughts she was having were voided. "What is success?" Benji asks.

"Living good," says burgundy bandanna.

"Getting rich," comes another.

"A house like on Real Atlanta Housewives and mad stuff," a cute Hispanic girl says.

"Okay." Benji nods.

"Lenae, look in the dictionary and read me the definition of the word success." A very familiar looking young lady flips through the dictionary until she finds her target.

"Success. One, favorable or desired outcome. Two, the gaining of wealth and fame. Three, one that succeeds."

"So basically everything our peers just said?" Suffiyah notices how he incorporates himself inside their group.

"I guess," Lenae replies.

"Why is it you guess? So basically you don't agree?"

"To some extent."

"Well what would you consider success?" Suffiyah watches the girl scrunch her pretty face up in consideration. Recognition sinks in for Suffiyah, this is Drama's girlfriend.

"Happiness." She finally comes up with. "I believe success is equivalent to happiness. You can have all the money, cars, homes and jewels, but that doesn't mean you're happy. I know if I had all those things I would be content, not happy. I want to quote a wise man, Benajmin 'Coop' Cooper." The class laughs. "Coop said. *'I fear love the most.'* That first day in my class when you said that, I didn't understand. Now I think I do. You fear love because love is happiness. To not know love is to not experience true happiness. So you never know what you're missing. So any semblance to happiness is sufficient. But once you've known love, true happiness, and then you lose it. Nothing outside of love can ever replace that emptiness."

"I had love and lost it, so why am I happy?" Benji asks.

"I never considered it 'til today and I figured it's because you found love again when you found us. That's why you were happy."

"Were? So I'm not happy no more?"

"Nope, you're happier because now you also love her." She points her pen at Suffiyah. "You have your favorable or desired outcome., which makes you successful."

"Aiight, group is over everybody. Lenae ruined it." Benji teases, sticking out his tongue. "Lenae you killed it shorty, I'm proud of you."Benji beams. "Next subject…"

"Allahu Akbar, Allahu Akbar Ash hadu Anla hilha illallah ash hadu anna muhammadar rashulullah hiya alas salah hiya alal falaah qaad qaamatis-salaat qaad qamatis-salaat Allahu Akbar, Allahu

Akbar la hilha illallah." The Muslims line up in ranks to offer the obligatory prayer. They wave the new convert to the front row, where the most blessings are said to reside. Munch makes his way to the front of the congregation mentally preparing himself to do this tough regiment five times a day. He will soon be targeted by his old cohorts, so survival skills have led him to a new security blanket.

"You surprised me. When Sufee said the most important part of your life, I assumed your mother. I never pictured you in that field. Watching you with those kids was so special. You were smiling and clowning. Can't nobody tell you, you ain't one of them," Lee says.

"That's true. 'Cause I am them, just a little wiser."

"I get that. Look at Mr. Benjamin. I mean, Coop." they laugh.

"I forgot how funny you were the last time you tried to castrate me."

"It's hereditary."

Lee Lee shrugs. "My father always said my mother was a ball buster." Suffiyah can only shake her head. "Anyway I have to be leaving you two. I'll check in every hour on the hour parole officer Cooper. No need to put any apb's out," Lee Lee states as she leaves.

"She was right, that was special."

"I'm glad you approve."

"Can I ask you something?"

"Anything."

"When Lee Lee said she assumed your mother, I kinda thought the same. How come you never speak about your mom?"

"What you tryna be depressed?" Benji jokes half-heartedly. "It don't be much to say. Me and my mother have a love/hate relationship. I loved her she hated me. Now she probably still hates me and I just don't acknowledge she exists."

"You don't think that's harsh? I mean given that she birthed you."

He shrugs.

"That ain't the prize you make it sound like. My mother's a bona fide junkie. If that were to be her only flaw, we could get through it. My addiction to the streets was just as compromising.

Difference is, she created my addiction. My father was her ticket out of Newark. She trapped him by getting pregnant with me, her words not mines. Seven months into her pregnancy he got murdered. So she lost her meal ticket and gained another mouth to feed. She felt like dude cheated her. When I was around two she started getting high. By then according to her, I looked so much like him that seeing my face was a constant reminder of why she was stuck in this city. I was cognizant of the abuse by nine. The more I hugged her, the more she whooped me. I mean for absolutely nothing. Bats, cords, sticks, I don't even know what a belt feels like. She'd lock me out the house barefoot in the cold, rain or snow. I mean for hours. When she came down off her high and let me in, there'd be no remorse. It wasn't the drugs, she had a dead heart in her chest. When I was ten she practically sold me to this dude named Do Rite. Told him I was going to hustle for him but the pay goes to her. I was just happy to not have to be around her all day, so I dove into my new position. Do Rite showed me the game and taught me to survive. So I thank my mother for him. But forget that. What do you think of my kids?" Suffiyah tries to unimagine the scene he described. But she understands now isn't the time for more questions.

"The way you treat them, the way they look up to you. They're amazing. Did you know that one of the boys had a gun on him?" he nods. "You don't feel that puts the other kids in jeopardy? Or you?"

"Nah. We're like a family. This is a place of trust. I allow them to be who they need to be now, to survive. So they can come to know what they want to be later, to live. Cause surviving and living aint the same." That statement makes so much sense to her. He has a way of simplifying the most complex of matters.

"The girl was Draymon's girlfriend right?"

"Yeah. Lenae."

"I thought so. She's more than a pupil to you. When she was giving her breakdown on success, you looked like a proud father."

"That's my baby." He smiles.

Later That Night

"Have you ever loved somebody so much that it makes you cry, have you ever needed something so bad you can't sleep at night, have you ever tried to find the words but they don't come out right, have you everrr have you everrr..." Ms. Emma knows this song backwards and forward. You would think Brandy lived here also as much as her voice is heard in there. It makes Ms. Emma sulk every time it plays because she knows her granddaughter is upstairs doing the exact same thing. It's on repeat for at least an hour every night. Ever since that boy was killed on the porch it's like so was her grand baby's joy. It's the soundtrack to her heartbreak. Upstairs Lenae stands in front of the mirror completely nude, fingering her locket. Inside is a picture of herself, Drama and Coop. It was a gift from Drama and she loves it more than her life. Her throat is constricted from weeping but she can't help it. As her bath water runs she wraps her hair and admires the confident young woman the men on her neck helped her become.

"Coop?" The text pops on his screen.
  "What's up, Nae?"
  The little thinking bubble pops up on his iPhone meaning she's typing. After about three minutes a long message appears.

> *"'If I had a father like you I wonder what life would have been? The day you walked in our class I was already counting the seconds until you left. Not knowing that I was dismissing probably one of the greatest gifts God has ever given me. I can't thank you enough for taking us in when even our families and teachers counted us out. You're a miracle. The tortured demon that God turned into his angel. That's why I never take this locket off, both of my angels are in it. Before you I felt like nothing, honestly now I feel worth more than*

the rarest jewel, beautiful. I love the skin I'm in. Thanks to you, I forgot what it was to be sad, til they took Draymon. Did you know I suffered from severe depression since I was around twelve? I was able to stop taking my pills thanks to you two but my heart hurts so bad right now though Coop. I mean HURTS! Smh. This is a sadness I can't shake, I haven't felt this weak in a long time. I hate myself for what I'm about to do to you (tears) but I'm tired. Try to understand, I love you Coop. Always Us Never them (Drama voice)"

A picture of the three of them pops on his screen. He attempts to text her back but Suffiyah has been reading over his shoulder the entire time. She understood the words like Benji never would, because she once thought them.

"Get dressed, call her now!" she screams while pulling on her sneakers and sweat pants. Benji presses call without hesitation.

She hates to interrupt Lenae's alone time but she's been holding her bladder for over an hour. Ms. Emma slowly climbs the stairs to the bathroom and knocks on the door. "Nae-Nae, I'm coming in. I have to pee something awful." She turns the knob and walks in. "No, No, No! Nae-Nae!" Lenae lays in the tub and looks like she's sleeping peacefully. Only thing suggesting otherwise is the red water and the razor next to her phone.

This entire scene feels like déjà vu. Same block, same house, same people. Only difference is Suffiyah is on the personal side of the event. The crowd parts as the paramedics descend the stairs slowly with the stretcher. Their lack of haste tells her they're too late. When Benji sees the sheet covered blanket, he breaks down. It's like all his strength is sapped. As if brittleness settled into his bones and crumbled from the joints. He drops to his knees and belts out a guttural sound. A pain deep from the pit of his stomach. All heads turn in their direction. Suffiyah drops down, unfazed by the attention and cradles him. Her mouth opened but words refused to form. What can she say anyway? Sometimes presence is more effective then spoken words.

CHAPTER 26

F OUR DAYS HAVE PASSED SINCE Lenae committed suicide. Outside of washing and going to brush his teeth, Benji hardly leaves his bed. Suffiyah does as much as possible to try to remove his mind from the gloom it resides in, if only momentarily, to no avail. He exhibits every sign of depression, but that's normal given the consecutive losses he's experiencing. What worries her is the lack of light in his eyes. Never has she seen a sign of weakness in him, even when he cried. He was still ever defiant. A true revolutionary to the core. Until now, at this moment he resembles a casualty of the harshest, coldest war man has ever witnessed. He sits with his back against the headboard in a tank top and pajama bottoms. The iPod plays through the earphones as he drowns out the world as if it isn't still spinning. She doesn't need to hear the song to know what he's playing. He's only been listening to one song for the past four days, as he holds Lenae's locket in his palm. Ed Sheeran made it as a song for lovers but Benji has made it into a haunting tribute to Lenae. She doesn't know the name of the song but the words will never be forgotten. They've left Benji's mouth thousands of time over the last ninety-six hours.

> *"Oh you can fit me inside the necklace you got when you were sixteen, next to your heartbeat where I should be, keep it deep within your soul and if you hurt me, well that's okay baby only*

*words bleed, inside these pages you just hold me
and I won't ever let you go"*

Benji? He can't hear her voice over the music, but he can read his name on Suffiyah's lips. *Benj?* She hasn't left his side or judged him throughout this ordeal. It would be so much easier to waddle into this dark place and curl up if she'd just leave. *Benji?* He pulls one of the bubs out his ear. "You couldn't hear me?" She sits indian style in just his football jersey facing him.

"No. What's wrong?"

"You have to do your monthly editorial. I know I'm no writer, but I was wondering if I could put an article in there this month?"

"Cool," is all he says and puts his ear bud back in.

Hours Later

Suffiyah wakes Benji up from his nap. "I don't remember falling asleep."

"It's okay, you needed the rest. I spoke to Mrs. Wise and she said Lenae's services start tomorrow morning at ten. I cooked dinner whenever you're ready to eat and I'm never leaving from right here if you need me," she says grabbing his hand. "Remember I told you I could be strong for you? That strength has a lifetime guarantee. You look like you're ready to quit on me. I haven't cried once, as bad as I want to, because I'd lose it and you need me. But as selfish as it might sound I need you more." Her mouth trembles as the first tears take form. "I haven't heard your voice really in over three days. I have never been with you and still felt alone. Please come back to me," she pleads. Her face showed dismay that reached the depths of Benji's being. He saw the scared baby girl going from foster home to foster home looking for something or someone to depend on. Then for the first time in days she saw his smile as he opened his arms. She nestled into him and sobbed.

"I'm here, beautiful. I'm so sorry." Her body just convulses as he holds her.

How did Suffiyah manage to find happiness while she was supposed to be suffering? All over the city bodies are dropping, some directly, for her sake, well the sake of her attention. She's been fired and robbed of any sense of security but she's happy? He's going to erase that smile, and if she still felt safe in her home, this will change that. The killer roams her apartment flipping chairs and breaking dishes. Clothes and papers are strewn everywhere, books litter the floor and he's opened all the windows. Her 'home sweet home' looks abandoned. He's poured water inside all of her television sets. Standing back admiring his handwork he can't help but feel something's missing. It doesn't seem like he's getting his point across. An idea comes into his mind. This will get her attention.

How do you measure strength? Is it by how much weight you can lift or how big your muscles are? Maybe you find combatants from all over the world and fight until one of the final two is the evident victor. On TV you see men who can pull trucks with their bodies! Because you can do all of these thing does that make you strong? The definition to strength, that I like is, the quality of being strong; ability to do or endure. I guess to measure strength you need to decide what's more important, physical or moral strength. I've seen men who can lift 500lbs but can't find the strength to lift a dollar from their pocket to feed the homeless. Strong enough to pull a mack truck but too weak to carry an infant from a burning building. How is their strength measured? Any coward can attain muscles but character is strength. Morals and principle are weightless but at the same time heavier than mountains.

People of moral and principle are a gift. Those who are broken down by their own problems yet they still shoulder the burdens of others with no complaints. Sees others trouble and walks towards it instead of away from it. Unable to bench press 500lbs but has the ability to lift their people. I've found one of those strong people. Who collects the unwanted youth and guides them. Takes less to give them the most. Risks death to ensure them the opportunity to truly live. I measure strength not by the ability to do but by the risk of actually doing. Anyone can do anything but not many will risk themselves to do what's important for others. So if you lose one in a fight to save millions, do you quit? The strength of a man is measured by his ability to be strong in his moments when he is at his weakest. Now my question is, how do you measure strength?

"So you tryna take over my magazine?"

Suffiyah blushes as she eats her dinner. She was nervous about Benji reading the article she'd written. She figured at worst, he would feel it was unworthy of being published and at best, he'll know how much she feels for him.

"Not yet. You like it?"

"I love it. See you was wasting your talent writing tickets for jay walking." He laughs.

"So I changed your mood?"

"Maybe."

"Whatever. I don't know if you noticed but we're a team now. So from here on out we go into all situations like that. Just know you aren't alone tomorrow."

"You trying to ask to be my girlfriend?"

"No. I'm telling you I'm allowing you to be my boyfriend. You're welcome." The tension from Lenae's death has decreased over the past few hours thanks to Suffiyah's persistence. Every fighter has to be reminded by their corner that they aren't in this fight alone. "After we eat can you take me to my apartment to get something to wear to the funeral?"

"No problem, shorty."

How much more swollen can one pair of feet get?

Sonya asks herself as she rest hers on the coffee table. The warm butter aroma coming off the popcorn causes her mouth to water as she lazed on the couch waiting for her movie to begin. She's been picturing this scene in her mind all day. Her shift couldn't have ended a moment earlier. Chubby fingers reach in the bowl and grab a handful of popcorn and pops it into her awaiting mouth. The chair rings and startles her. She grabs the phone wedged between the sofa cushions. "Fields." On her line is a frantic Suffiyah. She jumps up toppling the bowl of popcorn. "Okay, I'm on my way." She has to beat the Maplewood cops to the scene before they touch anything.

Suf-Fer Suf-Fer Suf-Fer Suf-Fer Suf-Fer Suf-Fer Suf-Fer

The monotony of the word is more menacing then the desecration of her apartment. The scrawled words on her full length mirror were enough to make her pee her pants. The mess was simply overkill. The sheer audacity of the mirror was like the killer's hand being on her shoulder. He made it evident that he could touch her at any given time. The fact that he was in her humble abode, destroyed its sanctity. Never mind her comfortability which had been removed. Benji stood with the officers giving them the just of the situation, while Suffiyah stood in the middle of the room wrapped in her own arms. The destruction looked like a child's temper tantrum on steroids. Bereft of any real consideration. But the writing was done with a goal in mind. That goal was to make his presence felt. But who would know she wasn't staying at home outside of her? Only Benji and Lee Lee.

"Sufee." She turned around to find Sonya standing there with opened arms. She rushed to them. "We're going to get this bastard, baby. I promise that," she says while rubbing Suffiyah's back.

Her pulse quickens after the initial shock of seeing their number one suspect in person for the first time. Benjamin Cooper, standing with the Maplewood police. *How did he end up here?*

"Sufee, is that? Is that who I believe it is?"

"Yes, but he was with me the whole time. Well, I was with him."

Son of a bitch. I said she might be working with someone, thinks Sonya. This is no coincidence, this was just blatant stupidity on Suffiyah's end. She was in such a rush to create this scene that she failed to cross her T's and dot her I's. She holds Suffiyah at arm's length and looks at her.

"As much as he was talked about, I've never heard you mention knowing him."

"It's a long story but at that time I didn't. Not like this. I can explain it to you later, but can you just trust when I say he isn't behind this?"

"Of course." This puzzle couldn't be coming together more beautifully if she was doing it with her own hand. Lewis is infatuated with Suffiyah which explains his hard on for Benjamin. He's found out about this little relationship and needs to intervene. Clearly his only option is removing Benjamin from the equation. As crooked as Lewis is, it's not far-fetched to see him pulling that off.

"I don't trust her." Benji gives his opinion on Sonya. "Her eyes held the look of an opportunist. She was holding you while scoping everything like a hawk." Suffiyah stands there undressing for bed. "And the way she looked at me," He shakes his head. "I'd rather sit in a cobras nest then put my life in her hands."

"Sonya's cool. What you saw was probably concern in her eyes and you misinterpreted it. She always been down for me." She feels the need to defend her friend.

"In all my years in the streets do you know what one of the realest lessons I learned was? It was, that it's easy for everyone to be down for you until it's time to show up. Put their self on the line, then you know who's actually down for you." When she was fired did Sonya speak up for her? Or did she hide like the others?

"I don't know. I just want to go to sleep so we could lay Lenae to rest tomorrow. Can we go to bed?"

"Put this number in your phone first. Mrs. Hawkins was at the Children's Home Society of New Jersey while you were there. She remembers exactly who you are and will only release any information to you." Benji passes her his phone so she could see the text message. "Figure out the dream, find the killer right?" He holds his hand up for a high five, she connects and locks their fingers.

"Right. Now put me to sleep."

6:00am

Boom! Boom! Boom!

Suffiyah and Benji sit up in unison as the banging at the door continues. Experience tells them both who it is at the door, but the question is why?

"Benji, get dressed I'm going to answer it," Suffiyah whispers while pulling on her clothes. She commences to the front door but stops at the window. There's a whole task force out there. Now she's scared. Continuing to the door she tries to gain control of her nerves. These are her old co-workers, so why is her hand shaking as she reaches for the lock? Soon as the door cracks the team swarms in.

"Miss, get on your knees!"

"What's going on?" Benji asks stepping through the doorway. All guns swing in his direction.

"Get down! Get down! On your fucking knees! Hands behind your head!" Suffiyah is stuck. Everything's happening so fast but it's like slow motion in her mind. "Benjamin Cooper, you are under

181

arrest for first degree murder, first degree felony murder, first degree conspiracy to commit murder…" By this time Suffiyah has lost all comprehension of the words being said as she loses her ability to speak. Everything is a blur now, black figures going left and right. Indecipherable words being screamed, things slamming, Benji cuffed and then all of a sudden complete silence. When Suffiyah gains a grip on reality, she's the only person left in the apartment.

Benji's mouth hasn't opened once. After being paraded shamefully in front of his neighbors and walked slowly to an awaiting car. He was whisked to 50 West Market Street and sat in the major crimes office where he declined questioning. From there he was taken to a cell. Another man sat in there also in street clothes. He was happy to have company, he started talking to Benji before the bullpen locked. "We just missed the bus. We gotta go to the county (jail) with the dudes returning from court. I hope they R.O.R me. I just did a three-sixty-four. B.O.N got me on Bergen. Twenty-three bags…" On and on he went, Benji never even looked his way. "Cooper?" After sitting for about two hours, an officer called his name. He was cuffed to three other men in green jumpsuits, to board the van to the county jail. All he could think about was not seeing Lenae one last time before being swallowed by the Earth for eternity. Before he knew it they were exiting the van to enter his new home. The other men were sent to their unit while he was put through processing. The intake bullpen was as cold as a deep freezer. The benches were metal and torturous. Four hours later, after being printed again, issued an ID band, stripped and violated, placed in a shower and trading his clothes for a musty jumpsuit he was housed in a filthier bullpen. Junkies were defecating and vomiting in toilets that were unclean five years ago and have only grown worse. It smelled like a zoo. Somehow the other man from West Market Street ended up with him and was still talking. "We go to CJP in the morning to get arraigned. We sleeping in here tonight though." Benji looked around the cramped bullpen and wondered where forty men could possibly sleep. "Let me get this bench," a young man demanded standing in front of

Benji. Everyone in his immediate vicinity scattered. Leaving the young man plenty of room, yet he stood in front of Benji.

"You too, old head."

"Bruh, I'm begging you to go lay down."

CRUNCH!

The sound of cartilage shifting sounds like thunder in the quiet bullpen. Punch after punch rains down on him before the lights turn out.

"Breakfast! Stay seated we'll bring it in," the C.O yells.

Benji removes his hands from his face and can't believe he'd sat like that the whole night. He blacked out last thing he remembered was someone grabbing his jumper. You'd think he was deranged the way every other occupant in the bullpen avoids eye contact. The young man sits on the other side of the room using his dreads to hide the bruises. Benji's concept of time is off so it could be anywhere from 6am to 11am, he just knows its morning thanks to breakfast. Which he won't be eating either. Once given the Styrofoam tray he takes it to the young man. Only way to teach people better is to show people better.

"Thanks bruh," the young man mumbles as he sits with a more humbled and reserved bearing. When CJP is called out hours later, they travel single file in bright orange jumpsuits. Over the course of two hours they are broken up and appointed into three separate bullpens. Then called out to see a judge on a video monitor. Benji smiles for the first time through this whole ordeal when they say he has family in the court. He could picture Suffiyah waiting on the benches in his mind. His smile recedes when he hears his bail set at $750,000 cash only, the same as his codefendants. *What codefendants?*

CHAPTER 27

$750,000 CASH SOUNDS LIKE A billion to a man with roughly $35,000 in his bank account. With very few options available to him, Benji tries to find some sort of comfort in what will probably be home for the rest of his life. Next he's led to the Quarantine Unit where he must be housed for three days pending a mandatory tuberculosis test. Once in his cell he realizes *Quarantine* is just a cute name for severe oppression. Twenty-three hours and fourty-five minute are spent in a cell with an addict going through withdrawal. The toilet is brown with used tissue paper stuck to the seat. The floor holds compacted dust in abundance and stains which are indescribable. I guess the ploy is to make you appreciative of where you're housed permanently after seventy-two hours of this. Or to keep you from complaining about only having fifteen minutes to use the phone and shower, because any reprieve from being in that cell is a blessing. When his fifteen minutes of fame finally comes he uses five of it to shower. Which leaves him to ten to call Suffiyah. After the long message she presses one to accept his call.

"Hello?"

"Hey, Sufee."

"Why are you just calling?" Her worry pierces the receiver.

"I'm sorry, I was out of it, I had to adapt. I only have ten minutes though so I need you to listen. I'm going to do a power of attorney form so you can clear my bank account. It's $35,000 in there. Take twenty to my lawyer so he can get on whatever this is and hold on to the other fifteen so you can be straight while I'm gone."

"Straight?" He can hear the smile in her voice and hopes he is mistaken.

"You sound amused, but I don't see the humor," Benji snaps.

"Sorry bae, but you just made my day. Me and Lee Lee had a conversation and she asked me what I was prepared to do and would you do the same for me? I told her it didn't matter I just needed to know you're good. And here you are in a situation where your life is in shambles, yet you find the time to make sure I'm good."

"You know it's a possibility I'm never coming home?" Benji needs to point this out. He'd hate for her to be here for months and then leave when reality sets in.

"Boy please. You'll be with me in a couple of weeks." She must be delusional from trying to remain optimistic.

"Ain't no bond on my bail. Unless you plan on taking that $35,000 to the racetrack, it ain't in there for me, gorgeous," he admits sadly.

"Nah, hold your money. I got us."

"You got us?"

"Didn't I tell you we were a team? If you're afflicted, I'm afflicted. Likewise if I'm straight, you're straight. Now, thanks to you unselfishly offering me your last, I'm more than straight. I was ready to sacrifice it all on a gamble of the heart, but you once again proved you're a sure thing."

"It's not much time left and I'm lost, shorty."

"Nobody knows but Lee Lee but when I got shot, I received a settlement. 2.2 million. So just know I'll see you soon. I love you." Now Benji is smiling.

"I love you more."

The traffic on route 1 to Trenton was bumper to bumper for some odd reason. It was as if the envoy of vehicles knew how anxious she was to get to her destination so they decide to be her obstacles.

"Girl! If you don't quit inching up to these unmoving cars. I swear if your bumper rubs theirs I'm siding with them. You've been driving like you're trying to kill us all morning," Lee Lee complains. Suffiyah can't help herself. This woman is the only possible answer to her many questions. So she doesn't care how much Alicia complains, she is going to get there as soon as possible. "Act like you don't hear me. I'll jump out this car and hitch hike." Suffiyah smiles at her.

"Alicia, if you don't hush. I'm going to calm down, okay?"

"Um-hmm, you better or you gonna lose a passenger. Do you think she can tell us anything vital to all this chaos?"

"That's what I'm in a rush to find out." The rest of the trip is accident free. After about forty-five more minutes they are finally parking in front of the Children's Home Society of New Jersey in Trenton. Nervousness settles into her stomach creating a feeling of queasiness.

"I can hear your bubble guts from here. It's too late to be nervous we've arrived. Pull your big girl panties up and let's see what we can learn and you bet' not poot." Suffiyah can't imagine what she would do without Lee Lee and her goofy antics. "Ain't nobody pooting, you retard. I just don't know what to expect."

"I do. Answers."

Benjamin Cooper has been arrested on a boatload of charges. Which are sure to keep him imprisoned for most of the foreseeable future. Suffiyah is all alone to deal with her own impending legal woes. Lewis is as happy as a fox in a hen house. Everything is going better than Sonya could have imagined, yet something seems wrong. She can't put her finger on it but something is definitely out of place.

Mrs. Hawkins is a beautiful fifty-ish black woman. Her face holds not a single wrinkle. Making her look more Suffiyah's age than her actual age. Only her salt and pepper hair gives her away. She sits and admires Suffiyah with a sincere smile on her face. "You have grown into a truly beautiful young lady. When you arrived here you were completely traumatized. You cried for the whole two first months you were here. You wouldn't allow anyone to touch you but me. I took on the role as your Godmother while you were in our care. Children like you, are the reason I'm still at this place today. This was just a summer gig for me, up until you came. Seeing a beautiful baby like you, *unloved*. Let me know I was needed here and it became my career.

Since then, countless little boys and girls of all shades come through these doors and I make sure they feel the love of home." The duo sit across from Mrs. Hawkins, hanging onto her every word. "I used to call Mrs. Richardson and check on you, but I never got more than, you're fine. Eventually I took the hint and let them raise you without my interference. I always think about you. So you can imagine my shock when I received a phone call asking about you? I had to see you. Now that's done, so what can I do for you?" The warmth emanating from this woman causes any previous nervousness to subside. This woman held a genuine love for her.

"Why didn't you adopt me?" The question is out her mouth before she knew she was asking it. From the look on Lee Lee's face she is just as shocked by what was asked.

"Suffiyah, I was only twenty-two. I could hardly take care of me let alone you and me. But I would have loved to have had the privilege of calling you my daughter."

"Thank you. I don't recall the things you've done for me in the past, yet I know they made a difference. But the reason I really came today was to find out about my first foster family. Is there anything you can tell me to help me locate them?"

"I can give you all I have, which isn't much. Really only their names and an address that might be outdated. But I don't know why you would want to find them, you cried for two months out fear of them."

"So why was I afraid of them?"

"Apparently they tortured you. Never physically, just psychologically. You were convinced your name was Suffer. Isn't that strange?"

"If you look around us what you'll see is a lot of people in fear. In fear of the world around them but more in fear of looking in the mirror and acknowledging what's in front of them. They fear seeing in the mirror anything other than the person they project to the world on the day to day basis. So you know what they do?" Lenae is so into what Benji's saying she isn't touching her food. *"They use the mirror for just the basics. Getting dressed, applying makeup, checking their bodies. All of these things while avoiding eye contact with their greatest enemy, themselves. Eyes are the windows to the soul. You can beautify the exterior all you wish. Drape it in the latest fashions, polish it til it shines. But an ugly soul is just that. God didn't create a make-up that can hide that. I could hide it from you but I can never hide it from me. You see how so many people in this restaurant are smiling with their lips only? Their eyes are devoid of any joy or happiness. Those are the soul hiders seeking to please the world with what they deem is acceptable. You're probably wondering where I'm going with this, so I'm going to get to the point. You are one of the few whose outside beauty matches their inside. I look in your eyes and see so much promise and undetermined greatness. But I also see a soul that's being neglected. You are so worried about the world's view of you that you've become imbalanced. Perfect self, first by acknowledging you are as perfect as you were created. Know that there are no accolades or*

compliments that the world can give you that will make you any better. It's only them finally being able to see the greatness that was Lenae form the start." She tries to stop the tears forming in her eyes from freeing themselves to no avails she looks down. Benji places his finger under her chin and raises her head. "Don't be ashamed to cry, it doesn't detract you of anything. Keep your head up and face the world. Some man cheated himself of seeing you grow up. If I had a daughter, I'd consider myself lucky if she was half of what you are. Matter fact, do you have a Godfather?" Lenae shakes her head no. "Now you do. Only thing keeping me from being your real father is different blood. But in my eyes, blood couldn't make us any closer."

Pools of tears collect in Benji's ears as he lays on his bunk looking at the ceiling. Memories of Lenae just float in his mind on their own. For everyone he wrestles away two more appear. It's the middle of the day, but thankfully he doesn't have a cellmate. His heart feels like it's in a vice that is being turned tighter every day. The bail source hearing to ensure that his bail money came about by legitimate means is set for two weeks. By that time he believes his heart will actually burst from the pain. This is the second woman he allowed in his world and failed to protect from it cold nature.

"Phillips. Richard and Antionette Phillips. The last address on file for them is 101 Asbury Street, but I know that's no longer accurate because I remember when that house burned down. It was all over the news, entire house was engulfed in flames. I suggest you Googling their names and see what that offers you. Could be a dead end but it never hurts to try," Mrs. Hawkins advises.

"Thank you, Mrs. Hawkins, I don't know what I would have done without you."

"With all the money I heard you paid to find me it was the least I could do. I don't even want to know how much the private investigator who called me charged you, if it caused three grand to find me. I just wish I could give you some of your money back."

"I wouldn't take it. You don't even know it but you're still providing me with information that is beyond value. If there is anything I can do for you ever, please don't hesitate."

"Well, there are two things actually. One, is to give me a hug and the other is to never lose contact with me again." Mrs. Hawkins gives her the type of hug that could only come from a mother. The love is in their embrace.

"I promise."

Files are spread all over Detective Sonya Fields desk. Each one thoroughly inspected for anything that might have been overlooked. It's usually that small piece which pulls everything else together. While looking through Ranesha Felders' file it was nothing of interest outside of her pictures. Her phone is crammed with videos of her and her various clientele in different acts that put some pornography to shame. A file marked with a post it bearing Suffiyah's address on it proves most intriguing. It's something that's not being said or at least not being shared with him. The filex are collected and arranged in the same order they were found. It would be hard explaining when Sonya comes in from her day off, wondering why her files were in disarray.

The day started off rocky but things were looking up by the moment. Suffiyah's smile couldn't be removed with a scalpel. Traffic was flowing perfectly. Another piece to the puzzle of her life was placed on the table. And in the midst of these turbulent times she discovered that she'd found her soul mate.

"If you're sleeping with someone and they give you $3,000, do that make you a prostitute or nah? Because that's what Google's saying, so I just wanted to know?" She looks at her best friend.

"Jealousy doesn't look good on you, boo. I saw your face. It takes a lot to impress Alicia. So I know I have a keeper now. Really though, it's crazy 'cause we really wasn't trying to give him a chance and look. Nobody tries to come through for us like him."

"Yeah, yeah, yeah. All I know is you better hurry up and bring my brother home or me and you going to have a problem."

"So ya'll siblings now?"

"I'm not about to front, he earned all my respect and more. I see men who spend $10 and want sex and recognition for it. Here is a man who spends $3,000 and not only doesn't feel entitled to something for it but also never mentioned it? It's so few genuine men around that we can't let them go when we find them and you have one. I truly can't think of anyone more deserving of him than you." Lee Lee's statement just improved on Suffiyah's already great mood.

CHAPTER 28

PHILLIPS IS SO COMMON A name that they've been at it for days now and are just making headway. Suffiyah and Dr. O'Malley sit in Starbucks nursing cappuccinos.

"I knew I was spot on about those dreams. Ha! Nothing but repressed memories," Dr. O'Malley gloats with a victorious glint in her eyes. "Don't misconstrue my excitement. It just makes it easier to solve a problem when you actually know what the problem is. Quiet as kept I'm working on a book. A compiling of case studies and repressed memories. I was beginning to feel defeated but you just mustered the fight back in me. The way you're asserting yourself to the task of solving this string of crimes is inspiring. Such a beauty and tenacity in this small package. Kudos. How did you react when she told you, what you thought your name was?"

"I didn't. As surprised as I was to hear her say 'Suffer', I believe a part of me already knew. I did think of the mirror in my house though. Who could know that?"

"After you come from seeing the Phillips today, I'm going to attempt to hypnotize you again. All the answers we need are going to be found within that nightmare. If I didn't have a session this morning I would come along with you for the ride. I really don't like you going places alone."

"Oh, I'm ok. Dr. Jackson volunteered to accompany me. He's familiar with the city and wouldn't take no for an answer."

"Ever the gentleman. Well, come directly to me afterwards so we can get started."

Suffiyah's derriere sinks into the plush leather seats of the Mercedes S550 sedan. The comfortability of this car surpasses her Honda by far, making her chairs feel like public transportation seats. This car fits him to the tee. Sleek, debonair, attractive and exuding a higher degree of class. The smooth jazz he's playing creates an air of ease and relaxation. This is the closest she's been to Dr. Jackson since the near incident in his office. A pinch of guilt touches her as she thinks of Benji. She's never mentioned Dr. Jackson to him, Dr. O'Malley on multiple occasions, but never Dr. Jackson. But why not? Was this intentional? Was she hiding him as a backup plan? If the shoe was on the other foot how would she react to this road trip? She would flip out. How could she tell him about this trip without ever having mentioned the phone calls? Now isn't the time to bring this up with Benji already being in a stressful situation. Adding unnecessary trust issues to his plate wasn't going to help their situation. She made a promise to herself that moment to tell Benji everything when he's released. "Are you okay, Suffiyah?"

"Yes, Im fine."

"You're abnormally quiet it seems?"

"I was just daydreaming. A lot of things on my mind coupled with the stress, it keeps me in deep thought."

"You know you can always talk to me, if you wish."

"I know, but I'd rather sit back and enjoy your company."

"Okay." The rest of the journey is made in silence as they float down the highway. Dr. Jackson warned her how rundown the block would be, but seeing it first hand was different. Words can't define the bleak sadness of the area or it inhabitants. A group of males stand idly eyeing the luxury automobile with envy. Imagine their surprise when it pulled in front of the most disconsolate house on the block.

"You trust leaving your car out here?"

"Not in the least. You go on in and I'll keep an eye on things out here."

"Okay." Suffiyah steps out the car and is bombarded by birdcalls and all sorts of misogynistic comments. She ignores them and keeps towards the residence. After ringing the bell she starts to feel the jitters. There is no noise or approaching footsteps. Maybe this house is abandoned now? You can't expect to strike gold on your first swing. She turns to descend the steps and the door opens behind her.

"Who you?" In the doorway stands a homeless man who look to be about sixty, well he can't be homeless because here he is in a home. But appearance wise? He's very convincing.

"Richard?"

"Do I look like fucking Richard to you?" The pungent smell of alcohol and funk smacks her face.

"I'm sorry. I was told I could find Richard and Antionette Phillips at this address. Do you know them?"

"You just keep asking questions. I believe I asked who the fuck is you?"

"Pardon me, I'm Suffiyah. I was their foster daughter when I was a little girl."

"Shit, you ain't lil' no more," he says while ogling her. "Richard's my brother. You want to come in?" Saliva is almost dripping from his mouth as he stares at her hips. She can read the perverted thoughts from his facial expressions.

"No thank you. I just wanted to come thank them for taking me into their home." This comment earns her a cough infested bout of laughter.

"Shit you would be the first person to ever thank them for anything except leaving."

"If it's all the same, can I speak with them?"

"They don't live here no mo'."

"Well can you give me an address or number to reach them?"

"I guess you're just as stupid as you are pretty, huh?" Suffiyah ignores the insult for the sake of answers. "Antionette is in Anne

Klein. She's been there ever since the murder and Richard resides on South Broad Street."

"Isn't Anne Klein a mental institution?"

"Where else would you put a nut besides a nut house?" Her patience is wearing thin with his smart remarks. Just one more question and she can leave.

"Can I have Richards' address on South Broad?"

"Sure, why not?" And he gives it to her with ease.

"Thank you."

"You know you can always come sit on your uncle's lap." She descends the stairs. "Suffiyah?" She turns around disgusted.

"What!"

"Richard will never talk to you, you nut."

"Why is that?"

"Because that's the cemetery. Richard's dead!" He laughs heartily as he slams the door shut. His last words knocked the wind out of her lungs.

"24...26...28..30." Benji drops off the pull up bar and assumes the push up position. This little bubble that the jail calls a gymnasium is his outlet. The only therapeutic remedy to this oppressive redundancy they call jail, is in this room. It has become the core of his sanity. The stories he has to unwillingly endure due to lack of being able to go elsewhere, are as outlandish as the people who are telling them. Never in his life has he encountered so many rich, broke people. When they were free, money was in abundance. But as soon as they entered this facility it all disappeared. Now these same men are unable to purchase a $20 bag of commissary. He can't decide which is more sickening the lies they tell or the people who line up to listen to them. He's been so far removed from this aspect of the streets that this was foreign to him. It felt strange unleashing his inner beast to roam this jungle after working so hard to tame him. But in this place being a man can only take you but so far. Detective Lewis has been down here twice doing his rendition of 'deal or no deal'. He's left unhappy on both occasions. Another week and this will all be over.

"Benji." He stops pushing up to look at the person addressing him. "I'm about to make something for lunch, Big Bro, you good?" Its turn-up. Chance places him on the same tier as one of his co-defendants. Through him he has learned the particulars of the crime, which only served to further confuse him as to why he's here.

"Just make me a small bowl."

"Got 'chu." He sets off on his task as if he was just asked to protect the president.

"Turn-up." He stops the young man. "I told you all that 'Big Bro' talk was unnecessary."

"Lay Low was my Big Bro and he told me you was his Big Bro. So what would that make you in my eyes?" Benji smiles. He never knew Lay said anything like that.

"Relax. Breathe. Take me to the attic." Suffiyah follows the far away bodiless voice. "Tell me what you see." Suffiyah climbs the rickety attic steps and surveys the goings on.

A little girl cowers in the corner of the attic, as the monster frantically searched for her. She silently prays to God that he doesn't look behind the boxes of clothes stacked in front of her. "Suffer! Suffer!" he screams as he flings objects out of his path. "Here you are!" But his voice is coming from across the room, directed at someone unseen. "Now you must suffer with me."

The girl peeks from behind the boxes as the monster lifts someone by the collar. "Where is she?" the monster barks. She sees a little finger point in her direction. The monster turns towards her with eyes the color of heated coal. The scrawny boy, in his massive hands, squeezes his eyes shut tightly. "You ruined a beautiful home, a beautiful family." Tears drip from his eyes and enhances the madness within them. His lips curl into a sinister grin. "So much pain, I suffer. Honest I do." He practically drags the boy behind him as he come towards the girl. His grin disappears. "But I won't suffer alone," he growls as he reaches for her hand. His grip almost crushes her tiny fingers as he slings the boy to the floor. He sits her on his chest and grabs her hands. She cries as he places her hands around the boy's neck and applies pressure. She can feel his breaths struggling to pass his throat as he's strangled. His feet kick out as he struggles. The man just smiles as he keeps on squeezing. "Now you suffer with me." Suffiyah pops out of her trance hysterical. "Breathe Suffiyah, breathe."

"Oh my God I killed him. I killed that little boy."

"You don't know that."

"I do. The man said Antionette's been in a mental asylum since the murder. I killed her son."

Alicia does a Google search of 'Richard Phillips of Trenton, N.J'. Outside of several miscellaneous things, there's an article from The Star-Ledger Mercer County section. She double clicks on the heading and opens it.

> *"Reports of an unendurable odor led authorities to 63 Asbury Street. The front entrance was slightly ajar on their arrival. After calling out for the residents and receiving no response, they entered the residence. Inside of the attic of the one family home authorities found the source of the smell. A days old corpse was found rotting in what seems to be an apparent homicide. The unidentified male was found strangled with the word 'Suffer' carved into his forehead. It's unknown whether he was an occupant of the address or a visitor. Authorities have declined to answer questions or identify the man until the family is notified."*

Curiosity sufficiently piqued, she clicks on the tab labeled 'Related topics'. To her shock it's the article Mrs. Hawkins spoke on. There is a picture of a house set ablaze. The article reads, *"In a suspected arson attack, a home on the one hundred block of Asbury Street was burned to the ground. The landlord said the house was being renovated and placed on the market. He was unable to provide any revelations as to a motive for the fire. But speculations from neighbors point to a victim found dead in another residence not too far from this address. He was identified as Richard Phillips, a 52 year-old plumber. Prior to the fire his body was discovered that morning. Sources state that up until a new proprietor purchased the property a year ago, Mr. Phillips resided in the recently fire bombed home. Whether mere coincidence or if the crimes are in fact related police are investigating all avenues in this incident.* "The two short articles are the only ones about the murder or the fire. Lee Lee screenshots each article and send them via text to Suffiyah.

"Benjamin? Benjamin?" Planted on the stool inside his cell is Sakinah. "You're letting yourself be beaten." He just stares at the apparition. "The Benji I knew would have never laid down." It's something wrong with her voice. "Maybe you're no longer my superman. You didn't save me after all." *I must be going insane.* "You're not crazy, just incapable. Incapable of being the man you convinced me you were." *How could she read my thought?* "Because I'm in your mind, it's the only thing you left me. I'm no longer a part of this world and now you've given another your heart. So what's left for me?" Its Sakinah's mouth but a symphony of voices are exiting it." You'll beat this," She shrugs. "It's written. Then the suffering ends and you'll be with me." "Me." "Me." Sakinah, Lenae and Drama now stand in his room. Is there any validity in dreams or are they just the nuance of a never resting brain? Coalesced with thought, memories and fear to make them seem believable? Or are they truly glimpses from God placed in your mind for a purpose? Benji ponders his dream and if it means anything. And if it doesn't why does his heart refuse to stop racing?

Destiny's Child's song *T-Shirt* blares in her ears as she whisks through the apartment cleaning thoroughly. All the stress of the past weeks and revelations are of zero relevance at the moment. Benji's bail source hearing is scheduled for the upcoming morning.

The lawyer has everything necessary to ensure Benji's release, so all Suffiyah has to do is wait. Her excitement is uncontainable as she anticipates being in his arms again. The forces of the world placed them together when it seemed they were both destined for a lifetime of loneliness. He'd been diligently tested and deemed befitting of her giving him her everything. Lee Lee's discovery can't even dampen her spirits. Alone she'd feel defeated, but with him in her corner there isn't a battle the world could throw at them that they couldn't conquer. A sharp pain takes her from her meandering as she stubs her toe on the leg of Benji's workstation. Toppling his folders and spilling the contents. She stoops to pick up her mess and sees a familiar photo. A nagging sense of curiosity causes her to settle down on her knees and check the folder. Each new picture is more startling then the last. She immediately dumps the remaining folders and searches for an answer to her questions. Her heart sinks to the very depths of her stomach as the pictures drop from her hands.

CHAPTER 29

NEVER HAS A NEW JERSEY Transit bus ride felt so luxurious. Walking down the ramp of the Essex County Correctional Facility to a barren parking lot was not what he envisioned. However, how could he complain after the small fortune that was spent in bail and attorney fees? If she wasn't down here to greet him she had to have her reasons. It was only almost 7:30 in the evening but as dark as midnight as he walked to his front door. All the lights in his apartment were off but Suffiyah's car was parked across the street. *She must be asleep.* He thinks as he climbs the steps quietly. Placing his key in the lock, to his surprise the doors are unlocked. His antennas are raised instantly.

"Sufee!" he says rushing in and switching on a lamp.

Suffiyah sits on the couch staring at him blankly. He lets out a deep breath of relief. "You scared me. I thought—" The sound of a pistol being cocked leaves the rest of the sentence in his mouth.

"Don't talk to me or touch me. I swear to God I will kill you, you sick bastard." The calm viciousness in which Suffiyah makes her statement chills him to the bone. "You were stalking me, I found the pictures. When I was leaving the house on Ridgewood, I *knew* I could feel someone watching me. But who would know I would be there except the person who sent me there?"

"It's not—"

"Shut. Up. One more word and I will squeeze this trigger until no bullets remain. You've been killing all these helpless woman for no reason outside of looking like me. Or rather looking like her." She tosses the nude photos of Sakinah on the coffee table. "You killed her too you psycho. I'm leaving and I'm taking these pictures with me. If you try to stop or follow me, you won't have to worry about the police. Stay away from me. Stay away from Lee lee. You've been warned. Move!" Benji stands with his hands up as she circles toward the doorway.

Once outside, Suffiyah breaks into a dead run as her bravado turns to fear. Seized by uncontrollable shivers as she gets in her car. Pulling out the space with no hesitation, she eyes the entrance to Benji's house. He set her up. Studied her moves and manipulated her thinking. She felt like a puppet or for the more sufficient title, a dummy. Her heart hurt with an inexplicable yearning that could never be accommodated.

Rage courses through Benji in tidal waves. Where he should feel sadness there is only anger. To think that she had the audacity to point a loaded gun at him, has him seeing red. Given the evidence against him, he can imagine how it seems. But to not even be granted the benefit of doubt or at the very least an opportunity to explain, how could she be so shallow? He knows exactly what to do.

Three Days Later

"You were wrong," Lee Lee says walking over to Suffiyah, "Look." She shoves her phone into Suffiyah's face. On the screen is a clipping from the obituary page. It reads about Richard Phillips and his funeral services. When she gets to his family, it says he leaves behind a loving wife and their only child, Ferming Phillips.

"I don't get it. But I saw him die in my dream."

"No, you saw him stop moving and equaled it with death." The pictures are damning, but Lee Lee can't quite put her mind to certainty when it comes to Benji. He may be a lot of things but psycho isn't one description that grabs her.

"So the child has to be Benji. That's the only thing that makes sense."

"How? Benji isn't high yellow."

"It could be that I'm just imagining his complexion. It doesn't have to be spot on accurate. The same way the man is a monster to me."

"Benji is younger than us."

"And?"

"You said the boy was a couple years older in you dream. It doesn't match."

"Well," Suffiyah searches for her words.

"He could be lying about his age, yeah, he has to be." The surety Suffiyah felt days ago dwindles daily. Nothing adds up in her mind but if she's wrong about this, how could he ever forgive her? Her initial thought was to take everything to Sonya and get her opinion. Something in her gut told her that was a bad decision. So her only other option was Lee Lee.

"So him and the entire judicial system are in cahoots about this lie?"

"No. What?"

"If you said he changed his name I could go with it. But his age can't be changed. The name and age he gave us was on the warrant. How do you explain that?"

"You aren't helping, Lee. Do you know how hard this is?" She asks as she nervously pulls loose strings from her sweater.

"If it's not him then what do the pictures mean?"

"Okay, all I'm saying is you didn't want to go to Anne Klein because you thought you killed her child. Now that we know that isn't the case, we can arrange to see her and hopefully get some answers."

Later

"She thinks I'm killing people who look like her. Even Sakinah."
Benji sits at the table explaining to a mutual friend of him and
Sakinah's. During the time of her death he was the key to Benji's
sanity. To the point he was the first call Benji made in the morning.
He eventually got his life back on track and moved forward to
become the Benji we know today. He successfully revamped his
life, with the help of this man. Whatever he can do for this brother
to attempt to repay him is never second guessed or questioned, it's
just a given. His debt to him is eternal. The tutelage and advice
he received was like his rebirth. So, whom else could he run to in
this state besides the one who guided him through the darkness
the first time? Not to mention, he's the only reason Benji knows
of Saffiyah. A police corruption scandal was brewing in the major
crimes department and she was a key suspect. Benji was hired to
record her routine and regular whereabouts on the day to day
basis. If anything irregular happened within her day that seemed
suspicious or odd, he was to report it. She passed with flying colors.
Which made her irresistible to Benji. "I don't know what to do. I
figured only you could help me." Benji stares into his friend's cat
like eyes wearing his emotions on his sleeves.

"Benji, you're like the little brother I never had. I was already
prepared to help you before you asked for it. Come by the house
later and we'll figure this thing out. Problems only come in two
sizes, a mountain or a mound. They're the same problem but you
know what makes the difference?" Benji shakes his head. "The
perception of the man. How we view it. A problem is only as big
as we allow it to be.

Once again we're in the comfort of Lee Lee's living room as her and
Suffiyah sit in front of the TV. "Neither are watching it but more so
using for the acoustics or the room would be eerily silent." Suffiyah
palms the hot mug of tea. It's burn seemingly ineffective to her but
she's inadvertently punishing herself. Her whole body feel numb

as if she's devoid of life. The sensation from the mug reaffirms her being.

"Okay, so I called out of work tomorrow. Our first stop is the nut house. If we don't get the right answers there, our only alternative is back to the brother's house. He's going to answer us by any means even if I have to let him feel your butt." Lee Lee smiles at her attempt to lighten the somber atmosphere. Suffiyah on the other hand doesn't show any sign of having heard a word from her friend's mouth. She just stares at the TV. In her mind though she clearly hears some of the wisest words she has ever heard spoken. *"I believe success is equivalent to happiness. You can have all the money, cars, homes and jewels, but that doesn't mean you're happy. I know if I had all those things I would be content, not happy. I want to quote a wise man, Benjamin 'Coop' Cooper. Coop said, 'I fear love the most'. That first day in my class when you said that, I didn't understand. Now I think I do. You fear love because love is happiness. To not know love is to not experience true happiness. So you never know what you're missing. So any semblance to happiness is sufficient. But once you've know love, true happiness, and then you lose it. Nothing outside of love can ever replace that emptiness."* Suffiyah smiles, a self-defeating gesture. "I let that girl die." She never looks away from the TV. The tears dropping into her tea audibly.

"What girl, Sufee?"

"Lenae. I was just thinking about the explanation she gave when we went there. She was so sad. That's how I recognized who she was, from her sadness. But I was so selfish I didn't recognize her sadness for what it was. Her entire soliloquy wasn't for the class, it was for her. She warned us that she was giving up on life and we were deaf to her warning."

"Sufee, I understand you feel depressed but you're not taking the blame for that poor little girl. Nobody appreciates the light 'til its dark. That's just the way of the world. We didn't understand her light."

"Lee?"

"Yeah, Sweetie?" Suffiyah looks at her for the first time in a hour.

"I need Benji."

Benji seals the envelope as he walks out the house. The only chance he has of Suffiyah hearing him out is Lee Lee. So he penned an explanation to Lee Lee touching on everything which needed saying. This letter to her and the advice he is on his way to go get are his only two chances at getting back love. He drops the letter in the mailbox.

CHAPTER 30

THE SUN IS SHINING WITH a warmth that penetrates the clouds and touches the earth. The wind factor is at a seasonal low. If this beautiful fall weather is any indication to the day's prospects for Suffiyah, than things are going to work in her favor. The beauty of the day lifts her spirits from the obscurity it manifested yesterday. As Lee Lee drives through Trenton singing along with the radio, Suffiyah mentally encourages herself. The GPS shows they will be at their destination in three minutes. Dr. O'Malley had a rapport with one of the doctors here and made this visit possible. A part of her wishes it didn't go through. The more she learns of her past the happier she is to have forgotten it.

"We're here, Boo." The scary movie vibe grips her as she looks at this jail for the mentally unstable. "You ready?"

"No. But I don't think I have a choice."

"You don't. But let's go get this over with." In the front they state their names and the nature of their visit. Dr. O'Malley allowed her colleague to know that Suffiyah was under Antionette's care as a foster child and wanted to extend her gratitude by visiting her. As they're escorted to the common, area images of Antionette dance inside both of their heads. Their eyes search the room for the wide eyed, wild haired woman they'd be meeting. The woman walked up to them briskly, carrying something in her hand and snickering. She held her two hands on top of one another as a child does when they catch a lighting bug. When she's right in front of them she reveals her treasure, shoving her hand in Suffiyah's face. "You see!" Suffiyah almost trips over Lee Lee's feet as she jumps backwards from the empty hand.

"Berta!"

One of the orderlies grabs her hand. "This isn't your visit." The woman allows herself to be pulled away pouting. A beautiful light skinned woman with pretty long hair stood watching in amusement by the window. She had the frame and gait of a maturing model as all 5'9 inches of her strolled towards them. The light played in her green eyes bringing you in the mindset of those of a cats. A keen intelligence rest in her gaze and not a hint of lunacy. "Ms. Antoinette, here is your company." The orderly introduces them like honored guest.

"Hello, Mrs. Phillips. I'm—"-

"I know who you are," she says waving them to sit.

"You do?"

"Of course. They said you're my daughter, how could I forget my daughter?" Suffiyah isn't for certain but she believes she has just seen lunacy peek her head out.

This has got to be the worst hangover in the history of the world. Last thing he remembers is being handed his first drink. His pulse sounds like a college marching band is performing in his head. Cotton mouth causes him to smack his lips together searching for some form of moisture. The hardest part is forcing his eyes open. For the life of him, Benji can't figure why he can't open his eyes.

The woman is familiar to Suffiyah. It's possible that the woman truly knows who she is too.

"What's my name?"

"Cigarettes."

"Huh?"

"Did you bring any cigarettes?"

Why in the world would she bring anything that could cause a fire into a mental institution?

"No. I don't smoke."

"Well that was mighty selfish of you, wasn't it? All this time I've been in here and all you're able to think about is what you want? You can fool the world little girl, but you can't fool me." She places her face just inches from Suffiyah's.

He's suddenly aware of the pressure around his eyes. It's something covering them. He lifts his arms to remove whatever's on his face. He can't. His arms are constrained by something also. So are his feet. From the way his body is positioned he can tell he's in a chair. The sense of panic begins to settle into his chest. He begins to hyperventilate as reality sets in. He's trapped. He doesn't know where and he doesn't know why. He hears a shuffling sound to his left, some movement.

"Yo?" It comes out like he has sand in his throat. Hands grab the back of his head. He squeezes his eyes shut and awaits the bullet to his head or the blade to touch his throat. Before he knows it, he reaches the light.

"Are you planning on sitting there quiet or are we going to talk?" Antionette asks sitting back in her seat. Suffiyah is trying to formulate a coherent thought when Lee Lee speaks up.

"Who am I?" The look of confusion settles over the woman as she stares at Lee Lee.

"You're my daughter." She replies.

This woman is as unbalanced mentally as they said. "I thought she was your daughter?" Lee Lee points to Suffiyah.

Confusion quickly is replaced with anger as she looks back and forth at them. "Listen you little cunts, I'm your mother. How dare you disrespect me? Where's Ferming?"

The blindfold drops from Benji's eyes as he blinks to adjust his vision. He hears wheels rolling as a chair is pulled in front of him. The answer sits in the chair and stares at him with a deranged smile on his face. "Ferm, what's all this bruh?"

"Hell of a night, Benjamin. Hell of a night. I like you a lot. No let me correct that. I love you like a brother. You've always been genuine with me, from day one. So why am I so angry with you, hmm?" Ferming laughs.

"Whatever this is we can get through this, Ferm. Just talk to me." Benji tries to keep a handle on an uncontrollable situation.

"I'm your therapist, Benjamin. Not the other way around. I do the mind fucking around here. You see, I had to confine you to this chair because I have two stories to tell you."

"What's wrong with my head?"

"Oh, that's just the drugs. It'll wear off soon."

"Why would you drug me?" The more Benji tries to understand the less he seems to understand.

"Would you let me tie you up without it? I didn't think so. You stole from me twice. How? You are nothing but an illegitimate seed that your mother should have swallowed. An everyday run of the mill thug with a smidgen of education." A look he's never seen on Ferming before presents itself. Danger. "Nevertheless. They chose you." *They who?*

The two girls look at each other. "It's me, Mommy. Suffiyah." Her face frowns up at the sound of the name.

"My Suffiyah? But you left me, you left us. Me and Ferming and Richie. How could you do that to us, do you know how much Richie loved us?" All Suffiyah could think to do was play along.

"Where is daddy?" Her face became stern again.

"You made Ferming kill him. He made me watch, said I could suffer with him. I never told anyone about y'all game in the attic. Oh, you thought I didn't know? You tried to steal both my men from my life. But you couldn't." She laughs. "Ferming still comes to see me. He told me he found you. But you don't look like no cop. You made my baby suffer so much he changed his name."

"I felt like a cuckold. All the time and energy I've put into trying to grab Sakinah's attention and in waltz Mr. Hoodlum. A wholesome young woman like her deserved the best, she deserved

me. Not some gangbanging scum from the bottom of the barrel."
Benji is impressed with the manner in which he's hidden this
hatred. Being from the gutter he usually detects any ill feelings
directed towards him. He never saw this coming. "The first time I
saw her face, it was like seeing a ghost from my past. I knew I had
to have her. So I turned up the charm and went for her, no days
off. Soon as I made some lead way she comes in talking about the
thug who picked up her books. So I befriended her and made the
doctor/patient relationship grow into a friendship. Do you know
how? By embracing you. All I had to do was concede to the loss
and embrace your relationship. Taking you in and treating you as
special as she felt you were only increased the bond between her
and I. To the effect she began to trust me to the point I became her
confidant. The day of your test she was actually going to *propose*.
She was going to *propose* to you." He shakes his head. "I lost it.
So I made up a story about buying an apartment by her job and
wanting her opinion. I only wanted her body initially, so I took
it. I made love to her. She said it was ok but the eyes never lie. I
saw she despised me and I knew those eyes could never view me
the same again. She reminded me so much of her at that moment
I couldn't let you have her. So I gave her to the most suitable one
for her, God."

"I'm going to kill you."

"I was right, a little bit of your world kills you, *Superman*." He
smiles at the reference to his letter. "But wait, there's more."

"Changed his name to what?" Suffiyah asks.

"Who?"

"Ferming. What did he change his name to?"

"Why would he change his name? What's wrong with you?"

"But you said—"

"What did they say about the cigarettes?" Suffiyah blows her
frustrations out.

They're talking in circles. "They said not right now. But what
did you say Ferming changed his name to again?"

"What did you say your name was again?" Antoinette asks.

"Suffiyah. My name's Suffiyah."

"Suffer." She giggles. "You're not Suffiyah, Suffiyah died."

"What did you call me?"

She leans in close to Suffiyah and whispers, "I don't even know who the fuck you are." The look she just gave Suffiyah sealed the deal.

"Shit!" It just hit her like a ton of bricks. She knows exactly why she recognizes Antionette. "Would you like to see a picture of my boyfriend?"

"Why would I—" Suffiyah turns he phone towards her. "That's Ferming." She smiles and reaches for the phone. "Can I have it?"

This intense staring game has been going on for minutes, neither man blinks. "Do you know why I didn't gag you?" Benji says nothing. "Exactly. I knew you wouldn't yell. I prepared for it in case you did by bringing you in the basement. Every TV and radio is on upstairs so you wouldn't be heard if you screamed, but I knew you wouldn't. It would go against your gangster's code of ethics." Benji has never been so sad that he was able to afford bail in his life. His thigh vibrates and illuminates through his jeans. "Let me get that for you." He retrieves Benji's phone. Suffiyah is calling him. Soon as it ends, she dials right back. He declines it. A text message appears immediately. "Please pick up! It's an emergency. I'm sorry!" he reads the text out loud dramatically for Benji. "That brings me to my second story. After the incident with Sakinah, I got a name change and a new job. I'm from Trenton, but I moved here to escape my past. But karma is such a conniving bitch that on the first day of my new job she brings me face to face with my past. It's a long story if you're interested in hearing?"

"You know where you can stick that story?" He ignores Benji.

"It started on a street in Trenton thirty odd years ago. My father was one of the most attentive providers you can imagine. I was their pride and joy, a miracle baby. My mother was told she couldn't have children but she carried me the full term. It was a high risk pregnancy but she pulled it through. But all her life she wanted her little boy and little girl. My father was determined to fulfill her wishes. They went to an adoption agency and were placed on a waiting list. In the midst of that wait he was laid off. He had just enough money saved to barely hold the three of us over. When I was five my mother was finally granted her daughter, a foster child named Suffiyah. By the time she came about my father was completely embittered. He kept landing one dead end job after another eventually finding himself stuck back in the unemployment line. He dived deeper and deeper into the bottle. My mother was collecting more money from welfare a month than he was able to accrue in half a year. I guess this emasculated him because it's around the time that the abuse started. He needed to feel and be looked at as the man of the house, so he had to break his competition. Me. So the attic games begin..." Ferming sits back with a faraway look in his eyes apparently reliving what he is recalling.

"You two make me sick," Richard says as he takes them to the attic for the first time.

"Everything was great before you came along and made life hell. Caused me my job and eat all the food I can buy. And as if you weren't bad enough," he says pointing at Ferming. "Somebody thought it would be funny to mail this little bitch to us." He slurs now looking at Suffiyah. "Then God is so fuckin' evil he makes me suffer. But it isn't enough to make me suffer, I have to be reminded of my suffering daily. Don't you think it's cruel that the first three letters of both of your names spell suffer? S-U-F." He points to Suffiyah then Ferming. "F-E-R. Big fuckin' conspiracy. The whole shitty worlds against me. When you hear me say Suffer I'm calling the both of you, to meet me here immediately or I gotta hurt you. Suffer!" Neither

kid moves. Fear has them frozen in place as they watch their hero meltdown. "Suffer!" The smell of urine fills the room as a puddle forms around Ferming's bare feet. This only further enrages Richard. "Ungrateful. Disrespectful. Bastards. I'm going to show you how it feels to suffer. I did it all by myself now you're going to suffer with me." Before either of them can react he has them in his grasp. They cry hysterically but it doesn't dent his heart. He knocks Ferming down and sits Suffiyah on his chest. Next he wraps her hands around his neck. Fear is all the little boy feels as he has the life squeezed out of him.

"…I always woke up later in my bed shaking and pissy. I promised I'd return that feeling of fear and suffering to him when I was bigger and stronger. I kept my promise. One day I knocked him down and forced my mother to choke him, but I forgot to let go of her hands. So I fled Trenton and started anew. I met Sakinah and it reminded me of my suffering, but we know how that played out. Ferming no longer existed after that. I figured with a new job and a new name it was no turning back. Then she walked in my office." The deeper this story goes the more content Benji is with death. There is no possible way he's confessing all these things and intending to let him walk with this knowledge. "What hurt the most is she didn't even recognize me. I knew her before the words 'Detective Suffiyah Adams' left her lips. All I asked you to do was follow her, but you couldn't resist. This was the second time you stole from me, there won't be a third."

The sound of Benji's voicemail once again has Suffiyah seething. She gives up and goes to Sonya's name and calls her. While she does this LeeLee drives recklessly back to Newark. Neither has a plan but both knows something needs to be done.

"Hello?" Sonya's voice comes through the speaker phone. Hope fills the car.

"Sonya! Where are you?"

"I'm at the office. Calm down and talk to me. What's wrong?"

"I've found the killer! I know who's been strangling all these women."

"You do? Where is he?!" Sonya went from telling her to calm down to becoming equally, if not more excited.

"Where is Dr. Jackson? I need you to go get Dr. Jackson!"

"He's gone, baby.He quit shortly after you left. But we don't need him honey. We can handle this." Suffiyah's hope sinks.

"We do Sonya. Dr. Jackson is the killer." Silence creeps through the phone at this revelation.

"You have to find him, Sonya. His cellphone is off. But if you catch him, I promise you have your suspect. Trust me. I'm on my way to his house."

"No! Me and Lewis are heading there now, Stay put until you hear from me." The call is disconnected.

CHAPTER 31

THE ENERGY SPRINGING OFF OF Detective Fields has Lewis more than interested. "No! Me and Lewis are heading there now. Stay put until you hear from me." This gets Lewis fully intrigued. Sonya hurries into her coat. "We gotta go, Lewis!" Any other time Lewis would be questioning her but he's already moving. Whatever is going on is big! As they wait for the elevator, she brings him up to speed. "Suffiyah figured out the culprit to the strangling's."

"Cooper?"

"Not at all, now that she brings him to my attention it makes sense. He fits the bill." Now Lewis is totally lost. *Who's this surprise suspect?*

"It's Dr. Jackson."

"Dr. Jackson?"

He asks as they enter the elevator. "Uh-hmm. Right under our noses." Dr. Jackson? It's always the light skinned pretty fellows who are the sickest. "We have to get to his house." Sonya jogs to their car. "Before Suffiyah tries to beat us there."

"You know where he stays?" Sonya doesn't have the breath to reply so she nods. "Okay. Drive."

Where could he be? There was no sign of life in Misfits. INC, and she used her spare key to check his apartment. He didn't even sleep at home last night. That thought alone causes a pang of jealousy.

But after the evening she took him through could she blame him? She has to find a way to fix her mistake or she'd regret it forever.

"Do you trust Sonya to catch him? I feel like this is something we should be handling ourselves." With Benji missing, she can't think of anything else more worth her time than catching Dr. Jackson. Just hearing Lee Lee suggest it proved her right.

"I trust that she'll give it her all, but it couldn't hurt to have re-enforcements."

Just a few more inches. Benji stretches his arm to its limit. He can almost grasp the hand reaching out for him.

Slap! Slap! Slap! Slap!

Sakinah disappears and a blurry Ferming stands in her place. "Whoa. I think I held you too long that time. I thought you were dead." Benji's strength is depleted. He's lost count of how many times he's been unconscious. Every time he begins to gather his wits, Ferming's hands again find his throat. "If you scream the suffering ends. All you have to do is yell." Benji moves his lips but his words are faint. "What?" Benji's lips begin to move again but his words are inaudible. Maybe his voice box is damaged. Ferming places his face close enough to hear him better.

'PFFT'

The glob of spit lands in his eye followed by a hoarse, "I said pussy." And he smiles. Ferming wipes the film from his eye with his sleeves and his hands are squeezing Benji's neck before he can react.

The sirens blare as Lewis and Fields race to Dr. Jackson's house.

"How do you want to approach the situation?" Lewis asks as Fields narrowly misses another vehicle. He regrets getting in the passengers' seat.

"We pull up with sirens hollering and ring his bell. When he comes out we act like we're a million percent sure of everything were saying. Lt. McFarland is in the process of trying to get us a search warrant. So it's our job to keep him stalled until it's signed." Lewis is mashing the imaginary brake on his side as they speed towards a red light.

"If we don't die before we get there." Fields gives him the stink eye from the side as she continues tumbling recklessly through the city streets.

Twenty Minutes Later

Ferming casts a furtive glance in the direction of the front door as the incessant banging timbre rises. "Dr. Jackson, its Detectives Lewis and Fields! Open up we can hear you!" He scrambles to the shelf over the fire place and grabs his car keys. Lewis had to have seen him trying to flee the go go bar. He grabbed his handgun. It was only a matter of time before their backup arrives and surrounds the house. He could shoot himself for ignoring the approaching siren. Cockiness always proves to be the downfall of man. The backdoor is his target. If he can get out of it and to his van he'll be in the clear. He's out! The van is less than thirty feet away. Throwing caution to the wind, he takes flight.

"FREEZE!"

He looks to his left and there stands Lewis. His gun points in Lewis' direction but Fields bullets fly into his back, knocking him forward the last ten feet. He slams into his van with a sickening thump, before sliding down its side panel. He felt the impact but there is no pain. *This can't be good*, he thinks. Lewis kicks his hand He's screaming but no words are reaching Ferming as he looks back and forth at both officers. Fields is barking commands in her cellphone. He can read her lips. How ironic? The person who just shot to kill me is calling people to come save my life. He smiles. His white teeth are covered in blood. This is funny. I think I'm the only one who knows I'm dying. No more suffering for me, but this is only the beginning of others. Look a light...

An ambulance and multiple police cars surround the house. Yellow tape extends around the side of the house and goes toward the back. Lee Lee parks and her and Suffiyah jump out. "They must've killed him," Suffiyah states more so to herself. She spots

Sonya and walks towards her. "Sonya!" Detective Fields looks in her direction and puts up a finger telling her to wait. Ignoring the gesture she keeps walking, she has to know it's over. A paramedic backs out the house pulling a stretcher. The sheet is over Dr. Jackson. Relief washes over her. It's really done. As they come down the steps his hand escapes the sheet. The world ceases moving and sound doesn't exist. She takes off at top speed running towards the paramedic. An arm wraps around her torso and it lifts her from the ground as she kicks and claws at the air. The pitiful yell leaving her mouth sets Lee Lee off behind her. Suffiyah finally wiggles free and hits the ground like a sack of potatoes. Her face is stuck in the grass as she cries the cry of a widow or a mother who's just lost her only child. She feels Lee Lee holding her but it's of no consequence. The paramedics speed up the process of getting to the ambulance. The caramel colored hand hangs limply as the sun twinkles off of the plain face Movado watch with the brown band. It takes hours to calm Suffiyah. At nightfall Lee Lee finally gets her to leave. The air is impregnated with her sorrow and distraught with her pain. As she leans back in the passengers' seat, she grips her phone. The message icon shows a number one, she presses it. A message from Benji, it's a video. She touches the screen for it to play and first hears a strained gurgling noise. Then it's Benji's face. His eyes bulge out of the sockets and a thick vein protrudes from his head as he's being choked. After the thirty second video are the words "Now you suffer with me." Everything goes black.

Three Days Later

Suffiyah opens her eyes and is no longer in the car. As the blurriness subsides she recognizes the look and smell of a hospital room. So did she dream everything? She looks to her right and there sits a puffy eyed Lee Lee. "You're finally woke!" Lee Lee never cries but here she is. "You scared me so bad. All you kept talking about is dying." Suffiyah opened her mouth to speak but her throat felt like it was coated with sandpaper. She pointed to the water. Lee Lee held the straw for her to drink. "We're going to get through this Sufee, I promise. You can't give up. You have to live for them."

"For who?" Either Lee Lee was losing it or her medicine was causing her to lose her grasp on comprehension. She looked down at Lee Lee's hands as they touched her.

"The babies."

She covered Lee Lee's hands on her stomach. She just looked at the ceiling, she was speechless.

That Night

Through all of the excitement that Lee Lee's been enraptured in, she's forgotten the responsibility of everyday life. This is apparent by the disconnect screen on her television. While playing Nancy Drew she's neglected to pay her cable bill. She heads out her apartment and goes to the mail boxes. In just a few days the mail has amassed significantly. She plucks through it on her way back to the apartment. Being that Suffiyah will be released tomorrow it was unnecessary to sleep in one of those uncomfortable hospital chairs. She sits on her bed and searches for this month's cable bill. Instead she finds a letter from Benji addressed to her. Immediately she tears it open and can hear his voice as she reads.

> Peace,
>
> *First and foremost pardon my soul for my intrusion into your day. It's likely that I'm the last person you wish to hear from. So I will be as brief as possible so as not to oppress your time. The look of things are deceiving in the sense that nothing can be judged on the face value. Take me for instance, when y'all saw me at the mall you believed you had me figured out. But on the contrary I was the*

polar opposite. Likewise, I'm being misjudged due merely to outlook. I believe that the only thing which speaks louder than a man's voice is his character. I also believe as an ally to Sufee you weren't interested in the words I spoke to her but moreover if my actions manifested those words. In hindsight I believe you now know that your approval of me is a derivative of the consistency of my character. I just wanted to clarify the way things seem. First, Suffiyah believes I was stalking her because of the photos she found, so I'll begin by explaining that. A friend of mines works as a psychiatrist in her department. He told me of a police corruption investigation that Internal Affairs needed his assistance with. He gave me her name and where I could find her at and I began my investigation. My job was to document her routine and notify him of any incidents that might raise any eyebrows. I kept tabs on her and informed him of all my findings. For the record I would have never given this information to a stranger but this is a man I trusted with my life. More like an older brother. Now, our run in at the mall was staged. It was the second day of my investigation on her and I wanted to see if, she proved to be as upstanding as I perceived her to be at first sight. To say I wasn't slightly infatuated with her after watching her would be an untruth. I built my courage up to approach her at the mall and chickened out. Bumping into her at the courthouse was purely coincidental in nature, but I believe it was fate. Onto the pictures of Sakinah. This letter came with another. The last page is a letter from her killer. I don't know who he is but he sent me the letter and pictures to taunt me.

As macabre as the pictures are. I couldn't make myself discard them. They were her in a time when she needed me most and I failed her. It was a reminder of my shortcomings and a motivation to hunt down the man behind this. Tossing the pictures, to me, symbolized giving up hope and failing her again. That's the truth as I know it but for you to decide if you are inclined to believe it. If you do and decide to speak on my behalf can you tell her something for me? Tell her love is an acronym to me which means loyalty overrides vain emotions. So to love someone means to put them before your own self. That being said let her know I adore her with all of me and it isn't a moment that I see her face and not thank god for his mercy. But if she's happier without me, then I'm for us never speaking again. Because I'd rather live everyday suffering alone and know I brought her joy. Then to be in her presence daily knowing I'm the source of her displeasure. Ten times out of ten her happiness trumps mines and that's how I measure love.

P.S. Don't blame Ferming for doing his job. If it wasn't for him there would have been no us.

Forever Real,
Benji.

CHAPTER 32

SAKINAH MUNEERAH ROGERS
The headstone reads in fancy script. A fresh dozen roses decorates the gravesite that's maintained with the greatest of care. "You have a beautiful name." Suffiyah stands over the grave rubbing her baby bump. Four months pregnant with twins she promises to show a love neither of their parents knew. "I googled the meaning of Muneerah, it fits you. It says "bright, illuminated light." It's more but it's all basically that. You are a light. No. A beacon. Even buried under the ground your guiding light refuses to be diminished. Your hope for Benji prompted a domino effect. Your light started at him and is being used to guide twenty renegade teenagers struggling to find their place in this world. Now even I'm following your light. Benji said he came down here for lunch almost every day to keep you company. So I made a promise to myself to keep his tradition firm. Starting with me and followed by these two. He wrote in a letter that he would sacrifice his happiness just to see me happy. Forever the altruist. In life the happiest he could ever be is with you, so that's why I placed him here in death. I know that if he followed your lead while he was here and it led him to such greatness. Then in death following those same footsteps could only lead him to Heaven's steps." She looks to her right where Benji's headstone lies. "You deserved him so much more than I did. But I appreciate the man you allowed him to realize he was. And I'm eternally grateful to have had him in my life, if only for a short moment. For him to

even compare me to you is an honor that humbles me. Sleep easy, Queen. Your king is next to you." In light of all that has transpired Suffiyah has made the decision to continue Benji's work to the best of her ability. The fact that she was unable to apologize to him forever doubting him, is something which will haunt her forever. She was practically begged to come back to work. She declined their offer. McFarland told her of the claims made by Sonya which led to his decision. Once again Benji read the situation precisely. That wasn't the life for her. So she would also find her way through the kids of *Misfits, INC*. But today she would put out the final issue of *Why We Bang?*

CHAPTER 33

THE PLACE IS ALIVE WITH energy. The walls repainted a bright white and on the furthest wall a portrait. Over it are the words *Misfits, INC.* and under it is an inscription. *Bodies die, but legacies live.* The portrait was taken from Lenae's locket and transferred to the wall where they will be forever. Suffiyah looks at the trio and gets a glimpse of the happiness this place created. Three people martyred for the betterment of a society.

Do Rite sits on the table looking at his group of Misfits. These sessions are the single most important thing in his life. This is his chance at redemption. The opportunity to rebuild a community he helped destroy. In front of him and the rest of the room sits a copy of the final issue of *Why We Bang?* It's turned to Benji's departing editorial. The background picture on the page is Benji, Lay Low and Do Rite on a porch on 11th Street.

My Moment

I wonder how life will be when I go? Will all the dreams I watched come to fruitions be reverted back to a figment of an overactive brain? Or will they exceed heights that even I lacked the foresight to imagine. Will my ideology be seen as a fallacy or a meticulous blueprint to an egalitarian world? Every step taken has a consequence which will either push it forward or backwards. Setting its leader in a role to be remembered throughout the pages of history as either a courageous general or delusional tyrant. Or the worst kind of leader. The one who chooses to mollify the masses by compromising the integrity of his group for the greater good of self. These are the things I wonder about happening when I go. But as we read the pages of this magazine we discover all the turmoil happening now. All over the "Free" world and in the prisons where men of substance fight for the opportunity to be seen as a man I again in contrast to the prisoner. While the subpar men struggle between understanding whether they are inmates or prisoners. Due to this lack of understanding they undermine the progression made by said men. Likewise women are being marketed as product to be sold and used at the leisure of cartels. Trafficked into the country and forced to give away their virtue for the price of two movie tickets. Children are being battered by un-wanting parents or kidnapped broad daylight. I wonder how life will be when I go? The answer is exactly as it is right now, today. Unless we do what's necessary to fix it. People will think what they want regardless of what we do. So live in the moment. It doesn't matter how things will be when I go, because I won't be here to change it. So I do my deeds now and you should also. Because we won't have to answer for tomorrow because tomorrow is theirs, but today is my moment.

Just Benjamin

ACKNOWLEDGEMENTS

First and foremost all thanks and praises to my Lord Azza Wajjal for providing me with this talent and the opportunity to display it. I'm eternally grateful for the blessings you continue to shower me with even when I was too ignorant to appreciate them. To my ummi, Doris and my kids Aasiyah, Rami, Haleem and Jada, I put this book in my real name so after all these years of shame that I brought y'all throughout my incarceration I can finally give y'all something to brag about me. This our accomplishment and I love y'all more than any words can ever encompass. To the Laboo boys, Kel, Meel, Riq, Niqua(insider Lol), Day Day and my two sisters Kareemah and Tasha thanks for believing in me. Through all my wrong decisions and heartbreaking actions y'all never left my side. Y'all loyalty is a rarity in today's world and I'm honored to call y'all my brothers. We on the road to greatness and ain't no traffic!!! To my Abu, Malik, thanks for providing me with my brothers. I'm forever indebted. To True2Life Al-Saddiq and Naim Banks, thanks for mentoring me throughout my life and showing me what it meant to be real, a lesson that will never be forgotten. To my nieces and nephews I love y'all! My grandmother and a host of aunts, uncles and cousins I can't begin to name out of fear of leaving some out, thanks for believing in me. Throughout the trek of preparing this book the faith in me never wavered and the encouragement saw me through to finish this project.

To my team at More Than Words Publications, Shay and Javonne, y'all did more for me than I can ever repay but I will never stop trying. When y'all look at this finished book I hope you feel the pride of all the effort that you put into making my dream a reality. Jazakullah Khairan! To Dashawn Taylor and his team at Next Level Publishing, thanks for your professionalism and help in seeing me through the steps of becoming a published writer. To my Baghdad Boys, the real and the few. They did everything in they power to break us and we never folded in front of them or more importantly on each other. Loyalty is royalty so I'm surrounded by kings! Without y'all their would be no me! To my 007 family, y'all adopted me as one of y'all own and embraced me. Never think that this move is a me thing, it's a we thing because we one and the same. From Baghdad to 007 the knots been tied! To everyone who reads this book, whether it's to find a reason to keep hating or for genuine support, I appreciate the purchase. I hope I didn't let you down! To Fat Charlie and K-Nutty it's forever FREE Y'ALL! I'll never forget my block believe that! My words grow short but never my love. Peace!

Book Excerpt from Upcoming Novel

Only Life I Know

By: Robert Laboo

Prologue

"Is my stubbornness a testimony to my strength or a sign of defiance in my character?" As the hot sun congeals the blood in my scalp and dries the excess that leaks down my face, I can't help but ponder this question. The certainty which is death causes me less fear than the thought of all my actions being for nothing. I've dedicated my short life to creating a pro-black environment. A small community of black owned grocery stores, laundromats, homes and educational institutions. But to build this community the present one has to be eradicated. Some would call me radical or extreme, but I prefer the term driven. Every man with sight isn't blessed with vision. That line might fly over the heads of some, but those with vision will grasp the concept. But what is vision without balls? All of these stoic faced eunuchs preaching a word that they don't practice. Not me though. That's why I lay here drenched in blood on the cusp of death, not overly excited but fully prepared to be a martyr for the only life I know.

Chapter 1

The crisp Autumn breeze pushes the leaves across the concrete in waves as eight year old Jahlil Wright walks to school. His face lights up every morning as he approaches 12th Avenue. He can still hear his mother's voice pointing out the unique quality of their little corner of the world.

"Look over there, Jolly." This was her nickname for him. "You know what makes our laundromat and store so special?" Jahlil shakes his head. "Majority of businesses around here have been overrun by every people except our people. But Ms. Virgil and Mr. Tony are a testification to our strength. They held on to their little businesses and refuse to sellout for a few measly dollars. This is how we keep our community a community. Those strangers will never love us or look out for us like these people. Why? Because they never struggled with us. When you look in their faces you see us. When you look in their eyes you getting a glimpse of our past. They're survivors. Veterans of a completely different war. One we didn't have to go overseas and fight. That store and that laundromat are their rewards for their fight. Making them worth more than any dollar amount you can imagine."

He looks at the grungy facades of the establishments and doesn't see how they can be worth so much.

"Even $1,000 Mommy?" She laughs, "Yup, Jolly. Even two thousand. Blood, sweat and tears are always worth more than money. Always remember that."

He did. That conversation took place two years ago. Ms. Virgil sits in the doorway of her laundromat speaking to all who pass by. She is a still a very handsome woman somewhere in her sixties. Her squat, portly frame fits her grandmotherly disposition. The sunlight glistens off of her salt and pepper curls which cover her round head. When she look his way and smiles he can practically feel the warmth. She has an angelic glow radiating from her. She is the heart of this community. He waves to her and continues on to Mr. Tony's store. The bell jingles over top of the door as he enters.

"That sounds like somebody who owes me money." States Mr. Tony.

"I don't owe money, Mr. Tony!" Jahlil exclaims.

"You don't?"

"No! I just want some Peanut Chews." Jahlil shows the two quarters in his palm.

"Oh, I apologize, Jolly. Now I owe you a juice."

Mr. Tony was about 6'4 and 260 pounds. He hardly smiled and was perceived to be mean. But, despite his intimidating appearance he was actually one of the kindest men you could meet. If Ms. Virgil was the heart of the community he was definitely its soul.

"Thanks, Mr. Tony!"

"No problem, buddy."

Seeing polite kids like Jahlil made Mr. Tony's heart smile. It showed him the future had a little hope left in it. In a day where there was so little love for the race shown, he took pride in the few people who did. He remembered the '65 riots, when blacks burned down the majority of stores on Springfield Avenue in the fight for civil equality. The black love was tangible. Thirty years later and black males are killing one another for getting dirt on their new sneakers. He glances across the street and sees Ms. Virgil shuffling back inside the laundromat. A smile creases his face. Him and Ms. Virgil are staples in this area and an example of what black love could accomplish, even here in Newark, New Jersey.

<u>Next Morning 6AM</u>

The burgundy Oldsmobile Cutlass sits in the middle of 7th Street between 12th and 13th Avenues running silently. The three heroin addicts inside impatiently await their mark. The air in the car suddenly becomes oppressive.

"One of you motherfuckers shit your pants?" Asks Sam.

He was the uncontested leader of the trio. The drugs didn't slim him down as drastically as it did others. He maintained a somewhat muscular physique, despite his habit, that only made his short temper all the more threatening. If possible, he was even more irritable today. He couldn't believe he was on this mission. Robberies were no foreign thing to him, but he was always a man of principles. This proposition was brought to him on multiple occasions, yet he readily denied. He couldn't fathom selling out his own neighborhood for a group of outsiders. Yet, here he is. The monkey on his back led him here. Fighting the physical illness of withdrawal and needing his daily fix has caused him to compromise his integrity.

"Sorry, Sam. I farted. I'm fucked up man! I need my dose." One of the men state.

Sam's bowels aren't faring much better, but he's attempting to hold himself together.

"Keep your cool, turkey. Our lick is on the way. Control both those holes sucka or you gonna have a third one in your head." Sam faces back forward. As if on command, a set of headlights penetrates the dusky morning and parks.

"Bingo!" Sam exclaims pulling on the thick '70's style ski mask.

"Remember, we're just robbing this sucka and wrecking the joint. Got it?"

"We hear ya, Sam!"

"Let's roll then."

The engine of the '92 Lincoln Towncar makes a ticking sound as it cools down. Mr. Tony steps from his car and inhales the brisk morning air. He doesn't officially open the store until seven each morning, but he likes to arrive early and enjoy the neighborhood. The peaceful quiet allows you to see the beauty that is still Newark, before the sidewalks become congested with drug dealers peddling their poisons. Before the streets are tattooed with burnt rubber from joyriders in stolen automobiles. Before the silence is disturbed by the never ending gunshots and police sirens. Before it becomes a hotbed of turmoil, you are granted the opportunity to view how beautiful this city is minus its blemishes. The slight pain he feels in his back as he lifts the gate over the store reminds him of his mortality. Soon he'll be too old and his son will have to takeover the store. He places the key in the door and flies inside.

As soon as the key twists in the lock, Sam shoves Mr. Tony with all his might. He slides headlong into the potato chip rack. Sam motions for his accomplices to cover the store owner.

He commisioned these two for this exact purpose. Not willing to risk Mr. Tony recognizing his voice, he's allowing them to commit the robbery while he vandalizes the store. He runs to the back knocking all the glass jars from the shelves. One of his team runs behind the counter and searches for money. The other reaches out for Mr. Tony.

The haziness from his fall starts to subside as he stares upwards at the three masked men. He sees their mouths moving but is too shocked to pay attention to what's being said. In thirty years of owning this store, not once has he ever been robbed. A tug at his pocket brings him back to the moment.

"...everything god dammit!" Is all he catches as he grabs for the hand on his pocket instinctively.

"Let! Go! Of! My! Hand!"

Mr. Tony's brain rattles with each mind numbing blow from the gun. Every word is emphasized with a strike from the pistol. He's seconds away from losing consciousness.

Sam runs to the front of the store and sees Mr. Tony being beaten savagely by his cohort. He hauls off and sucker punches the man while he attempts to hit Mr. Tony again.
BWAH!
The gun roars as the punch connects and knocks the man over sideways. "What the fuck is wrong wit' 'chu man?!" Sam screams as his friend attempts to stand up. "Don't ever put your hands on 'im again or I'll kill you!"

"Sorry, Sa-"

"Shut the fuck up and get the-"

Sam looks in Mr. Tony's direction. He holds his throat like he's attempting to strangle himself. The blood pours through his fingers and around his hand while his right foot twitches emphatically. Everything just went wrong, Sam turns and flees the store without warning.

Pandemonium. That's the only word to describe the scene outside of Tony's Grocery Store. Dozens of police weave through the growing crowd of somber onlookers. The milieu has the feel of a funeral, a very sad funeral. Jahlil's mother's heartbeat speed increases the closer she gets to the crowd. She spots a friend on the fringes of the group holding her fist to her mouth. Tears stream down her face as she stares at the store.

"Vera, what happened?" She notes the slight cracking in her own voice. She's on the verge of tears and she doesn't even know why. Maybe she's just identifying with the sentiments of the collective. Vera points as she speaks, "They, they shot Mr. Tony."

Her heart that was speeding on her arrival, has just dropped to the pit of her stomach.

"Who? Why? We gotta get to the hospital!"

Vera shakes her head. "He's still in there. Melissa, they ki, killed Mr. Tony." She cries.

Everything begins to blur and spin out of control. Jahlil's mother never felt herself hit the ground.

UMDNJ (University of Medicine and Dentistry of New Jersey)
Melissa looks at all the people in her hospital wing fretting over her and becomes embarrassed. She's never fainted before but it isn't worth all this fuss. Especially given the fact that Mr. Tony lost his life. Everyone's attention should be on that tragedy.

"Mrs. Wright? Your husband is on the way up." A nurse informs her.

"Thank you."

She feels so selfish. Her mind hasn't once considered how her husband will take this. Knowing him he will want to retaliate. When he was released from prison, Mr. Tony gave him a job in the store. Then arranged for him to be employed at the warehouse where he currently works. She doesn't know what her family's financial situation would be without Mr. Tony. But, they are eternally indebted to him. The news of his death will crush her husband.

"Melissa, are you okay baby?" She starts crying immediately upon hearing her husband's voice. Physically she was perfectly fine. But her heart hurts from having to be the one to tell her husband about Mr. Tony. He hugs her to his chest. "What hurts baby?" Concern oozes from his words.

"Mis, Mr. Tony's dead. Sam somebody killed Mr. Tony!" She cries. "Who would kill that sweet man? Fucking animals!"

Her husband is speechless, his only response is to hold her tighter.

"Why, Sam? Why?"

Sam's silence causes her to become all the more distraught, because he usually always has the answers.

- Book Coming Soon -

SUFFER
With ME

A NOVEL BY:
ROBERT LABOO

Made in USA - North Chelmsford, MA
1101682_9780578406534
05.08.2020 1341